EDGE OF REGRET

Recent Titles by Janet Woods from Severn House

AMARANTH MOON

BROKEN JOURNEY

CINNAMON SKY

THE COAL GATHERER

MORE THAN A PROMISE

THE STONECUTTER'S DAUGHTER

EDGE OF REGRET

Janet Woods

This first world edition published 2008
in Great Britain and the USA by
SEVERN HOUSE PUBLISHERS LTD of
9–15 High Street, Sutton, Surrey SM1 1DF.

British Library Cataloguing in Publication Data

Woods, Janet, 1939-
Edge of regret
1. Homeless women - Fiction 2. Inheritance and succession - Fiction 3. Edinburgh (Scotland) - Social life and customs - 19th century - Fiction 4. Love stories
I. Title
823.9'2[F]

ISBN-13: 978-0-7278-6626-4 (cased)

All Severn House titles are printed on acid-free paper.

Typeset by Palimpsest Book Production Ltd.,
Grangemouth, Stirlingshire, Scotland.
Printed and bound in Great Britain by
MPG Books Ltd., Bodmin, Cornwall.

One

The slap Robert Gilmore gave Kenna Mackenzie propelled her into the leather chair that had once been her father's. Her fingers touched against the flaming patch on her cheek as she stared up at him, shocked. With tears filling her eyes, she told him, 'No amount of bullying will make me marry Rory Challoner.'

Across the room stood Robert's new bride, her arms folded across her chest and a smirk creasing her face. Agnes, pretty with her dark hair and bold, dark eyes, had been the housekeeper up until yesterday. Kenna had never trusted or liked the girl, though her late sister had been unable to see anything wrong with her. But then, Jeanne hadn't possessed a mean bone in her body, whereas Kenna seemed to be filled with them.

'Hush now,' Jeanne had said to her when she'd criticized Agnes's forward manner. 'You're too passionate, Kenna. Agnes is good to me, and so is Robert.'

While it was true that Robert had been good to his wife – and Kenna had been given no reason to suspect that her brother-in-law didn't cherish the ailing Jeanne – he'd made sure that his dislike of Kenna had been carefully concealed. But from the moment Agnes had stepped through the front door Kenna had suspected her relationship with Robert was more than that of master and servant. It had been a suspicion she couldn't reveal to her suffering sister, but one that had proved to be true.

It had also become clear when the will was read that Jeanne's trusting nature had been manipulated in life. Everything had been willed to Robert, except for an amount of money for herself – money which had represented half of the value of the estate at her father's death. That trust was administered by her brother-in-law, who had once been a clerk in the law firm her father had founded.

And so Robert had ended up with everything: the business; the house in Ainsley Place and its contents; plus control of her own money and her life. Worse was to come. Six months after Jeanne's death Robert had secretly wed Agnes over the anvil. Now, Kenna found herself a guest in the home she'd grown up in, and totally under Robert's control.

He stared at her now, the dislike he felt for her a flame burning in his eyes. 'You'll do as I tell ye, because you'll not be staying here for much longer.'

'I turned Rory Challoner down when I was eighteen. I haven't changed my mind.'

'Aye, and you've turned down every suitor I've found for you since. Well, Rory Challoner has got more patience than most. He's been waiting for you to find some sense, and so have I.'

'My father would turn in his grave if he knew how you'd cheated and manipulated my sister. Now you're trying to do the same to me.'

He shrugged. 'Don't you say such a wicked thing, girl. Jeanne was my wife. I'll never love another as well. If I could, I'd bring her back and die in her place.'

Agnes's smile faded.

'Yet you hate me, her sister. Why?'

'I don't hate you, Kenna. You're a part of my life I could well do without, that's all. You're a nuisance. Jeanne married me because she needed me to manage the affairs of the house and business. She used me, but for all I did for her she always neglected me and put you first in her life.'

'You were jealous of me, her sister?'

Taking her by the shoulders he pulled her upright and gave her a little shake before releasing her, saying wearily, 'For all her delicate airs and graces, Jeanne was a fool. I spent four years at her beck and call. You'll be a bigger fool if you cross me, Kenna Mackenzie. Rory Challoner will be coming to collect you in the spring. Make up your mind to it. If you refuse him again I'll toss you out on to the street and you can stay there until you change your mind.'

'You should throw her out anyway,' Agnes said spitefully.

'I don't want her living in my home. And when will we go to London to see the sights? You keep promising, but when are we leaving?'

'Stop nagging. We'll go as soon as I've dealt with some business I have at hand, and when I decide I have the time to spare. As for Kenna, I've dismissed all the servants, since I can't see the sense of paying them when I'm not here. Kenna helps with the work, and someone will be needed to keep an eye on the place.'

'The neighbours could do that.'

'I've never encouraged neighbours. It doesn't pay to let strangers know your business.'

Kenna's ears began to burn as Agnes's gall sunk in. '*Your* home, is it? This house belonged to my parents. I was born here, and I grew up here.'

'Be quiet, the pair of you. This is my house, get used to it. Agnes, go about your business. I want to talk to Kenna in private.'

'I'm not the housekeeper now, and don't you forget it,' she said on her way out, slamming the door so forcefully behind her that smoke billowed from the chimney.

Kenna's face stung from Robert's slap. 'Say what you have to, Robert.'

He sighed and perched himself on the edge of the desk. 'I promised your sister I'd look after you and see you settled when she'd gone, but you're making it very difficult. You always argue, and you constantly push me past the edge of patience.'

'I'm twenty years old, a grown woman. I can't see why I shouldn't have a say in my own future, that's all.'

'What's wrong with Rory Challoner? Your sister approved of him as a husband for you. In fact, he was her suggestion.'

To tell the truth there had been nothing really wrong with him, except he'd been inebriated and had acted accordingly. 'He seemed immature. He couldn't keep his hands to himself, his remarks were personal and I hated his unkempt beard and wild hair.' She shuddered, but because Robert had taken the trouble to meet her halfway for once, she told him the truth. 'I want to marry a man I can love and respect.'

'You'll grow to love and respect Rory Challoner. Glenchallon is a large estate with a fine house . . . it just needs managing properly and a few repairs doing to it. He's a laird. You'll have a title. Lady Challoner. I'll have to bow to you. You'll like that.'

She laughed, she couldn't help herself. 'I don't give a damn about his title or his estate, and I don't want a man who wants me for the money I bring, and looks upon me as a chattel. He drinks too much, has no manners and is . . . unintelligent.'

Robert gave a faint smile. 'He drank because he was nervous. He won't make the mistake a second time. But yes, I'm inclined to agree with you that the laird has more brawn than brain. He's a well-proportioned man who would give you handsome children, though. A clever woman could change him. As for his lack of sophistication, he's from the southern uplands and he's not used to the city. He'll be more comfortable on his own ground. You'd have him wrapped around your finger in no time.'

'I'd rather not. I want a husband who will respect me and deal honestly with me. I also don't want to live in the wilderness. Give me my inheritance so I can leave here. If you find me a nuisance I promise I won't bother you again.'

He came to where she stood, touched his fingertip against her cheek and said quietly, 'I'm sorry I slapped you, Kenna.'

It wasn't the first time he'd slapped her. 'You should learn to take control of yourself rather than to seek to dominate me.'

'An intelligent man will always seek to dominate a woman, that's why Rory Challoner would suit you. He's not used to city women, he'd be in awe of you.' He slid his finger down her cheek and under her chin. 'You're lovely looking, you know, Kenna. You have your sister's delicacy of feature, but you're more robust in body and fiery by nature, like malt whisky set against white wine. I've always wondered what it would be like with you. It would be like making love to your sister before she became too ill to love me in return. If you'd allow me a certain privilege I would loosen the purse strings on your allowance a little . . .'

She took a step backwards. 'Are you saying you'd hand over my inheritance?'

'Don't take me for a fool, Kenna. I'm not about to do that.

You'd just spend it, then you'd have no dowry at all. You're only twenty years old. If you don't marry you won't get control of any of it for another five years, anyway. No, I meant that I'd give you a little more to spend.' He filled the space between them. He was perspiring, and Kenna could feel the tension in him when he stroked her arm. 'I could prepare you for your wedding night, show you what's expected of you.'

She only just managed to suppress a shudder. 'I know what's expected of a wife on her wedding night.' Agnes was probably listening at the keyhole so Kenna raised her voice. 'Are you telling me you'd be unfaithful to Agnes?'

'I've always admired you, Kenna, and I'd be discreet. Agnes wouldn't know. Besides, an anvil wedding isn't worth much in legal terms. It hardly rates any respect, at all, which is why I've insisted it be kept a secret for the time being. If I tossed Agnes back into the gutter, she wouldn't have any recourse.'

'And do you intend to do that?'

He shrugged. 'Agnes is useful to me in many ways. She's a whore in bed, and she keeps me amused.'

Kenna blushed, then raised her voice to cover her embarrassment. 'You're suggesting that I become your . . . your *slut* too? Even if I agreed, how ridiculous of you to imagine I'd allow you to pay me for my services with my own money!' She tossed a scornful laugh at him. 'You're scum, Robert Gilmore. I won't marry Rory Challoner, and nothing you can do will make me. Now, get out of my way.'

She pushed past him and opened the door, nearly knocking Agnes over in the process. The woman's face was like thunder. 'People who listen at keyholes deserve to hear bad of themselves. You two deserve each other,' Kenna told her as she walked past.

'You witch!' Robert shouted after her.

Kenna had calmed down by the time she reached her room. She sat on the bed she'd slept in since childhood and stared at herself in the mirror, trying to remember when she'd last felt happy. She wanted to cry, but wouldn't allow herself to indulge in feminine weakness. How nasty a man Robert was, now he'd shown his true colours.

There, on the bedside cabinet, was a portrait of her mother set in an oval frame. Kenna experienced a flare of love for her. Though she could hardly remember Teresa Mackenzie, both she and her late sister resembled her. Looking at her, Kenna felt less alone, as if her mother had entered the room to comfort her.

'I can't wed Rory Challoner,' she whispered. 'But what other option is there?' For certain she wouldn't give in to Robert's demand in exchange for her allowance being raised. She could leave Scotland, she thought. She could go as far south as she could and find herself employment as a governess or a maid. That way she could support herself until she was old enough to claim her inheritance.

Downstairs an argument was raging. After a while, the front door slammed shut and there was peace and quiet. Robert had stormed out. He'd become unpredictable since Jeanne had died. He might sleep at his club, or return home, his ugly mood heightened by liquor, to demand his dinner. Never before had he made personal advances towards her, and she was perturbed by it, though suspected it might have been to frighten her into marrying the laird, rather than from any real desire on his part.

The light had gone from the day, and the grey sky wept tears. From outside came the clop of horses, and the sound of wheels over the cobbles cut through the quietness. What if Robert did turn her out? Where would she go? It wasn't wise to make an enemy of Agnes, because from the sound of things she had her own set of troubles coming up. Perhaps Kenna should try and make amends.

She found the woman sitting at the kitchen table peeling potatoes. Agnes's eyes were full of malice as she glanced up. 'What do you want?'

'I thought I'd help you with the dinner.'

'Did you, indeed?' She stood, her eyes red-rimmed from crying. 'Do you think you're going to sit at my table and eat dinner, after what you did?'

'I didn't start the argument, Agnes, and you can't hold me responsible for what Robert said.'

Agnes still had the knife clutched in her hand. 'I can and I do. I was good to you and your sister, despite your fancy ways.'

'I appreciate that, Agnes, but you were paid to be. You were a hired servant, after all. We were good to you, too. I always treated you kindly despite knowing Robert was unfaithful to my sister with you. He loved her, and used you for his baser needs. I suspect that you were lovers long before you came here.'

'What if we were?' she said, and chuckled. 'Don't look so shocked. He set me up in a room over near the docks. When your sister was taken ill it was more convenient to bring me into his home, to save him having to explain his absences. When she died, he married me. We were both drunk at the time, but if he thinks this marriage isn't legal just you wait and see what will happen if he tries to wriggle out of it. I know too much about him and his schemes. His name will be smeared all over Edinburgh if he crosses me. And now he knows it, because I've just told him so.' Her smile was smug. 'I've got witnesses to the marriage, see. The blacksmith and his sons.'

It seemed Robert had bought more trouble than he'd thought with Agnes. Good luck to her, Kenna thought. It was about time someone got the better of him.

'Well, Miss Kenna Mackenzie. Now it's your turn to discover what it's like to be down and out. Who knows, you might have to sell your body to fund your next meal. Perhaps you should have let Robert have his way with you, after all.'

Kenna's mouth dried. 'What are you saying?'

'You're not deaf, are you? You can go – you can get out this minute, and in the clothes you stand up in, just as Robert said.'

'It was said in temper. He didn't mean it.'

Agnes began to walk around the table, the knife held out in front of her. 'Aye, but he *did* mean it. You might think he's taken a fancy to you, but he hasn't. He's taken everything you've got, except for one thing.'

'Which is?'

'Your innocence. He said he made advances to you because it would be the ultimate humiliation before he threw you out. If you're still here when he gets back it's likely he'll take you by force.'

Kenna gasped.

Agnes smiled. 'He said you need teaching a lesson.'

'Robert wouldn't dare.'

'Aye, he would dare, because that's how he took me. By force. Only I'm not going to allow him that personal satisfaction with you. As far as I'm concerned you can fend for yourself until the first day of March, by which time – if you've survived the streets – you'll be more than ready to marry Rory Challoner. I for one will be glad to see the back of you.' She jerked her thumb. 'There's the door.'

'But where will I go? I've got no money.'

'I don't care. I'm sure you'll manage. Try scavenging in the alleys and begging outside the public houses. Or there's always the hospitality at the poorhouse. Nice types they get in there, dying from all sorts of sickness. As a last resort there are plenty of medical students who will pay you to lift your skirts.'

Her crudeness made Kenna shudder. 'It's cold out, Agnes. I need to get my cape.' Once upstairs, she could lock herself in her room until Robert came back, so she could talk some sense into him.

Grabbing Kenna's shawl from a hook, Agnes threw it at her, and, coming up close to her, placed the point of the knife against her throat and screamed, 'I'm not stupid, so don't try and fool me. Get out now! If you don't I'll cut that pretty face of yours to shreds. Then we'll see if Robert still admires you when he comes back!'

Backing away from her, Kenna turned and ran out into the rain. The door thudded behind her and the key turned in the lock.

For a while, Kenna huddled in the doorway in the rain, shocked beyond measure. It was freezing. When her brain began to work she decided it was best to go in search of Robert. Agnes might throw her out but her brother-in-law surely wouldn't stoop so low, wife or not.

She didn't know any of Robert's friends. Since she'd known him, Robert had never allowed his social and home lives to intertwine. They were entirely separate. He'd always been secretive and dictatorial, although charming; even when her sister had been alive.

Lord, but Jeanne's death had changed him. Kenna now

realized that she'd never been encouraged to have friends. She'd cared for Jeanne as her condition had weakened her, and that had kept her effectively at home. Yet the sisters had been like stars around Robert's sun. Both of them had lived for his praise, and his charm had always got him what he wanted. Now, she was beginning to believe he'd worn it as a mask.

He wouldn't have gone far, surely, and at least walking would keep her warm. She began to traipse the nearby streets.

Two hours later, soaked to the skin, Kenna gazed through the steamed-up window of a tavern and saw Robert seated at a table not more than a few inches away from her.

Robert looked up when she banged on the window. A swipe of his hand cleared a space to look through and a frown creased his forehead when he saw her. He downed his drink in one gulp, then stood up, clutching at the table to steady himself.

He was still unsteady when he reached her, and in an ugly mood. 'What do you want?'

'Agnes has thrown me out of the house.'

'Aye, and I don't blame her.'

'Robert, I'm cold . . . I want you to come back home with me and make her see sense. She threatened me with a knife.'

He began to laugh, a harsh barking sound. 'So Agnes actually did it, she threw you out? Well, Kenna Mackenzie, I daresay it serves you right, and it might teach you a lesson. I have no intention of living in a house with two sniping women. You can come back when you decide that you'll wed Rory Challoner.'

Her hands went to her hips as her temper flared. 'That will be never.'

'So be it. Remember that it's your choice.' He hailed a passing cab. 'I'm off home for my dinner. Are you sure you won't change your mind, Kenna?'

The savoury smell of cooking wafted through the air and her stomach growled. 'No,' she said stubbornly.

'Then don't bother coming home until you do, because you won't be allowed inside.'

'Robert,' she cried out, and put a hand on his arm to restrain him as he climbed into the carriage. He pushed her away so she stumbled backwards.

Fingers closed around her arm. 'Is this woman bothering you, sir?' a voice said.

'She was begging for money.'

'Move on, girl,' the constable said gruffly, and fumbled in his pocket. He handed her sixpence. 'Here, that should buy you a bowl of soup.'

Kenna watched the cab disappear into the traffic with Robert, then shrugged, though she felt like weeping. 'Thank you, sir. That's kind of you.'

'It's a raw night. Get along with you now.'

Where could she go? Kenna began to walk aimlessly through the drizzle.

Dominic Sterne watched the constable deal with the girl. He hadn't been near enough to hear what was said, but she seemed to know the drunk who'd got into the cab.

He was on his way home from the medical school. This was his last week in the job. His replacement was a skilled physician who'd been doctoring for three decades and was willing to impart his knowledge to the many students who passed through the Edinburgh systems. They would receive a solid training, for the exams were tough, and only the best and most dedicated of men survived the courses.

He was looking forward to moving back to England, to the milder climate of the south coast, where he and his daughter could be part of a family once again. He should have left earlier, shortly after he'd been widowed – but he'd been obliged to work out his contract . . .

The girl didn't quite know which direction to go in. She gazed aimlessly up and down the street. When the constable propelled her with a gentle shove in the back she kept going in that direction, along wet pavements that reflected the light and towards the poorer part of the city. She seemed uninterested in the men who noticed her, the whistles and shouts from soldiers and low remarks from businessmen. Without thinking, Dominic began to follow her.

After a while she came to a lane. Dominic swooped in a breath when he saw her face in the light from the street lamp. Her features were exquisite. Just a glimpse, he had, for it was then that she became aware of him – and aware of the empty streets. Eyes wide with alarm, she turned and ran into the darkness of the lane.

'I won't hurt you,' he shouted, and followed her into the darkness, with the intention of giving her a shilling or two.

But she must have quickly found a hiding place – and no amount of coaxing was going to bring her out of it. He stood for a few moments, just listening, then he shrugged. She probably lived in one of those mean houses that backed on to the lane.

As for himself, he must get home to see his daughter before she went to bed.

Heart pounding, Kenna crouched behind a fence. The man was a tall dark shadow. They were so close it was a wonder he couldn't hear the muffled harshness of her ragged breathing. What seemed like hours later, when her body was frozen to the bone and aching from being held in the one position, the man turned and walked away, humming to himself.

Not far from where she'd been crouching, she discovered a shed at the end of a vegetable garden. She had no idea where she was, but the house the garden belonged to was in darkness. The shed door was well oiled, and it didn't make a sound when she opened it.

The interior smelled earthy, and she didn't want to think about spiders. Shivering with cold she groped behind the door and found an oilskin coat hanging from a nail. She used her shawl as a pillow and, making a space on the bench, curled up under the oilskin to try and get some rest. One thing: she would not return home to be exploited by Robert Gilmore; she'd rather die. In the meantime she intended to look for work with accommodation.

It was to be the first of many long, cold nights. But for now the clawing ache of hunger and the exhaustion that came with it had only just made themselves known. Worse was yet to come – the despair of finding every door closed because of her poverty, and knowing that nobody cared whether she lived or died, except perhaps for Rory Challoner, the laird who wanted her for her money.

Rory Challoner, she thought wryly. Ha!

*   *   *

From the edge of the forest, Rory Challoner gazed down at Glenchallon House. It looked solid and handsome in the morning light, the bluish-grey facade picking up the illusion of warmth from the yellow dawn. The mist was beginning to rise from the surface of the loch. It would rise as high as the roof and stealthily surround the house, as if seeking its way inside.

He laughed at his fancy. There were many ways inside, through the broken tiles and windows and down the empty chimneys. It only had to follow the draughts.

The smell of warm blood rose to his nostrils and he looked down at the red hind, dressed in her greyish-brown winter coat. How quickly her soft eyes had lost their shine when the heart stopped beating. He swung the creature up over his shoulders by her legs and headed down into the glen, the hind's head bouncing against his hip. The animal was young, and would be tender. The stags would have fought over her come the autumn rut. The strongest stag would have won her and would have thrust himself inside her in a frenzy of bellowing and biting to plant his seed, whether she wanted him to or not.

The stag's loss was his gain. The hind would keep them in meat for the next week.

When he reached the house he hung the carcass in the scullery from a hook and slit her open from chest to groin to remove the entrails. He threw them out into the yard for the dogs to fight over and placed the offal in a bucket underneath, which would also catch the blood. Maggie would give him hell if it dripped on to the floor and made more work for her. The kitchen was the only room that she kept really clean. Rory couldn't afford staff. Maggie was old and had nowhere else to go. Besides, the woman was Challoner blood kin.

Maggie must have seen him coming down from the hill, for when he went through to the kitchen she was frying eggs for his breakfast, instead of the usual oatmeal. And there was a slab of bacon to go with them, streaked through with sizzling fat. His mouth watered as she sawed a thick slice from a loaf of barley bread and threw it into the pan to fry.

'Is my grandfather up yet, Maggie?'

'No, he isn't, Master Rory. He finds it hard to rise these cold mornings.'

'I'm going down tae the village for some lamp oil after I've eaten. Is there anything you want me to fetch?'

'Aye, some salt, and some scrubbing soap. And we need some oats, but the store won't give us any more credit.'

'We'll see,' he said comfortably. 'If the Challoner can defy the bastard English by hiding Bonnie Prince Charlie at Glenchallon, we can persuade the village shop to extend our credit to cover a sack of oats. Otherwise, McTavish will get the barrel of my rifle aimed at his arse the next time he poaches one of my hares or helps himself to a trout.'

'You and I both know that Donald McTavish will have gone off early to market, it being a Thursday. And you know Fiona will be minding the shop. Just you be careful it's not you who gets a rifle aimed at your backside one of these days.'

'I dinna know what you're talking about,' he said with great innocence.

'Aye, you do. Now, don't you go fooling around with the shopkeeper's daughter. If the Mackenzie girl has changed her mind – though she may have married someone else by now – she'll not like having a rival.'

'Her brother-in-law promised her to me. She made a fool of me, then,' he said reflectively. 'I'm older now. Once the ring's on her finger the woman will do as I tell her.'

'That was two years ago. If she had a mind of her own, then she still will have.'

Rory grinned and pulled on his beard. 'She had a scolding tongue, at that, and I was struck dumb by it. She said I was a dirty ruffian who smelled of drink, and she slapped me when I tried to kiss her. She said she'd rather wed a donkey. Told me to come back in two years when I'd grown up. Then she stalked off, her tail twitching from side to side so I felt like smacking it.'

'And you all of twenty-six then.' Maggie cackled with laughter. 'The lassie was probably telling the truth. You shouldn't have gone courting with drink fermenting inside your brain. And you should have told her that you were *the* Challoner, Laird of Glenchallon, and that she'd be a lady.'

'I did; it made no difference. I should have smacked her arse like I wanted to. She was a sonsie lassie though, Maggie. She set my thoughts scattering in all directions, and right uncomfortable it was. I couldn't sleep for a week.'

Maggie hooted with laughter. 'It wasn't your thoughts that were uncomfortable, I'll be bound. Have you nae wondered why she was offered to you along with her fortune, when all you've got is an estate that's crumbling down around your ears and a title you set no store by? Because she's a scold and nobody else will take her, that's why. You should forget the city girl and put the ring on Fiona's finger. That's what she's after.'

Rory shrugged. 'Aye, I would, but Fiona has no money. As for Kenna Mackenzie, I might have made Glenchallon House sound better than it was. But she's not one to let such things impress her. Once we're wed and her money is in my purse, things will look up. I'll be able to pay off some of the debts, do some repairs, and stock the place with sheep. Likely she'll give me a son or two. Besides, she's a Mackenzie.'

'Oh, aye, and what's that got tae do with anything?'

'It was a Mackenzie who killed my great-great-grandfather. Cut his head clean off and sent it back to my great-great-grandmother.'

'He should be glad that was all he lost. The Mackenzie caught him in his wife's bed, so it serves your ancestor right.'

'Aye, but Mackenzie stole the woman from the Challoner in the first place, and from under his nose in front of his men, making him look a fool.'

'Likely he *was* a fool if you're anything to go by, since the affliction seems to have been passed down.'

'When Mackenzie made off with her, my great-great-grandfather vowed to regain his honour.'

'You're not thinking of doing the same thing to this lassie you're after, are you? Laird or not, it's likely you'd be made to dance on the end of a rope for your trouble.'

'Wheesht! Woman, I'm not that stupid. I'm well aware that the Challoner's head is old history. I'm just saying that she's a Mackenzie, and a Mackenzie severed a Challoner's head.'

'This one might cut off your manly parts if you're not careful.'

Rory began to laugh. 'Get away wi' you, Maggie. I was just saying, that's all.'

'Aye, I know full well what you were saying. Best you stop talking about the lass and go and get her if you want her.'

'I'm waiting for the word from that lawyer brother-in-law of hers.'

She set the plate down before him. 'So that's why you're going into the village . . . to see if the word's arrived as well as warming yourself under Fiona's skirt.'

'Aye, I might see if there's a letter for me as well,' he said with some annoyance, for he hadn't given it much thought. Maggie was a nosy old biddy who sometimes twisted him up in knots to find out what she wanted to know. He speared his knife through an egg and spread the yolk over the crisply fried bread. 'Satisfied?'

'Aye,' she said. 'Now, stop your clack and eat your breakfast before it gets cold.'

Two

The door at the back of the hotel opened to momentarily spill light across the yard. Kenna held her breath as a man tipped scraps on top of the rubbish pile, and tried not to cough when she expelled it.

A ham bone, and it still had plenty of meat attached to it! She edged forward when the alley dimmed to the sputtering illumination of the gas light above the door and she reached out for the bone.

A rattling growl menaced her. Fear froze her to the spot when the shadow of a dog loomed on the wall and began to leap and dance in the flickering light. Barely able to breathe, Kenna slowly turned her head, then smiled. Though his head was held low and his slavering mouth was curled back to reveal a row of sharply pointed teeth as it took a stance between herself and her prize, the dog was much smaller than the shadows suggested.

'You don't frighten me. You can snarl all you like but that bone's mine. I saw it first and I haven't eaten for two days,' Kenna said, as firmly as she was able. Not that she was hungry, but food was fuel and her energy was swiftly waning.

But neither had the dog eaten, for even his dull black and white patched coat couldn't hide the ribs nudging against his skin, and the stomach that hollowed into his sides. But when he cocked his head to one side and pricked one ear, he didn't look fearful, just a scared and hungry dog who had recently left his puppyhood behind.

Risking a savaging, Kenna picked up the bone and shoved it in the pail she carried, then began to rummage through the rest of the leftovers. There was a wedge of stale bread. The dog sank down on its haunches in defeat and gave a little whimper. She hardened her heart.

'By God, it's so cold,' she whispered. Pulling her shawl more tightly around her she hooked out a couple of potatoes and the stump of a cabbage and added it to the pail. She found a thick slice of beef smeared with congealed gravy. The dog kept its hopeful eyes on her. Although Kenna's stomach was empty, it roiled against eating the beef, telling her she wouldn't be able to keep it down. The animal was salivating, and his pleading little whimpering noises filled her with pity, despite her earlier resolve not to weaken. They were in the same predicament. She should be charitable. Pulling the beef into two pieces she held a piece out to the dog. 'Here.'

Delicately he removed the scrap from her fingers, then mashed it apart in two bites and wolfed it down. His tongue slavered over his snout, seeking out every last drop of gravy. He gave a gentle belch and gazed at her again, one paw held up.

'You have good manners,' she said, and his tail whipped from side to side. Kenna felt light-headed and sick, so she gave the dog the remainder of the beef.

Quickly she sorted out the rest of the salvageable scraps, then hurried away down George Street, across Charlotte Square and into Ainsley Place. She knew where the spare key to her former home was hidden and she wanted to check, to see if Robert and Agnes had finally left for London. Kenna intended to take advantage of the empty house. Despite her defiance and her need to prick Robert's conscience, she knew she was just about at the end of her tether.

But once the cold she currently suffered from had improved, she could look for work. At least she could lay low for a while, take a bath and change into the clean clothes she'd been forced to leave behind. And she had things she could sell to provide her with money for food.

If Robert and Agnes were still in residence she intended to beg them on her knees to allow her back in, otherwise she'd have no option but to make her way to the poorhouse. Only a fool would choose to perish from the cold on the streets.

The dog had followed after her.

She rounded on it angrily. 'Get away with you. I can't feed myself let alone a dog.'

Its tail curled between its legs.

She began to cough, sucking in harsh gasps of the cold air and hugging one arm across her chest. Although her face burned she could hardly control her shivering. Each cough brought pain and weakness and set the blood pounding in her ears.

There was a burst of laughter as a group of young men spilled from a house and surrounded her. 'What do we have here?' one of them said, and, grabbing her by the arm, spun her round. The contents of her pail spilled across the pavement. 'I'll have a kiss for luck from you, sonsie lassie.'

She shook herself free and eyed the mess on the pavements, breathing heavily. 'Look what you've done to my dinner.'

'Call this dinner?' A brown-booted foot slid across the scraps and kicked them in all directions. The dog darted forward, risking a kick in the ribs as he took the opportunity to snatch up the bone. He settled in the gutter with it and began to rip off shreds of meat.

One of the other young men caught her by the waist and twirled her round, her skirts flying out. Her shawl fell into a puddle. As she lashed out at them she saw an amused pair of eyes on her, and an older, very English voice drawled, 'Kissing the dog would have more appeal. Put the dirty little urchin down, Richard. She looks as though she needs a good wash.'

'What a good idea, but we'll leave the dog for you to kiss, esteemed tutor.' They bore Kenna off round the streets, cursing and laughing good-naturedly. She was jostled back and forth as they all tumbled down the grassy bank, slipping and sliding in the frost that crunched under their feet. Taken by her hands and legs she was swung between them. At least they didn't intend to violate her, she thought as she flew into the air, even knowing she didn't have enough strength to struggle. She hit the Waters of Leith flat on her back. The sudden cold of the dowsing against her overheated body robbed her of breath.

By the time she'd crawled out, spitting water and mud from her mouth, the young men had gone on their raucous way. The water dripping from her began to freeze in the raw air, and Kenna burst into sobs when the dog thrust its head into her lap. She asked the creature, 'Now, what am I going to do?'

The Englishman came to squat beside her. 'I'm sorry – that was my fault.'

'Aye,' she agreed miserably. 'You look old enough to know better.'

'I am. They're students, celebrating new year.'

'A nice way to celebrate Hogmanay, trying to drown a complete stranger!'

'They were only trying to clean you up.' He gave a quiet chuckle. 'High spirits. Most of them have passed their final exams and the New Year sees them start out in their professions.'

'And what might that be? No, don't tell me, doctoring, I imagine, since Edinburgh is full of medical students. I suppose they'll be let loose to practise their craft on the unsuspecting sick.'

'Rest assured,' he said curtly, 'they've survived several years of the most rigorous training, which will render them well qualified for the task ahead of them, despite their high spirits.'

She managed a scornful snort, which hurt her chest and made her cough. Tiredly, she croaked, 'Stop being so pompous. I could have drowned.'

'The water isn't deep enough to drown in, unless you happened to be a child, or unconscious, of course. Neither applies to you. I'll see you home.'

Kenna had been on the streets long enough to recognize an opportunity to beg for the money for a meal. 'I haven't had a home since my brother-in-law took a new wife. Though he promised my sister on her deathbed he'd look after me, he had other ideas. When I argued, his wife threw me out in the clothes I stood up in.'

His mouth twitched. 'I'm not interested in your sob story, since most of you street women have one and I think I've heard them all. I admit, though, yours is more inventive than most.'

Damn him! If the Sassenach didn't believe the truth when he heard it, he wouldn't believe the rest of it, either, so she might as well save her breath. She eyed his expensive evening suit. This was typical thinking from a man of his ilk, who had never known poverty by the looks of him. He was too eager to think the worst of people. Her blood rose, but her efforts to argue brought about a violent coughing fit that left her exhausted.

He gazed sharply at her. 'Where do you sleep?'

She'd found an empty house which was in such bad repair that the door had fallen out of its frame when she'd pushed on it. The place was full of mice and cats, and stank of bad drains. Most of the windows had been broken, or were boarded up. Mouldy plaster fell from the ceiling and the stairs to the upper storey were rotten. But Kenna slept downstairs in the kitchen and at least she was out of the rain. And sometimes, if she found enough dry wood she'd light a fire in the grate. She'd stolen a horse blanket from a stable, and slept on an old sofa that had been left behind.

'Would I be stealing food from rubbish bins to survive if I had a room with a bed to sleep in? And if I was a street woman I'd have offered you the use of my body by now, I daresay.'

'I wouldn't want the use of it. I've got more respect for my own body.'

'Aye, well so do I, and you're making an unfair assumption.' She shivered and gazed up at the dense, slightly menacing mass of the castle. 'As for where I sleep, at the moment that happens to be anywhere that will keep out the damp and cold. She rose, her muddy and bedraggled skirt clinging to her legs, her stomach hollow and the cruel ache of cold in her bones competing with the dizziness hunger bought with it.

Suddenly despair flooded through her and she staggered. Her knees turned to water and she sank down again, all the fight gone from her. This was it; she could go no further. As her cheek lay against the cold earth she experienced real despair. Her teeth rattled in her head as she began to shake and she whispered, 'I'll go to the poorhouse when I find my strength.'

The dog dropped the bone he'd brought with him, laid his head on Kenna's side and whimpered, reminding her that she was still alive. She'd like to think it was the comfort of friendship, but the dog was as desperate as herself. Perhaps he was waiting for her to die, so he could make a meal of her. A smile touched her mouth. She was so thin now that she'd barely provide him with a decent mouthful, nor he her. She fondled his ears, feeling a kinship with him.

Nearby, a cheer went up, then came the wail of a bagpipe and the bells began to ring in the new year of 1860. It was a burst of joyous sound in the crisp night air.

'Happy New Year,' the man said, his tone so ironic that Kenna found the strength to lift her head and gaze at him. His eyes pricked back the light from the moon, which rode high over Edinburgh, and they gleamed with a mercurial brightness.

'Aye, mister,' she whispered wearily, 'and a toast to Auld Lang Syne while we're at it, only we've nothing but Water of Leith to sip on, and that's none too clean. Leave me to die in peace, would you? If anyone asks I'm called Kenna Mackenzie.' Her body was wracked with another coughing fit that left her even weaker. Her face heated and she began to shiver so violently that her body jerked and her teeth rattled.

The Englishman pushed the dog aside and knelt, reaching for the pulse at Kenna's wrist. Then he smoothed back the lank hair from her face. The back of his hand was cool and soothing against her burning forehead. Opening her bodice he laid his head against her bare flesh, and she didn't have the strength to protest against such intimacy.

It wasn't long before he buttoned her up again. Bringing a silver flask from his hip pocket he unscrewed the lid, and, supporting her with the other arm, he held it against her chattering teeth, forcing brandy into her. A warm glow trickled through her innards.

Removing his evening cloak he wrapped her in it, then pressed the flask into her frozen fingers and stood. 'The door to St Cuthbert's will be locked against you at this time of night. Sip from the flask if you get cold, but not too much. You have enough problems without adding drunkenness to them. Wait here, I'll be back for you shortly.'

Aye, Kenna thought, *I'll wait, for I've got nothing better to do and not the strength to take myself to anywhere else.* The earth was cold and clammy here by the Leith. *Like the grave*, she thought, and shuddered. But no, although it was tempting to fall asleep and hope she'd never wake up again, the will to stay alive was still flickering somewhere inside her.

The dog pressed like a smelly furnace against her back. She imagined that she smelled just as bad, and felt ashamed. She couldn't remember the last time she'd had a decent wash. No wonder the man had thought she was a street whore.

Coming round to her front the dog pushed into the comfort of her body, out of the wind. It was nice to have company, even if it did have four legs. The creature should have a name, she suddenly thought. She rasped out the first one that came into her head. 'Good boy, Hamish.' He whined and his tail flayed against her hip.

The cold began to eat into her bones. The wind had strengthened. It keened over the ground and cut through her like a knife. She must make the effort to move, find shelter from it. She tried to crawl but was hampered by the cloak. Remembering the brandy, her stiff fingers fumbled with the stopper on the flask.

When someone snatched it from her hand she gave a thin scream of surprise, and Hamish growled. She heard him yelp as a foot connected with his rump and a voice said roughly, 'Sod off, ye mangy lump of fleas.' Hands fumbled with the cloak she wore. 'What else have ye got, lass? I'll have the cloak off ye, to start wi'. Like as not I'll get a siller sixpence from the pawnshop fer it, or it'll make a bonnie wee blanket for my bed.'

Hamish plucked up enough courage to stand on the other side of Kenna and rattle menace from his throat at the intruder. His teeth were an ivory snarl in the dark. But it was obvious he was more bark than bite.

Kenna was rolled out of the cloak and on to her back. She protested feebly when the man fumbled under her clothes. 'Shut your whimpering, now, lassie. There's nae people about to hear ye, and I'm looking for yer purse.'

'I have no purse. I have nothing of worth.'

His groping became more personal, his breathing heavier.

'Nae, lassie, but you do. You're a skinny one, but I might have a quick piece of ye, the while.'

Fear shot through her and she muttered defensively, 'I've got the disease.'

'Aye, so have I, so it daesna matter much.'

He was fumbling with the fastening to his trousers when she heard the sound of a carriage coming at a fast clip.

'Help!' she cried out, and the carriage slowed to a halt.

'Take this for leading me on and getting me all pricked up, ye dirty cow.' Her assailant kicked her in the stomach. Drawing up her knees Kenna began to retch, even though she had nothing inside her to bring up.

There came a shout from the direction of the carriage and the man was gone, his boots pounding across the grass. Putting on a show of bravery Hamish chased after him into the darkness, kicking up a ruckus.

Her Samaritan knelt by her side. 'I'm sorry I took so long, I had a job finding a cab. Are you all right?'

'He kicked me in the stomach . . . I'm winded . . . give me a minute.' When she recovered some breath she told him, 'I'm sorry, he's stolen your cloak and your flask. I didn't have the strength to stop him.'

'It doesn't matter. The flask is engraved so I'll ask the local constabulary to keep a look out for it. Will you be able to walk up the bank to the road with my help?'

'Aye, I think so.' Hamish came trotting back looking pleased with himself and wagging his tail. 'You're a brave boy, Hamish,' she said.

Kenna was of average height, and her head just reached the hollow of the man's shoulder. His body felt hard and strong as he half carried her to the waiting cab. As she sank exhausted on to the seat she felt as though her life was draining from her. The cab was blessedly warm and smelled of tobacco, leather and sweat.

When the man closed the door behind them Hamish set up a howl and scrabbled against the door to be allowed inside.

He cursed soundly, then apologized, before asking, 'Is the dog yours?'

'Aye,' she lied, feeling a sudden attachment to the creature. 'We can't leave him behind, he saved my life.'

'That's yet to be proven.'

Fear leaped into her heart. 'What do you mean?'

'Amongst other things you seem to be suffering from a severe bronchial complaint. Had I left you on the street you'd have been dead in a couple of days. You still might be.'

He'd confirmed her own intuition, and it sobered her. She didn't want to die young, but just at the moment life didn't seem worth living. 'Why are you helping me?'

"Why?' He shrugged. 'How do I know why? Put it down to insanity if you harbour a desire to be grateful.'

'I am grateful. Are you taking me to the hospital?'

'There are no beds available. You'll have the dubious pleasure of being looked after by myself. I'm a doctor and my name is Dominic Sterne. It's several years since I cared for a living patient and I need the practise. I only hope you'll oblige me by surviving, since to die would be a huge blow to my self-esteem, as well as bad manners on your part.'

His wry words brought tears to her eyes, for he was not as awful a person as she'd first thought him to be. 'I'll do my best to live.'

Offering her a wintry smile he opened the cab door to Hamish and when the dog had settled, said to the coachman, 'Drummond Place, and as quickly as you like.'

Briefly, Kenna wondered if he *was* insane, but she was too exhausted to ask him and decided she must take her chances. She fell asleep before the cab reached the corner.

Dominic Sterne's house had already been sold, but he didn't have to vacate it for eight weeks. Which was just as well, he thought, for he'd need that time to get this lost scrap of humanity back on her feet.

After that he'd make his way south, where, in May, he'd be taking up a partnership in the seaside resort of Bournemouth. His partner was an established general practitioner whose current partner was due to retire. The practice was too big for one person to handle, since the town was growing rapidly, mostly with retired people who'd moved to the chines for the sake of their health.

Dominic was looking forward to the move south, and to getting away from the teaching post which had held him captive in Edinburgh for the past few years. He'd enjoyed it, but he'd been of the mind to get back to real doctoring for some time now.

He carried the Mackenzie woman inside, her dog slinking after him in a manner that suggested he was hoping he wouldn't be noticed. Kenna, she'd said her name was. She was light in his arms, like a child. As well as suffering from malnutrition and pneumonia she probably had parasites – and if she plied her trade on the streets she could quite possibly have one or more of the more serious diseases women of her type suffered from. He hoped not, for there was something about the girl he liked; a gritty sort of courage. She deserved to live.

Trying not to make a sound that would rouse his housekeeper he gently heeled the door shut behind him and began to carry his burden up the stairs.

Light flooded as Mairi's door opened. She smiled. 'Guid morning, and a happy New Year to you, Doctor Sterne.'

'I'm sorry I disturbed you, Mairi.'

'I've just had my bath, and I wasn't asleep.'

'Stayed awake waiting for the coming of the first footer, did you?'

Mairi chuckled. 'Aye, even now I live in hope of a tall, dark and handsome stranger crossing the doorstep just after the stroke of midnight. Unfortunately you qualify in all ways but two. First you're a doctor, so that daesna count. And second, you're much too young for me. Now, what's that you're carrying, and who owns that cringing wee beastie hiding behind you?'

'This is a poor, sickly girl I found on the street. She's seriously ill and badly needs my help. The beastie is Hamish, her dog.'

'The smell?'

'Both of them, I'm afraid.'

Kenna began to stir. She gazed from one to another through eyes the colour of ancient amber. Fear touched them.

Dominic lowered her feet to the floor. 'It's all right, Kenna. You're in my home. I'm a doctor, and this is my housekeeper, Mairi Lennox.'

Comprehension flitted across Kenna's face and a tear trickled down her cheek, but she looked less alarmed.

A resigned sigh issued from Mairi. 'Another waif and stray, Doctor? The last one you brought in for a good meal emptied the housekeeping box before he left.'

'Let's hope the money bought him good health and happiness, then. Don't scold, Mairi, I couldn't leave the young woman to die on the street, now, could I?'

Her expression softened. 'You're a kind gentleman, I'll say that for ye. You'll nae be putting the girl in a bed in that dirty condition if I can help it, though. I haven't emptied my bath yet and there's plenty of hot water on the stove to add to it.'

'A bath wouldn't go astray.'

Raising her voice as if she were talking to a deaf person, Mairi said, 'If I bathe you, will you behave yourself, lass? Nae doubt you won't be used to taking a bath, but I'll need to wash your hair to get the mud out of it. Now, I daresay you won't mind using my water, since I wasn't dirty to begin with and there's plenty of clean to rinse you off with.'

Dominic's mouth twitched, for he was having a hard time containing his amusement. His eyes met those of the girl and she gave a little grin. He quirked his eyebrow. The expression was gone in a moment, replaced by an impartial one more fitting to his profession.

'Thank you,' Kenna whispered, as though the thought of having a proper bath sounded appealing.

'Guid. Bring her through to the kitchen and set her in my rocking chair by the stove, where it's warm, sir. I'll see if I can find her something to wear.'

'My late wife's clothing should fit her. I'd intended to ask you to donate it to the poor after I leave, and she looks to be about the same height, if nothing else.'

'Aye, but a nightdress and robe will suffice for now, and a wee pair of slippers for her feet. If you fetch them I'll put them to warm on the guard round the stove. Just leave them outside the door and give a knock. Oh, and a hairbrush wouldn't go amiss.'

The dog began to take up position on the rug in front of the stove. 'Don't think you're staying there getting in the way, Hamish lad,' Mairi scolded. 'You reek something cruel, and will be going into the tub after your mistress.'

Giving a casual yawn Hamish slunk off under the table, and curled into as small a ball as he could make himself.

Dominic felt grateful for Mairi's help as he went off upstairs and entered one of the rooms. Holding up the candle he'd lit he gazed around him. It had been a long time since he'd been in this room, which had a window facing over the cobbled road into the pretty railed communal garden square.

This was the room in which his wife had lost the fight for her life when giving birth to their stillborn son two years previously. Harriet had been middling fair, and quiet. She'd turned out to be a good, god-fearing woman with a domestic nature and an inclination to be prim. The marriage had been one of convenience rather than a love match. Dominic had found a safe, dull sort of contentment within it. Sometimes he'd wished she had more passion, but she'd given him Evelyn, and for that he was grateful.

Opening a drawer he took out a nightgown made of flannel. It buttoned up to the neck and had long, cuffed sleeves. It struck him then that in the five years of their marriage he'd never seen his late wife naked.

Everything of monetary value such as jewellery had long since been removed from the room. It was packed away for when Evelyn was old enough to appreciate it. The bed had a new mattress and Mairi had kept the furniture dusted, in case the room was needed for a guest. He'd put the girl in here, he thought. The room was next to his and if she needed anything during the night he'd be at hand. After taking the nightclothes downstairs he fetched up some coal and kindling, and lit a fire in the grate to warm the air. He found some bedding in the blanket box at the foot of the bed and made the bed up, grinning at the sight of the crooked blanket. No doubt Mairi would remake it with mathematical precision, giving him pointed looks as she clicked her tongue in despair of him.

At a loose end, Dominic assembled a few things he might need to ease the girl's condition, though all that could really be offered was palliative care. The outcome of her illness depended very much on her constitution and her will.

Nevertheless, he filled a kettle with water to warm on the trivet. And he placed a bowl and water jug on the bedside table. Then he collected some towels to make a steam tent, which would help to loosen the phlegm. He added some peppermint oil and wintergreen ointment to the tray.

From there he went into his daughter's room, which was situated on the other side of his own. Evelyn had inherited his own grey eyes and dark hair. Her nose was small like her mother's had been, and her mouth had the same curve, only her lips carried more flesh and were wider and more mobile. How sweet and innocent the four-year-old looked in sleep.

Stooping, he kissed her soft cheek and smiled when her dark eyelashes fluttered. Evelyn would miss Mairi when they left, and so would he. But at least his housekeeper still had a job, since he'd arranged for the new owners of the house to keep her on.

Mairi Lennox was vigorous in her application of soap and warm water, but the girl didn't protest – indeed, she seemed to relish it. And why wouldn't she? Mairi thought. The poor wee beggar lived on the streets and would enjoy the warmth and pampering, as well as the feeling of being clean. While Kenna was soaking, Mairi whipped an egg into a glass of milk, and held it to the girl's lips.

'Nae, lassie,' she said when the girl turned her head away. 'You'll drink every drop, for you look like death warmed up, and you'll need the nourishment to help you get well.'

It was a slow job getting it into her, but it stayed inside her. When Mairi finished she dried the patient with a bath sheet, helped her into the nightclothes and seated her by the fire. She took a brush to her hair, which fell to her waist. It was pretty hair, mid-brown and shimmering with chestnut streaks. The girl's eyes began to droop as she relaxed, and she fell asleep.

There was a knock at the door and the doctor entered at her bidding. He stared down at the girl for a long time, as though he was seeing her for the first time.

'She's a bonnie one,' Mairi said.

'Is she?'

'You know she is. You might be a doctor, but you're a man all the same.'

He grinned at her. 'Forget your romantic notions, Mairi, you haven't managed to marry me off yet.'

'That bairn of yours needs a mother,' she pointed out as the doctor picked up the sleeping girl. Her head flopped against his shoulder and she turned her face into his collar, as if she belonged there.

'I think you'll have to agree that an ailing street girl wouldn't possess the necessary qualifications to become Evelyn's stepmother.

'Aye, well, you'd know best about that, Doctor, but there's many a treasure hidden under the muck. I managed to get an egg and some milk into her,' she said.

'Good,' he said approvingly. 'I need to examine her, Mairi, and I'll need you present while I do it.'

'Aye, 'tis only right,' she said, following him up the stairs. 'I'll tell you one thing, though, Doctor; the lassie doesn't have any lice or other wee pests hiding about her parts.'

Which would save him having to inspect those parts too thoroughly, since Mairi was sharp-eyed.

The examination didn't take long and the girl was unresisting. The congestion in her lungs was well established, but not as widespread as he'd feared. His hopes rose that she'd pull through.

Mairi straightened up the blankets as the doctor made a favourable humming sound in his throat. 'Now, you relax and try to sleep, dear,' she said, gently patting the girl's hand when her eyes opened. 'I'll look in on you before I go to my bed.'

'Thank you,' the girl whispered wearily, her eyes filling with tears. But sleep quickly claimed her again.

'She's learned some good manners along the way.'

The doctor sounded preoccupied when he told her, 'She's in better condition than I expected her to be.'

'Aye, and the clothes on her back were of guid quality. There's more tae this one than meets the eye, you mark my words. I'll be off to wash the wee hound now.'

'Why don't you leave him till morning?'

'And waste the warm suds? He'll soon dry off in the kitchen. Besides, the bairn is going to want to make a fuss of him in the morning, so he's got tae be clean. I'll give him the oatmeal that was left over from breakfast tae eat, that should stick to his ribs.'

'Do dogs eat oatmeal?'

'Beggars eat anything. They have no choice.'

True, he thought, feeling a sliver of guilt as he recalled the mess of leftovers in the girl's pail. He shuddered, and hoped he was never that desperate.

'Get yourself off to bed now, Doctor. You'll need your rest if you're going tae look after the lassie. She's going tae get worse before she gets better. I'll make an oatmeal and mustard poultice to put on her chest in the morning, it will help draw the poisons out. '

'Who's the physician in the house, you or me?' Dominic said with a grin.

'Och, there's nothing to doctoring. All you need is good dose of horse sense.'

Dominic fell asleep, grinning to himself as the dog's protesting yelps reached his ears.

Three

Evelyn Sterne slipped out of bed. It was still dark and she thought she could hear a baby crying. It was coming from beneath her, downstairs in the kitchen. Perhaps her mother had come back with her baby brother from Heaven.

Her nightlight was out and the fire in the grate had become ashes. But she wasn't allowed to light a candle anyway; she wasn't old enough. There was enough moonlight coming through the window so she could see her way down the stairs.

She still felt sleepy, and the air on the stairs was cold. When she reached the bottom she was tempted to go back up again, for she could hear the moan of the wind, and the branches of a shrub tapped against the window in the parlour, as if someone wanted to be let inside. Fear of the unknown made her tremble and she turned to go back to her bed. But the whimpering cry came again. Her bare feet were cold against the floor as she reached for the doorknob and opened the door to the kitchen. She'd forgotten her slippers.

'Mamma,' she whispered, 'is that you?'

There was quiet for a moment, then feet pattered across the floor, a wet nose nudged at her ankle and a warm tongue curled around her hand. She gave an excited giggle. A puppy . . . her father had bought her a puppy!

'Shush,' she whispered when it began to give small yips of excitement. 'If you wake Mairi up she'll be cross, because it's too dark for me to be out of bed. Come upstairs with me, doggie.'

The dog followed after her, stopping for a moment to scrabble at the door of the room her mother used to sleep in. 'No, this is my room,' she said.

She closed the door and climbed into bed, patting the covers.

The animal jumped up beside her and wriggled under the eiderdown with a sigh of bliss. Evelyn smiled happily as she snuggled up to him.

Dominic was woken by the sound of coughing. Turning up the oil lamp he pulled on his robe and went through to the sickroom. The girl's cough was tight and dry, her thin shoulders heaved with the effort of each spasm. He held a glass of water to her lips, watching as she gulped it down, and catching the trickle that ran from her mouth with a towel.

'I'm going to rub some wintergreen ointment on your chest. It will help you to breathe easier and loosen the phlegm.'

'Thank you,' she whispered, and sank back down on the pillows, her eyes closing in exhaustion.

Dominic filled the kettle with water and set it to steam on the trivet, then he loosened the front of her nightgown and smoothed the aromatic lotion on the soft exposed skin.

Her eyes flew open wide as the pungent smell assailed her nostrils. They glowed like amber as if the unguent had polished them brightly from within. He'd seen eyes like that before, but he couldn't remember where.

'It might heat your skin a little but you'll be used to it in a while.' He removed his hand from the gentle rise of her breast, wiping the residue on a towel. He then picked up the bottle of lemon and honey cough linctus he used for Evelyn. Dominic poured a measure into a glass and supported her head with his arm while she swallowed it. 'That will soothe your throat a little,' he said, and wrung out a towel in water to cool her face with.

'I'm going to leave the kettle on the trivet. The steam will help loosen the congestion. We need to get you coughing if we can. There's a jug of water and a glass by the bed in case you become thirsty. Is there anything else I can do to help make you more comfortable?'

She shook her head. 'You've been kind enough already.'

'I'll say goodnight, then.'

'Would you leave me the lamp?'

'Of course.' He turned it down and departed, closing the door quietly behind him.

Throwing back the covers Kenna swung her legs out of the bed, though she was loathe to desert its warmth. She was light-headed and her legs wobbled as she pulled the chamber pot out from under the bed and relieved herself. This had been something too intimate to ask him to help her with, doctor or not.

When she got back under the covers she was shivering from head to toe, yet her body was hot. On the trivet the kettle began to sing as steam trickled from the spout and made the lid rattle. It was a comforting sound. The dim light didn't reach the far recesses of the room; even so, the room had a feminine feel to it. The nightgown she wore was his late wife's, she recalled. This must have been her bedroom.

'I doubt if you mind me wearing your clothes,' she whispered, in case the woman's presence was still in residence and she was disturbing her. A kind man like Dominic Sterne would have only married a woman with a heart as charitable as his own.

Just as she began to fall asleep, with the smell of wintergreen sharp on each painful inhalation she took, Kenna suddenly remembered the caress of Dominic's hand against her skin.

Her face heated and her body began to prickle with perspiration. She threw off the covers, but a minute or so later began to shake with the cold, despite the fire in the room. Her teeth were chattering as she pulled the covers over her again and curled into a shaking ball. Damn! she thought. She was feverish.

Dominic was woken the next morning with a kiss, and the weight of his daughter sitting astride his body. He smiled and said, 'Good morning, my precious Evelyn, but I really don't want to wake up yet.'

There came a giggle and another kiss, which was followed by a sharp intake of breath. 'Ugh! You have horrid prickles. Thank you for the surprise.'

Surprise? When several feet stomped over him and a wet tongue rasped down his face he hastily opened the other eye and sat up, tipping his daughter and the dog backwards. Animal and child rolled around together in the dip between his legs, Evelyn giggling and Hamish yelping excitedly. The dog regained his feet and his tail whipped back and forth.

'How did that creature get in here? He's supposed to be in the kitchen.'

Evelyn gathered Hamish defensively against her. 'He was crying in the night because he was lonely by himself in the kitchen. And Papa,' she said, her eyes wide with wonder, 'I think Mamma has come back. I heard someone coughing in her room, but I was too scared to look in case she was a ghost.'

He smiled and sought to assure her. 'People can't come back once they've gone to Heaven. It's not your mamma in there, my dear, and it's not a ghost. It's a poor sick lady I found wandering the streets with nowhere to go. She needed help and I'm going to try and make her well. And that little dog belongs to her. His name is Hamish.'

One of the dog's ears pricked and his eyes came alert. He was a young dog, and rather appealing now he was clean, Dominic thought.

Evelyn's face mirrored her disappointment as she sighed. 'I thought you'd brought him home for me.'

'We'll be leaving here soon, Evelyn. I'll consider getting you a dog when we're settled in Hampshire. In the meantime you can look after Hamish for Miss Mackenzie until she recovers. Take him down to the kitchen now and ask Mairi to let him loose in the garden for a while. Otherwise he'll wet on the floor and she'll be cross.'

'Can I say hello to Miss Mackalenzie?'

'Not until she begins to get better. You might catch her infection, and I don't want two invalid young ladies on my hands.'

'You'll tell her I'm looking after Hamish though, won't you?'

'Yes, I will. I'm sure she'll be very grateful. Off you go, now. I want to shave and get dressed. Tell Mairi I'll need a mug of hot water to shave with.'

Evelyn went dashing off, Hamish skittering after her.

When Dominic was dressed and shaved he went through to see his patient.

The nightgown she wore was damp with sweat, her hair

a mass of tangles from where she'd tossed and turned. Her eyes were bright with fever, but she managed a wry smile when he felt her pulse.

'Can you eat breakfast – a small portion of oatmeal, perhaps?' he asked her.

She shook her head. 'I'm thirsty though.'

The jug of water he'd left her had been emptied, though some had been spilled on the bedside table and the floor.

'It's important that you drink plenty of fluids, even when you might not feel you want too. And you must try to take a little broth and some milk, if only a couple of mouthfuls.'

Tears swam in the depths of her eyes. 'I'll try, but I feel so weak. I'm hot, but when I throw the covers off, then I get cold and can't stop shivering.'

'The fever is caused by your body fighting off the infection in your lungs. Lean forward.' He listened to her chest, chatting all the time to keep her mind off the intimacy of his hands on her flesh. God only knew how many other men had pawed her, though. Goose pimples razed along her skin as the cold air touched her. She began to shake.

He tucked her back under the covers. 'No doubt you'll be pleased to know that Hamish is being well looked after by my daughter, Evelyn. She's quite taken with him. I must admit, he's an engaging little chap.'

'Hamish?'

'Your dog. I'll send Mairi to tidy you up now, and will be back in a little while.'

'Doctor?' she said weakly when he reached the door. 'Thank you for your help. How will I ever repay you?'

'Just get well, Kenna, that will be payment enough.'

'Will I get well?'

She was no fool, as the intelligence in her eyes proved. He went back to the bed, gazed down at her and smiled. Despite the burning fever patches on her cheeks she was lovely, and in an innocent sort of way. It was hard to believe she'd lived a life of degradation. And although she was free of disease now she wouldn't remain so for long if she stayed on the streets.

All the same, some reassurance might help her to fight the progress of the disease. 'While it's true that your body has been weakened by malnutrition, your constitution is strong. I see no reason why you shouldn't recover if you have the will. You do want to live, don't you?'

She nodded.

There were several reasons why she might not survive, he thought. There was a danger of her fever going too high. If that happened, her brain would overheat and she might convulse, go into a coma and die. Alternatively, if her lungs became too congested by fluid she'd be unable to inhale enough oxygen for her heart to pump it around her body, then her heart would fail.

He patted her hand and turned away. 'Try not to worry.'

Mairi cornered him later that morning. Dominic was pleased to note that she'd forgotten the oatmeal and mustard poultice. 'In case you want to know, the girl managed to piddle last night.'

Dominic tried not to grin. 'Thank you, Mairi.'

'Aye, and so did the dog, and right by the back door. Still, I'll give the wee beastie his due, he did it as near to the garden as he could get, I suppose. He swallowed the left-overs from last night's dinner, too. The bowl was as clean as a whistle when he finished.'

He couldn't imagine why Mairi was cornering him in his den about this nonsense. 'Is there something else, Mairi?'

'Aye. I gave her clothes a good wash and I found this pinned inside the pocket.' She slid a brooch on to his desk. A gold bar supported a heart-shaped, hinged pendant edged in pearls and engraved with initials on the back. There was a miniature of a man and woman inside.

'She looks a bit like the woman, I ken.'

Dominic could only see a passing resemblance to the subject of the tiny painting. 'You're seeing what you want to see, Mairi. The girl probably stole it.'

'If she'd stolen it, wouldn't she have sold it and bought herself a lodging for the night and a square meal?'

'Not while there are fools like me around for opportunists to take advantage of.'

'You're closing your eyes to what's under your nose, Doctor. That girl is not what she first seemed.'

He chuckled. 'Mairi, she may well be Queen Victoria in disguise for all I know. The fact remains that Kenna Mackenzie was living on the streets when I found her. Therefore, I can only draw the conclusion that she's a street girl.' He threw the brooch into the desk drawer. 'I'll make sure she has it back when she's well enough to leave. Where's Evelyn?'

'With Hamish. She's getting too attached to that dog, but it keeps her out from underfoot. Just as well with your *guest* to look after as well.'

So that was it! 'I've been thinking that I might hire a woman from the agency to see to the girl's personal needs for the next week or so. I don't want to wear you out, Mairi.'

Mairi's smile was touched with a slight edge of alarm. 'Och, it's nothing, Doctor. I'm glad I can be of extra service to you for a few weeks.'

'Then you must allow me to pay you a bonus when I leave.'

'Aye, well, I can't say I'd refuse the offer of a bit of extra cash to put away for my auld age. That's a generous man you are, Doctor. I'll go and fetch your coffee, shall I? Then I'll take Evelyn and Hamish out for a walk in the park before it rains. It's cold, but a wee bit of fresh air won't hurt either of them.'

Fiona McTavish was a bonnie handful, Rory thought, gazing at the valley that divided her swelling buttocks as she bent over. He wished she didn't have a skirt over them.

When she straightened, she placed the candles on the counter and smiled at Mrs Young. 'Is there anything else you need, Cathleen?'

'Aye. I'll have some sugar, and some flour.'

Fiona's glance came Rory's way as she weighed the goods, and her blue eyes hooded over. When the woman had gone she came around the counter and locked the door. Hands on hips and breasts thrust out, she whispered, 'And how can I be of service to you, Rory Challoner?'

Rory handed over his list.

'My pa said if you can't pay for the goods, you can't have them.' She began to gather his purchases together anyway.

When she'd finished, Rory pulled her close. 'You've got a fine pair of breasts on you, Fiona. Let me see them.'

'I will not.' Going back behind the counter Fiona climbed a ladder and reached for something on the top shelf, giving him a glimpse of her ankles. He began to run his hands up her legs.

'And what do you think you're doing?' she said huskily.

'You know very well.' His hands slipped higher and reached the silky skin of her thighs.

'You'll have me off this ladder in a minute,' she said breathlessly, and turned to seat herself on the top step.

'Aye, that's what I'm after doing.'

'My father might come home early while you're taking liberties wi' me.'

'All the more reason fer hurrying.' His fingers slipped into the wiry bunch of curls and he tickled her.

'Rory Challoner!' she squealed, and opened her thighs to him despite her protest.

'Come away down now, Fiona,' he coaxed, and each hand cupped a bare buttock.

She gave a girlish scream as he lifted her down, even though she was no longer a girl, but older than himself. Her arms came around his neck and her legs around his waist.

He took her into the storeroom where they tumbled on to a pile of sacks. He flicked up her skirt, then managed to undo her bodice and got a mouthful of breast through her petticoat while he fumbled with the flaps on his trews. His shaft sprang from the opening and he slid it into her, exposing his bare buttocks to the cold while they bucked together.

Fiona squealed like a mare as he thrust, but he was careful not to spill himself inside her. She looked as though she wanted more, and he wasn't about to keep her waiting.

Undoing the rest of her buttons he placed his palms on her white breasts and fondled them before he kissed each brown-stained button. His hands went to work, and soon she arched upward with a loud cry and a shudder.

As he pushed into her again she whispered against his ear, 'You do love me, don't you, Rory?'

'Aye, who would'na? You're a right nice handful, and accommodating.'

He was just about to satisfy himself when someone rattled the shop doorknob, distracting him. 'Damn,' he muttered, and was about to withdraw from her when Fiona bit his ear and arched herself against him. Desire overwhelmed him as her muscles tightened around his shaft. Unable to hold on to himself, the blood pounding in his ears as well as where it mattered, he let loose like a cork from a bottle.

'Are ye there, Fiona?' a woman called out.

Rory cursed again when his raging senses had quieted. 'What did you do that for, you silly mare? If you get knocked up, dinna go blaming it on me.'

'I was afeared it was my father. He suspects something's going on. We should find somewhere else to meet. Besides, who else would I blame it on?' she said. 'I'd never been with a man until you had your way with me, as you very well know.'

'Aye, I ken that.' Looking down at her he smiled. 'We could use the lodge to meet in, though it's used as a storeroom now. It's back off the loch and ye can get to it from the trees without being seen from Glenchallon. Meet me there on Monday.'

'We'll see. I might nae be able to get away.'

The door rattled again. 'Where are ye, Fiona? I need some flour.'

A few seconds later Fiona was on her feet, her bodice buttoned to her chin. Tidying her skirts she went off to open the door, a smug, self-satisfied smile flitting around her mouth as she scolded, 'Can't a body take their ease for a few moments?'

When the customer had gone Rory returned to the shop and gazed uneasily at Fiona, wondering if she'd slipped up on purpose, or in the heat of passion.

When the next customer came in, Fiona smiled at her. 'I won't be long, Alison.' She placed Rory's goods in a box. 'Will that be all, Laird?'

'Aye, lass. Put it on my account, would ye?'

'Oh, wait a minute, I nearly forgot. A letter came for you the day before yesterday,' she said, and handed it over. 'It's from some fancy law firm in Edinburgh.'

Rory's heart began to thump as he read the contents.

'Anything important?' Fiona asked casually, and both she and Alison gazed at him in expectation.

Folding the paper he slid it into his pocket and tried not to grin as he thought to himself that all his troubles would soon be over. 'It's private estate business, and nothing to do with you.' Slinging a sack of oats over his shoulder and picking up the box of goods, he shambled off, leaving them with disappointed looks on their faces.

Fiona's father was coming up the road in his horse and cart. 'I hope you've paid for those goods, Rory Challoner,' he called out.

'Och, shut your clack, mon. The next time you have venison on your table you could ask yourself whose estate it came from. Ye'll get paid soon enough, ye always do. I've got some money coming my way before too long.'

'Oh, aye . . . from where, may I ask?'

'You may, but that doesn't mean I'm going to tell you, Donald McTavish. It's private business between myself and my lawyer.'

Donald's face adopted a sour expression. 'Fiona remembered to give you the letter, then?'

'Aye, which is more than you did the last time I was in the shop. She's an obliging lass is your Fiona – right obliging.'

Rory strode off with a grin plastered on his face.

Four

Mairi's homespun observation proved to be right. The Mackenzie girl did get worse. Two days later her temperature soared.

Dominic caught his housekeeper piling blankets on her bed. 'What are you doing?'

'We should burn the fever from her, Doctor. I'm going to put a mustard poultice on her chest, build up the fire and make a blanket tent over her bed.'

'Mairi, I appreciate your help but please don't make decisions as to her treatment. Do you understand?'

'Yes, sir. I beg your pardon, I'm sure,' Mairi said, a trifle stiffly.

'Uncover her then. I want to examine her before you apply any old-fashioned remedies.' Pinching the girl's dry skin gently between a finger and thumb, Dominic observed the time it took to return to normal. His eyes went to the water jug, which was still full enough to make his eyes sharpen. 'Has she taken any fluids today?'

'Just a wee drop or two.'

'Urinated?'

'I helped her on to the chamber pot myself. She managed a trickle, but it was dark-coloured.'

Dominic nodded. He saw no need to use his thermometer since the heat emanating from Kenna was obvious. Besides, the gauge was too big, and it took too long for the body temperature to register. He wished someone would invent a more efficient one.

Eyeing the blankets piled up on his patient, his lips pursed and he gave an annoyed little hum. Kenna was hotter than hell already and the fevers and chills were following the all too familiar morbid process.

'She's already dehydrated. If she heats up much more she'll be in real trouble. Remove the blankets now, Mairi. I'm going to try and cool her body down. And I'm going to get some fluids into her.'

Mairi's hands went to her hips. 'And how will you do that, pray, when she won't open her mouth or swallow what goes into it?'

'I'll insert a tube into her oesophagus – her gullet,' he thought to enlighten her with.

Mairi turned pale. 'The things you doctor's get up to. You should let the poor wee girl die in peace.'

'That's your learned opinion, is it?'

'Aye, it is,' Mairi said defiantly.

'Then you're less intelligent than I imagined you to be.'

Mairi gasped at the sharp rebuke.

Kenna gave a moan and her eyes flickered open. They were glassy with fever, but cognizant.

Dominic leaned over her, took her hand in his and gazed into her eyes. He said calmly, 'You're not going to disappoint me by wanting to die in peace, are you?'

The expression in the eyes that met his contained so much trust that it humbled him. She managed a slight shake of her head.

'Good, because you've reached a crisis.' He gave her a shake when her eyes closed. 'Stop your mind wandering away and listen to me now, Kenna. To save your life I'm going to need you on my side. I'm going to try and cool you down. The process will make you cold and you'll shake with chills, so it will certainly be uncomfortable.'

Her eyes remained locked on his for another moment and he couldn't tell whether she'd absorbed what he'd said, or not. Then they flickered rapidly and rolled up in her head. She began to convulse. He managed to get a handkerchief over her tongue, and tied the ends under her chin. It would prevent her from biting it, and would make the passage of the tube easier when the convulsion stopped, for she was bound to fight the insertion of it.

While his patient jerked and moaned, he said to Mairi, 'Fetch me up a jug of lukewarm water, and the willow bark. I'm going to need you to help me. Are you up to it?'

'Aye, Doctor,' she said, and scurried off.

Dominic removed his coat, rolled up his sleeves then took a length of tube from his bag. By the time Mairi returned Kenna was still and the tube was in place. Dominic dribbled water infused with a teaspoon of powdered white willow bark into it, which would help reduce her fever.

'Is Evelyn asleep?' he asked Mairi.

'Aye, I checked on her on the way up.'

'Good.' Ignoring the need for propriety and Mairi's shocked gasp, Dominic began to strip the nightgown from the girl. When she was naked he picked her up. 'Place that rubber sheet and some towels under her, Mairi. I'm going to wet her, including her hair. Then we'll allow the water to dry on her body in the hope some of it will be absorbed. When it does dry, I'm going to keep repeating the process until she's cooler. And I'm going to dribble a glass of water through that tube into her stomach every half an hour. Not too much at a time in case she's sick. She might convulse again, and she'll certainly shake. I expect to be up all night. I don't suppose it will take two of us so you can go to bed if you wish, once the process has started.'

'Nae, Doctor,' she said, bustling about to do his bidding. 'You'll need someone to fetch and carry. And you'll likely need some refreshment to keep you going. I'm sorry I tried to tell you what to do earlier.'

He smiled up at her. 'And I'm sorry I was so sharp with you. You meant well and you didn't deserve it.'

Honour appeased for both of them, Dominic gazed down at his burden. Kenna Mackenzie was light in his arms. Although she was thin, her small, jutting breasts were firmly fleshed, the nipples like ripened hazelnuts set inside the brown blush of the aureole. Her hips were shapely, the dark triangle of hair at her groin giving just a hint of the delight that lay under it. Long, firmly-muscled legs ended with slim ankles and small, neat feet.

Just before he laid her on the bed, the male in Dominic appreciated Kenna's exquisite loveliness, and reacted accordingly. There was a moment of surprise, for he'd not been with a woman for some time and had learned to control his appetites by keeping himself out of temptation's way. Now, he was being reminded in no uncertain fashion that he was as fallible as the next man, for the sight of this naked young woman had aroused him.

Then he remembered her occupation. He sighed as he ruefully laid her on the towels, wondering what sort of existence he was trying to save her for.

Picking up the cloth he sopped cool water over her warm body, feeling guilty when her stomach hollowed to escape it and she sobbed a protest. The water pooled, then when she took in a breath overflowed over her mound then trickled under her body hair and into the crease. She gave a small shudder and sighed.

He continued with his task and watched her skin begin to contract into goosebumps before he placed a thin sheet over her – for his own sake rather than for Kenna's modesty. When he squeezed water against the burning furnace of her scalp she gave a mouse-like squeak. Her long, dark eyelashes flickered and then she began to shake. Her teeth chattered loudly.

Mairi turned away, tears scalding her eyes. 'I'll go and make you some coffee.'

'Thank you. After that, you can go and get some rest – no . . . I insist,' he said when she was about to protest. 'I don't see the point of us both being tired tomorrow, especially when Evelyn will need looking after. I can call you if I need you.'

The night seemed to be one long uncomfortable blur for Kenna. Her head was filled with bad dreams. She was in a windswept ocean being tossed in the waves. The next minute she was tied at the stake and being prodded by demons with fiery forks. As she writhed in agony the fire was dowsed in a hiss of steam. Perspiration slicked her body.

She protested, lashing out at these creatures. 'Leave me alone . . . I want to die.'

A face appeared, hollowed and gaunt with fatigue, one she had seen before. Grey eyes looked into hers, impaled her. 'You're too stubborn to die and I'm too stubborn to let you.'

'Who are you?' she whispered. 'God?'

He began to laugh, an odd sound that was muffled like bubbles. The next moment she was plunged under water again. But this time it was a calmer flow, like a river. She went with its current until the water became shallower, then she washed up on a bank. The mud was soft and damp under her and she could feel the chill of morning.

On the other side of her eyelids, dark gradually lightened to grey, then to white. All noise had hushed. She wondered if she was dead, because the frantic tension in her body had ebbed, too, and she felt quite peaceful. But her head and neck ached and her mouth was as dry as a bucket full of sand. Her body felt emptied out and cold, so she shivered.

When Kenna opened her eyes she saw Dominic Sterne. Seated in the armchair, his head had lolled to one side as he slept, so his dark hair was half-buried in a blue brocade cushion. It must have restricted his breathing, because he gave a little snore and moved. She stared at him for a long time, at his high cheekbones and generous mouth, slightly open as he breathed. There were bruised patches under his eyes, yet he was handsome in a lean, taut sort of way.

Kenna made a noise in her throat, like a grunt. His eyelashes fluttered open and he stretched his long body, making pleasurable little noises at the ease it afforded him. She must have come into his vision then, for he stared at her, but without comprehension for a moment. Awareness hit him. His eyes began to shine and a smile swept across his face as he completed his stretch, then he relaxed. 'Good morning, Miss Mackenzie.'

Kenna realized she was almost naked. Giving a little cry she reached out for the blanket, but her groping hand found only a damp sheet. Then she found she couldn't breathe and she choked and struggled for air, her fingers clawing at her throat.

He was with her in an instant. 'Calm yourself, Kenna. Lean back a little, relax. That's right. Try to breathe naturally through your nose while I remove the tube from inside you. It will take just a moment.'

She gagged a couple of times, then coughed and spluttered when some water came up. A minute or so later she was wrapped warmly in a soft blanket and seated in the chair he'd just vacated. His warmth still lingered on the cushions and she snuggled into it.

He seated himself on a footstool. 'How do you feel?'

'Empty, as if I could float away,' she whispered. 'And my head is aching something fierce.'

'No wonder. You've been fighting a dangerously high fever and convulsions for the last couple of days and nights. I thought we might lose you.'

'And now?'

'You're far from well, but your condition has stabilized and you're out of danger. It will take at least four weeks to clear up the congestion in your lungs. In the meantime we can begin to build up your strength.'

Her eyes sought his. 'Why are you doing this?'

The expression in his eyes told her he was asking himself exactly the same question. Finally he shrugged, then grinned at her. 'Because I was there when you needed me, and because I took an oath to preserve life.'

'Is that all?'

'No. I wouldn't have liked myself if I'd walked away, and would have wondered for the rest of my life what had happened to you. Had there been a bed at the hospital I'd have taken you there.'

'But one might have become vacant since. Have you enquired?'

'No,' and he chuckled. 'I told you at the beginning I needed to practise. I'm enjoying having a patient to look after.'

'A good enough reason, and an honest one. Thank you, Dominic Sterne.'

She'd remembered his name. A good sign. 'There's no need to keep thanking me.' He stood. 'I'll go and ask Mairi to come up to see to your bed and find you a clean nightgown. After than I'm going to try and start loosening the poisons in your lungs with inhalations of steam and by using the cupping technique.'

'What's that?'

'It's something I learned from my father, who was also a doctor. I'll cup my hands and bang them against your back and sides, like so.' He demonstrated on the side of the bed. 'The percussion of air against your body will help loosen the congestion, though some doctors consider it a waste of time. But I have time to waste at the moment and I can guarantee it won't harm you.'

The whiteness of the light and the quietness puzzled her. 'Why is everything so bright and hushed?'

'It snowed last night.'

'Ah,' she said. 'I dreamed of devils with pitchforks. Then when I woke up everything was so white and peaceful I thought I was in Heaven . . . and then I saw you asleep in the chair and knew I wasn't.'

He chuckled. 'A rude awakening, indeed.'

'Indeed it wasn't. I was relieved to see you. I've no desire to find out what's on the other side yet, and I knew you were alive because you gave a little snore. You looked nice, like a sleeping child. I had an urge to kiss your cheek.'

He appeared to be slightly abashed for a moment, then ran a hand over his morning crop of whiskers, and chuckled, making light of it. 'More like a baby ape with these on my chin. I'll send Mairi up to tend to your bed, shall I?' Stooping, he brushed his mouth across her forehead, then he was gone.

Warmth had curled into Dominic's stomach at her words, for Kenna's own vulnerability had been achingly apparent to him over the course of her crisis. Had she been left on the streets she'd be dead by now. Her body would be lying unclaimed in the morgue, an object of desire for students eager to bloody their shiny new scalpels by dissecting it.

He put the vision from his mind as he joined Evelyn for breakfast in the warmth of the kitchen. Hamish placed a paw on his knee and beguiled him with a look. Dominic looked round to see if Mairi was watching, then dropped a piece of bacon into the dog's waiting mouth.

Evelyn's eyes sparkled with excitement. 'It's snowing. Will you help me build a snowman after breakfast, Papa?'

'I have to see to Miss Mackenzie and give her some treatment first, but afterwards, I will.'

'Is she feeling better?'

'She's out of danger now.'

'Can I go and see her then?'

'Not yet, Miss Curiosity. She's too weak for visitors, even

little ones like you. I need to build up her strength before she can entertain. And it's "may I", not "can I".'

'May I send her a letter, then?'

'Ah, so you've learned to write, have you?' he teased.

'Only my name. But if I tell you the words you can write them for me.'

He laughed. 'All right, as long as it's a short letter.'

Dear Kenna Mackenzie,

Hamish is a good dog. I really love him and wish he were mine. My dearest papa is looking after you, and he said I'm not allowed to visit you yet. Perhaps in a week's time I'll be allowed.

At first I thought you were my mamma's dead spirit. It's exciting to have a guest in the house, and I hope you soon get well so I can visit you. Don't forget to eat all your food. It will give you strength and help you get better.

Yours truly,
Evelyn Sterne (Miss)

PS. You can write back if you like.

Kenna smiled at Dominic. 'Did she really think I was her mamma's spirit?'

He nodded. 'Her mother died when she was two, giving birth to our son. He was stillborn.'

'I'm so sorry.'

'Harriet was a good woman. Turn over on your stomach, would you?' He began to pound against her back and sides with his cupped hands. The sensation wasn't unpleasant, and after a while he stopped and said, 'Take some deep breaths in and out, would you?'

She was unprepared for the spasm of coughing that attacked her, and she felt drained when it was over.

He waited until she caught her breath, then said, 'We'll repeat this procedure before dinner tonight.'

She grimaced. 'Must we?'

'We must. I know it's unpleasant and you're embarrassed by the procedure, but it's doing some good because it's helping you to expel—'

'I might be a laymen in the medical world, but I really don't need to be told the effect your treatment had on me.'

His chuckle was unexpected. 'Sorry, I'm used to explaining procedures to students. I must go now, I promised Evelyn I'd help her to build a snowman.'

She laughed. 'You can build snowmen as well as save lives?'

'I'm a man of many skills. Can you manage some breakfast?'

To her surprise, Kenna felt hunger in her, and she nodded.

There was a small bowl of oats, a glass of milk, and some toasted bread spread with butter. She drank the milk, but the edge of her hunger was blunted before she could finish the porridge. Overcome by lassitude, she lay back on her pillow and listened to the fire crackle in the grate.

'Poor wee girl,' Mairi muttered to herself as she took away the tray with the remains of the breakfast. 'It might have been kinder to let you die, for what will be become of you after the doctor's gone?'

What would become of her indeed, Kenna thought. She could not go back to live on the streets. She'd have to go to Robert, eat humble pie and throw herself on his mercy. One thing she knew about him: he would not allow Agnes to dictate to him, wife or not.

Evelyn had watched the comings and goings for two weeks now, and had listened to her father and Mairi talking about Kenna Mackenzie. Curiosity burned in her.

'I'm extremely pleased with Kenna's progress,' her father had said that afternoon, just before he'd gone off to meet one of his colleagues for dinner.

Evelyn had heard the woman and her father talking, though she hadn't been able to make out the words. Sometimes the woman coughed, and sometimes both she and Evelyn's father laughed.

'It's not fair,' she whispered to Hamish. She heard Mairi coming up the stairs and leaped into bed. Hamish tried to flatten himself under the eiderdown. 'Don't make a noise,' she instructed.

Placing a tray on the dressing table, Mairi brought Evelyn

over one of two glasses of milk. Her eyes lit on the lump under the mattress and she frowned, saying sternly, 'That dog has to sleep in the kitchen, you know that.' Her plump arms gathered Hamish up and she scolded him. 'Now look what you've done, made me go all the way down to the kitchen again.' She went off grumbling at Hamish and leaving the other glass of milk on the tray.

It would soon go cold. Seizing her chance, Evelyn jumped out of bed, picked up the tray and headed towards the room where their guest slept. She put the tray on the hall table whilst she opened the door, and her eyes were drawn to the woman in the bed. Evelyn sucked in a deep breath. She had lovely pale skin, and looked pretty with her hair spread all over the pillow.

Picking up the tray Evelyn carried it in, being careful not to spill the milk.

The woman gazed in astonishment at her, then she smiled in a way that made Evelyn like her immediately. 'You're not old enough to be a nurse, so you must be Miss Evelyn Sterne. I'm Kenna Mackenzie.'

Shyness crept over Evelyn. 'Mairi forgot about your milk, so I thought I'd bring it before it gets cold. You won't tell my papa I visited, will you?'

'Not unless he asks. Thank you for the letter. It was kind of you to think of me. You have a very pretty name.'

'It was my mamma's second name. She's in Heaven. Have you got a mamma, Miss Mackalenzie?'

The woman smiled at her. 'My mamma went to Heaven when I was small, just like yours did. Perhaps you'd like to call me Kenna? It would be much easier.'

'Papa said it's rude to call grown-ups by their first name, but you can call me Evelyn if you like. Is that why Papa found you on the street, because your mamma died and you had nothing to eat?'

The woman hesitated. 'No, dear, it was because my sister died and her husband married again, and I had no family left to look after me. You'd best go now because I'm tired.' When Evelyn reached the door the woman said. 'Is Hamish behaving himself?'

Evelyn felt a smile speed across her face. 'Oh, yes . . . he's the best dog in the whole world. I wish he were mine.'

Hearing the kitchen door open and close, she said hastily, 'I've got to go to bed before I get into trouble with Mairi.' She skipped off as fast as she was able and was sitting up in bed drinking her milk by the time the housekeeper arrived.

Mairi looked around her. 'D'you ken where I put that tray?'

Finishing her milk with a gulp, Evelyn swiped her tongue across her upper lip for the froth, then crossed her fingers and said, 'Perhaps you took it into Miss Mackalenzie's room?'

Mairi shook her head. 'I can't remember doing that. I must be getting forgetful in my old age.'

Because she'd deceived Mairi, Evelyn guiltily hugged her tight after she received a goodnight kiss. 'If Papa died and I was left all by myself you wouldn't throw me out on the street, would you, Mairi?'

'What an odd thing to ask me. Of course I wouldn't. If I couldnae find your kin, I'd look after you as though you were my own bonnie bairn, so don't you go worrying your head about it.'

'I wouldn't like to be a beggar on the street without anybody left in the world to love me. That's what happened to Miss Mackalenzie, so it was good that Papa found her, and brought her home,' she said sleepily.

'You must have listened to other people's conversations to have learned all that.' Tears came into Mairi's eyes.

'Oh, no, she told me herself.' Evelyn gave her a hug. 'Don't cry, Mairi. We should be happy that Papa saved her life.'

Mairi's eyes narrowed. 'Aye, girl, that may be so.' But would the good doctor swallow his pride and come to believe it? Mairi wondered.

After that, Evelyn never seemed to get the chance to visit their guest again, though she could hear an occasional bout of coughing. Then, even that stopped.

'Has Miss Mackalenzie died and gone to Heaven?' she asked her father, who was packing books into a wooden crate, ready for when they moved. He smiled and shook his head.

That same evening Kenna came downstairs to eat with the family in the warmth of the kitchen. Hamish wagged his tail at her, but he'd attached himself firmly to Evelyn now and stayed by the girl's side, watching her every move with adoring eyes. He followed her everywhere, his tail wagging back and forth.

'I understand you've met my daughter before, Kenna,' Dominic said, his eyes twinkling.

'How did you know?' Evelyn said indignantly.

'Mairi told me. She was worried that Miss Mackenzie could have passed her illness on to you.'

Looking at the crestfallen face of the child, Kenna said, 'I'm sorry, Evelyn. I didn't mean to break a confidence, but when your papa asked me if you'd visited it would have been wrong of me to tell him a lie.'

'It's all right, Miss Mackalenzie.' Seemingly infused with the confidence to handle the situation, Evelyn climbed on her father's lap and hugged him tight. 'You're not cross, are you, Papa?'

'Not this time, because no harm was done. Remember this, though, young lady. The next time I say no to you it's because I love you and don't want you to suffer any harm.'

A loud kiss landed on his cheek. 'I love you too, Papa. You're the best papa in the whole wide world.'

Dominic caught Kenna's eyes and they shared a smile at this blatant demonstration of feminine adoration. When the smile became one of shared intimacy the breath caught in Kenna's throat and she tore her gaze away, thinking that Dominic's wife must have absolutely adored him.

Later, Kenna realized that she too had come to adore this quiet man, and it would tear her heart out when they had to part.

Robert had decided to leave Agnes in a boarding house in London.

'I don't see the point of paying both our train fares back to Edinburgh. I'll be back in London within a couple of weeks to finish our holiday. If I'm not, it'll be your fault for throwing Kenna out. I'm hoping she's gone back home. She knows where the spare key is kept.'

'It was you who said you'd throw her out. How was I to know you didnae mean it?'

Gazing at the rumpled bed, Robert wondered what he'd

ever seen in Agnes. Apart from the fact she was good-looking, she'd merely been a convenience afforded to him through his late wife's illness. All the same, he felt compelled to lie to her. 'It was a threat to get her to wed Rory Challoner, you fool. I've written to the man telling him to come for her on the first day of March, so I'll have to be there. What will I do if he turns up and finds I'm not there, and neither is his intended bride?'

'She wouldn't have gone far. Kenna's nae tough enough to fend for herself. If she's not at home she'll likely be in the poorhouse. It'll teach her a lesson she'll never forget.'

And make her more malleable to the marriage. 'Aye, there's that to it, but I'm worried about the lass. In all conscience I have to find out if the girl's all right. Her father was good to me and he trusted me with the welfare of both his daughters.'

'More fool him, then. After what I overheard you saying to Kenna I certainly can't trust you any more. Just remember that I'm your wife.'

Not for much longer, Robert thought, his hands twitching as the urge to strangle her hit him. 'You don't think I'm going to spoil Kenna's chance of making a good marriage, do you? Besides which, I was married to her sister, so cohabitation would be against the law. Rory Challoner's no fool. He'll expect her to be delivered intact, and he'll also expect me to hand over her fortune. No, Agnes, you're not coming to Edinburgh with me, and that's that.' Stooping, he kissed her pouting lips and laughed. 'I'm paying you a compliment. You'd prove to be too much of a distraction when I need to keep a cool business head on my shoulders.'

Predictably, Agnes gave him an arch smile and allowed the sheet to fall from her body. The sight of her didn't stir him at all. Her attraction had gone – and so had the blacksmith, who he'd paid to perform the ceremony over his anvil. Gently he pulled the sheet back over her breasts. 'There's no need to act the whore at the moment. I haven't got time, since I have a train to catch. I'll be back early in March, whether I find Kenna or not.'

'I wonder what she'll do when she learns that most of her inheritance is gone.'

Robert didn't answer, just shrugged into his tweed overcoat, placed his top hat on his head then picked up his documents satchel and a travelling bag. 'I'll leave my trunk with you until I come back. I've paid the rent in advance for the month, and there's some spending money on the dressing table.' He smiled again and gave her a final kiss goodbye. 'Remember, you're a respectable married woman now, Mrs Gilmore, so make sure you conduct yourself accordingly.'

Robert stepped out into the foggy air and strode towards the cab stand at the end of the road without looking back. 'Euston Station,' he told the driver.

Five

'Check.'

'And mate.'

Dominic chuckled when a pair of sparkling amber eyes gazed at him in triumph. 'You're too good for me, Kenna. Who taught you to play chess?'

'My father. He was the lawyer, Andrew Mackenzie. He died five years ago.'

Silence followed her words and she gazed up at him. 'What is it, Dominic?'

'When we first met you told me your sister had died and your brother-in-law's new wife had thrown you into the street.'

'That's what happened. After my father died Robert took control of my inheritance and became my guardian. When Jeanne died Robert inherited everything. He hired Agnes to look after Jeanne, but it was soon clear that they'd *known* each other before.'

'And they threw you out?'

'Agnes did. Robert backed her up.'

Dominic's amused expression told Kenna he was indulging her. 'For what reason?'

'Robert had arranged for me to marry a southern uplander when I was eighteen, a laird. I refused and told him to come for me when I was twenty, and Robert said I was not to go back home unless I agreed to the marriage.'

Dominic raised an eyebrow and grinned.

'It's true. Besides, Robert had made it clear that he . . . *liked* me.'

'Liked you? In what way?'

She frowned, for it was obvious Dominic didn't believe a word she was saying. 'Do you have to act so dense? In the way most men like most women, I imagine. I reminded him of Jeanne, he said. He loved my sister, but she was frail. Whereas I'm not.'

'What did your sister die of?'

'I'm not sure. She had stomach trouble, a growth inside her. She was in a great deal of pain when she died.' Noting the sceptical look in his eyes her hackles rose. 'You didn't believe me when we first met, so I don't expect you to believe me now. Let's drop the subject. I can't bear the thought of my sister's memory being sullied.'

He placed the chess set to one side. 'I didn't say I didn't believe you, Kenna. It just seems to be a flimsy reason to throw you out of your home. If this brother-in-law is your legal guardian then he's responsible for your welfare. Why did he allow his wife to do this?'

She heaved a sigh. 'It's all very involved. He wasn't there at the time – and although I tracked him down to a public house he was drunk and abusive. I didn't go back because I wanted him to worry. There had been an argument about me before. I'd asked for my inheritance to do what I liked with, you see. I thought I might be able to travel to England, buy a small house and teach music, or something. When he stormed out of the house Agnes drove me out, with the point of a kitchen knife. I slept in somebody's garden shed that night. It was so cold.'

His lips twitched. 'You have a vivid imagination. Have you ever thought of writing a novel?' Her cheeks had heated during the exchange. Now he gazed at her with concern in his eyes. 'You're not feeling feverish again, are you? Fever can cause people to hallucinate.'

'Damn you, Dominic Sterne – don't you recognize the signs of a good old temper tantrum coming on?'

He fetched his stethoscope and gazed calmly at her. 'All the same, I'd better make sure you're not about to have a relapse. Open the buttons on your nightgown.'

'They're open.'

'Lean forward, then. You should know the routine by now.'

She did, until her head was almost against his shoulder. His arm slid down the back of the nightdress and the stethoscope touched against her back. She automatically took breaths, but he was taking his time, being thorough. Barely an inch away from her mouth was the tantalizing curve of his jaw where it joined his ear. There was an irresistible urge inside her to place a kiss there. She wondered how he'd react if she did.

'Good,' he said, and she gave a tiny chuckle.

He withdrew his arm, his eyes engaging hers. 'Why the laughter?'

'You answered a question I was thinking.'

'Which was?'

'I was wondering how you'd react if I kissed your ear.' She couldn't believe she'd said that, and her eyes widened. 'It was as if you read my mind.'

'It's possible you may have read mine.'

Her heart began to thump. Had she heard that correctly?

As if he hadn't said it at all, he advised her, 'You seem to be in good health now, Kenna. You'll tire easily for a while, and will need to regain a little more weight.' He slid the stethoscope inside the nightgown and brought it to rest just over her heart. 'That's beating very nicely.'

She plucked it from his fingers and spoke into it. 'Liar, it's jumping about like a frog in a ditch. If you hide behind this thing again I'll strangle you with it. Did I read your mind?'

His fingers accidentally brushed over her nipple as he removed his hand from inside the fabric. He made no apology, just grinned as he pulled the instrument from his ears. Grey eyes engaged hers. 'Let's just say I'm not as immune to you as I should be, Kenna. But in a week or two I'll be gone so I can't afford to get involved in a love affair. We'd better stick strictly to chess from now on.'

'You're a poor loser, Dominic. I was only offering to kiss you on the ear, not indulge in a love affair,' she grumbled when he reached the door.

His hearing was acute for he turned, two strides bringing him back to the bed. Laughter danced like the devil in his eyes as he sat on the edge and turned his head slightly. 'In that case, kiss my ear then, and be damned to you! The rest can remain in my imagination.'

Her mouth found the little hollow just under and behind his ear, and her lips touched against it with the gentlest of caresses. She felt him shiver, then he turned his head and brushed his lips across her cheek until he engaged her mouth. She wanted to die from the rush of pleasure his kiss created inside her.

He pushed her gently back until she relaxed against the pillow, said, 'Kenna, if you have any regard for me at all you must keep it to yourself.'

'How can I not hold you dear to my heart when you saved my life?'

'You needn't be embarrassed about what you feel. It's natural under the circumstances. It's gratitude, and I don't want you to mistake it for anything else.'

She touched her palm against his face and was rewarded when he cupped his hand around it and turned to kiss the palm. Then he entwined her hands into his.

'Dominic,' she murmured, 'what are your feelings towards me?'

He was sorry she'd asked, for his feelings were highly ambivalent. She raised the most tender of emotions inside him, the need to care for and protect her. And she raised feelings that reminded him that he'd long needed a mate with whom he could share the most intimate of loving relationships.

But not this mate, this woman he'd scraped from the streets of Edinburgh and brought back to life, for only the best would suffice for his daughter. Yet part of him wanted to investigate and find the truth in her tale of woe. But he knew from experience that street women were accomplished liars, and deep in his heart he didn't want to prove Kenna's story false. He'd rather leave with the illusion that she'd learn from her mistake and go on to live a productive life.

He could take advantage of her now, slide under the blankets of this bed where he'd once been a dutiful husband to Harriet, a woman he'd never seen naked.

But he shouldn't compare this exquisite girl with Harriet. The two were nothing alike, one so pious and worthy, the other . . .?

He gazed into the glowing amber eyes of this temptress, and the feeling that he'd met her somewhere before came on him again. But the memory was illusive. No . . . she was nothing like Harriet, and no – it could not be this girl . . .

He didn't want to spoil this moment with the ugly names her profession attracted. Yet because of it he wanted to enjoy her while he could – then he could walk away without conscience.

She'd asked what his feelings were. He skimmed the surface of them, refusing to expose the deeper levels to himself. 'You're a beautiful liar, you amuse me and I like you a lot. I'd be lying if I said I didn't have any feelings except those of a doctor towards his patient, and under different circumstances . . . But you're right, Kenna, I am a poor loser. I should have just left it as a kiss on the ear,' he said, and was gone.

'And I'm definitely damned,' she whispered, pressing her hands against her glowing cheeks and wondering what it was about Dominic that made her be so bold.

The snow had melted away and the evening was crisp and dry. Dominic's household goods were packed. Most of the furniture had been sold with the house, except for his desk and chair, which had been crated for the journey.

Evelyn had gone to stay the night with Mairi's daughter and her granddaughter, who was nearly the same age as Evelyn and was hosting a farewell tea for her, an important engagement on Evelyn's social calendar judging by her insistence on wearing ribbons in her hair.

Now and again Hamish took up position on the chair, his front feet on the back rest as he peered out of the window to check the street for signs of Evelyn's return. He gave yawning sighs and grunts of discontent as he waited. His body now filled out, he was a handsome dog.

'Evelyn will miss Hamish when we leave,' Dominic said.

'He'll pine for her, I expect.' Kenna's heart suddenly sickened. She would pine for Dominic and Evelyn too, every day for the rest of her life, for she'd grown to love the lonely little girl as much as she loved her father. Blinking tears from her eyes she offered, 'If you'd allow it, Evelyn can take Hamish with her. He's a nice, small size for her, and has a pleasant disposition. You'll just need a basket for him to travel in.'

'But he's your dog.'

'I'd never seen him before the day you rescued us. He was a street stray, like me.'

He stared at her in surprise. 'But Hamish was guarding you.'

'Only because I was covered with food I'd been foraging for.' She laughed when he shuddered. 'I should have told you, I know. But Hamish was lonely. He needed somebody, and I couldn't bear to think of him being left to starve on the street.'

'As we all need someone, Kenna' – he crossed to where she stood, gazing down at her, reflectively – 'How will you manage when I leave?'

Her heart sank at the thought of it, but she told herself she'd get over him in time. She'd have to. She touched his cheek. 'Don't worry. I'll throw myself on the mercy of my imaginary brother-in-law.'

He gave a faint smile. 'I'm being serious. I'm concerned about your future. You can stay here for a few more days until the new owners move in. However, if you want to play games, as your doctor perhaps I should meet this brother-in-law, just to make sure he's aware of his responsibilities regarding you.'

That was the last thing Kenna wanted, even though it would prove to Dominic that she was telling the truth. She might be able to talk Robert around herself, but her brother-in-law would resent taking advice from a stranger.

'Robert's in London. Let's not think about parting, Dominic. You've been more than kind to me, but I'm not your responsibility. Mairi has left us a casserole for dinner. I'll go and heat it.'

He gave her a look that said he was sceptical. She couldn't force him to believe her so didn't try and persuade him further. What was the point when they'd never meet again?

He said, 'We can have the casserole tomorrow. Let's go out to a restaurant and have dinner. It will do you good to have an outing after being cooped up indoors for all this time.'

The dress she was wearing was dark blue. It had a fur-trimmed velvet jacket for warmth. Harriet Sterne had not been a slave to fashion. Her wardrobe was one of subdued colours with a minimum of decoration. The skirts were less full than those of today, but Kenna didn't need corsets and hoops to fit into them with room to spare. She wore her hair parted in the middle and pulled back into a net, for she had no time to arrange anything more elaborate.

Dominic tucked a rug over her knees in the cab.

The restaurant, though small and out of the way, was crowded. They were given a small table in a corner. Oddly, it was the restaurant whose alley had provided her with the ham bone on that fateful day. The meal was a substantial roast, the wine a robust red. A small band played in the corner and the waiter seemed to know Dominic. Several people nodded to him and a couple of men stopped to be introduced. When that happened he didn't encourage them to stop and chat. In fact he made it plain without saying anything that they weren't welcome to intrude. It was sad to think he was ashamed to be seen with her.

'Can we walk home?' she asked, when they got outside.

'Are you sure you won't tire?'

'I'm the healthiest woman in Edinburgh, you've made sure of that. Indeed, I need the exercise.'

He surprised her by saying, 'You're also the most beautiful woman in Edinburgh.'

'Why didn't you want your friends to stay and talk, then?'

He looked surprised. 'Was I that obvious? It was because they were people who would have talked about medical issues, and although I'd normally enjoy that, I wanted to enjoy your company undisturbed.'

His answer brought a smile to her heart.

As they walked home through the darkening night Dominic took her hand and tucked her arm through the crook of his elbow. 'I enjoyed your company tonight, Kenna. I'm going to miss you.'

You don't have to miss me, she wanted to cry out. *Take me south with you!*

The night was clear and provided them with a show of stars, into which the shape of the castle – which had sheltered countless regiments of Scottish fighting men – loomed.

'Tell me about yourself, Dominic,' she murmured.

'You know about me. I'm a widower with one daughter

to care for. Shortly, I'll be taking up practice with a physician and surgeon in Bournemouth.'

'Why Bournemouth? Does your family live there?'

'They do. I grew up in Southampton but my family moved to Bournemouth eight years ago, shortly before my father died. I now have nieces and nephews.'

'What's it like there?'

'It's a small seaside town with a small population made up of mostly the elderly – for the air has therapeutic values. And there are summer visitors who find the sea and sand to be invigorating. But there are plans afoot to attract people to the area, and I believe the town and its people will grow rapidly over the next few years.

'Why did you come to Edinburgh, where doctors are as numerous as fleas on a dog?'

He winced. 'Most are here to train, and there's no finer place. A professor I'd studied under offered me a temporary job, tutoring. He was incurably ill and he arranged for me to marry his daughter, who I'd met on several occasions before. The house belonged to him. When Harriet died I stayed on to fulfil my contract.'

'Did you love Harriet?'

There was a slight hesitation, when she thought he might tell her to mind her own business, for she knew she'd stepped over the boundary of good taste. Then he sighed. 'Not as much as she deserved. Harriet was a good wife and mother and I grew very fond of her. Sometimes, that's better than love.'

'How do you know? Have you ever been in love?'

He laughed. 'When I was thirteen I fell in love with my friend's sister.'

'How old was she?'

'Nineteen, and engaged to a soldier. She scorned my declaration of love, then laughed at me and broke my heart.'

Kenna giggled. 'She must have been insane. What was her name?'

He cast her a sideways look. 'I really can't remember. You're much too inquisitive, you know.'

'How else can you learn about people?' She made a face at him. 'You're quiet, calm and dependable on the surface,

Dominic. But I suspect that you're seething with life and wickedness underneath. You just don't know how to express it.'

'An astute observation, but I must correct one assumption; I do know how to express it but I prefer to control it. Edinburgh is a staid city. A reputation here is hard to live with when you have a responsible position and a child to care for. If you like, I'll dance in the street?'

'Then I'll dance with you. We'd better wait until we're off the main thoroughfare though, if you're frightened we'll be arrested.'

'That's a challenge if ever I heard one.' Taking her in his arms he danced her around in front of some astonished onlookers until they were both laughing.

A group of students cheered and applauded.

Dominic had surprised her, and her next words were more of a heartfelt plea than a question. 'Oh, why are you leaving Edinburgh?'

'Apart from the need to return home, I have the urge to put into practise what I've been trained to do. Evelyn is lonely. So am I. You must have noticed that she's begun to attach herself to you.'

Kenna swallowed a lump in her throat, because she knew what loneliness was like. 'Is that such a bad thing? Evelyn said she wants me to be her mother. I tried to distract her, but she said she loves me. I'm sorry, Dominic. I'm trying not to encourage her, but I don't want to hurt her feelings because I love her too, you know. She's a child who does you credit.'

'We both need family around us. Once Evelyn gets to know and love her grandmother and cousins she'll forget about you. I want her to be settled by the time she attends school.'

His words twisted inside her like a knife. 'I won't forget you so easily. I hope you'll both be happy, and I'll think of you often.'

'Thank you.' He squeezed her hand and they walked on in companionable silence.

When they reached home Hamish fell upon them with welcoming yaps, turning himself inside out. Shedding her jacket, Kenna fed him. He settled down, curled up in his basket within the warm glow the kitchen stove put out.

Dominic built up the fire in the drawing room, opened the bottle of wine he'd bought at the restaurant and poured them both a glass.

'I'm already light-headed,' she told him.

'I don't usually have that effect on people.' He fished in his waistcoat pocket and brought out a tissue-wrapped package. 'I've bought you a gift, a token to remember us by.'

'As long as it's not a stethoscope.'

His laughter joined hers as he unwrapped a gold bracelet. 'See, it's a magic bracelet. I've had all our names and the date we met engraved inside it – and our names are joined by sprigs of rosemary for remembrance so you'll always think of us when you wear it.'

She turned her eyes up to his, laughing with the happiness of receiving such a gift. 'Even Hamish has been immortalized.'

'It was Evelyn's idea.' Picking up her hand Dominic slid the bracelet on to her wrist. He still held her hand cupped in his, and the fingers of his other hand traced over the lines. 'If you're ever in need of a meal again, you can always sell it.'

The tension between them stretched. So this was goodbye, she thought. She had nothing to give Dominic to remember her by. But then, he'd shown no interest in wanting to remember her, until now.

She had herself, she thought. Dominic wanted her, she could sense the desire in him. Why should she save herself for a stranger, a husband she didn't want and didn't care about? If she married Rory Challoner he would get her inheritance. No doubt she'd bear him children. And she'd love those children, because they'd be hers as well. They would need her, and would love her in return. Perhaps it wouldn't be so bad.

But she'd rather surrender her innocence as a gift to the one she loved. Dominic was a gentleman, but not so much a gentleman that he wouldn't take her into his bed if she encouraged him. 'I'd rather starve than sell the bracelet.'

He gazed up at her and sighed. 'I know, Kenna.'

Now she'd thought it she found the words, and they left her mouth as a plea. 'You don't need to fight what you're feeling, Dominic. I feel the same.'

A smile curved, his eyes met hers and he raised her hand to his lips. 'Am I so damned obvious?'

Obvious? Never! He'd sneaked up on her like a fox. She shivered when his lips brushed against her palm, shivered even more when his mouth closed over hers. *Now* he was obvious, his body warm against her, thighs firm, his strength and need all too apparent when he finally lifted his head to whisper against her hair in a defeated manner, 'Will you allow me this one night with you?'

She'd give him her life if he needed it, and she nodded.

He took a half-step back and began to undo the buttons on her bodice, stopping to place a kiss against the flesh he uncovered. The intimacies grew bolder, then she was down to the thin cotton chemise she wore next to her skin. He took the pins from her hair and ran his hands through it, lifting it from the scalp so it tumbled over her shoulders.

Hardly able to breathe with the nervous excitement she was experiencing, Kenna gave a little groan when he touched each sensitive breast with the tip of his tongue.

Suddenly, he picked her up and headed for the stairs. Kicking open the door to his own room, where the lamp burned low, he placed her on the bed then began to strip off his own clothes. Even in the dim light he appeared lean and well-muscled, and his organ sprang rampant from his linens.

She gazed at him, fascinated by his lack of self-consciouness and inhaling the musky scent of his skin. Her eyes widened with the enormity of what she was about to do, and with the pleasure of seeing a man naked for the first time.

She wanted to touch him, and did, reaching out while he removed the chemise from her body. His skin was taut and silky, hot against her exploring hand.

Now it was his turn to groan. 'Not too much, at once. It's been a long time . . .'

She wanted to tell him it was the first time for her, but she knew he wouldn't believe it and the moment would be lost.

He slipped into bed and pulled her under the covers with him. Mouth filled by kisses that rendered her helpless and trembling, she enjoyed the sensation of his hands and fingers exploring her body. His touch was exquisite. She trembled and fell before it, mewing with delight as she relaxed to him. Then he was astride her, pushing against her wetness and sliding into her. She felt her own resistance, the moment of pain when he pushed firmly through it in a manner that made her draw in a sharp breath.

He withdrew partly, paused and gazed down at her, posing the question, 'Am I going too fast?'

She didn't know whether he was or not, all she knew was that she didn't want it to end. Both of their bodies were slick with perspiration. She smoothed her hands lightly over his taut buttocks, which firmed against her palms as she pulled him back into her, then, because it felt right, she locked her legs around his waist, keeping him there.

Half-hooded, his eyes met hers and he began to move slowly in and out of her. Kenna rose to his rocking movement. Then his eyes closed and so did hers as the pace increased. Towards the end his breath came in harsh gasps and she arched towards him, shuddering as waves of sensation overtook her. There was a prolonged groan of pleasure from both of them and he relaxed against her.

'Hell, that was over too soon.' The chuckle he gave was one of relief as he pressed a kiss against her hairline. Rolling on to his side he cuddled her loosely against him for a while. She liked the feel of him naked, of being in his arms. She touched his hair and traced over his face with a finger. He took it in his mouth, sucked.

Instantly her body began to react. Soon they were engaged in a much more intimate and prolonged lead up to the explosive heights of passion.

Afterwards, his voice licked seductively against her ear. 'Perhaps I should take you to Bournemouth with me.'

Her heart leaped.

'I could set you up in a little house and dress you in silks and satins. It might shock the residents, though.'

Her heart sank again with a bang, and she felt like dying. Was that all the regard Dominic held her in? He still thought of her as a street woman, one who sold her body. She wouldn't sell herself to any man, especially him. The intimacy she'd allowed him had been motivated by love.

Even so, she was tempted by the thought of being with him. But what about afterwards, when he'd tired of her – what then? And what if they produced children between them? They'd be bastards, shunned by society. Better she wed Rory Challoner. At least then her children would have a father's name to give them pride in their existence. The thought grew on her and she convinced herself it was right.

Downstairs, the clock struck three.

Waiting until Dominic was sound asleep she gently kissed his cheek and whispered against his ear, 'Remember, I will love you always, Dominic.' Carefully, she untangled herself from his loose embrace and eased out of their nest.

Once in her own room she dressed in the clothes she'd arrived in, now washed and repaired. Creeping downstairs she gathered up her discarded clothing, took it back up to hang neatly in the wardrobe. Best not to leave the garments downstairs for Mairi to draw a conclusion from. The housekeeper didn't miss much. Besides, they were the clothes of Dominic's former wife, not a future mistress.

As she rumpled the bed covers so Mairi wouldn't suspect what had taken place between them, Kenna thought about how Dominic had taken her into his own bed, avoiding the one that had belonged to his wife. He'd thought her a street woman to begin with. Her behaviour had now confirmed it for him.

Quietly, Kenna let herself out of the front door. It was raining outside, a light drizzle that merged with the tears trickling down her face. She ached where Dominic had pushed through the barrier of her maidenhood. His passion hadn't allowed him to even notice it. But oh . . . how she wanted more of him.

Stop your weeping, she told herself sternly, scrubbing her tears away with her sleeve. *You made the decision, now you'll have to live with it.*

But she'd miss him, and she'd miss Evelyn, the little girl she'd grown to love.

She stole through the streets in the early hours of the

morning, frightening a couple of cats, but seeing nobody. There was a sense of going into the unknown to the morning. It was too early for workers, too late for drunks. Her former home in Ainsley Place was in darkness. Were Robert and Agnes still away? Retrieving the key from under a loose flagstone she quietly let herself in.

She should have come here sooner, before her heart had been given to Dominic.

The darkness didn't bother her. She'd grown up here and knew every corner, every snap of wood, loose floorboard and creaking stair. The tick of every clock was a comforting sound, as were the scrabbling feet of the mice in the attic. The sad feel of the spaces bothered Kenna, though. Those she'd loved had died here, but they'd left no room for her, the youngest of the family, to join them. She felt alienated. Robert, with his charm, had sensed an opportunity. He'd walked into their lives and taken it all, and nobody but herself had seen it happening. And what Robert got his hands on, he kept.

She should warn Rory Challoner about him, she thought, then gave a quiet laugh. The laird was just as bad. He only wanted Kenna for the money that came with her. Well, he wouldn't get a bargain, she'd made sure of that. Dominic would remain a secret she kept close to her heart, no matter what he thought of her now.

Standing there listening to the noise within the silence Kenna sensed that somebody else occupied the house, for the clock on the mantelpiece had been wound. There was a prolonged snore, then a slight creak of bedsprings as somebody turned over. *Robert!* she thought.

She stomped loudly into the hall and up the stairs, and before she went into her room and locked the door, yelled furiously into the darkness, 'You've won!'

She heard the scrape of a match coming from along the hall, Robert's curse as he tripped over something, and his door opening. The light from a candle flickered along the crack under her door.

'Who's down there?' he shouted. 'Show yourself!'

'Nobody's down there. Go back to bed,' she said from her side of the door panel.

He rattled the door handle. 'Where the hell have you been, Kenna? I've been looking for you for over a week. I was about to report your disappearance to the police.'

'You knew where I was, since the pair of you threw me out.' A sob caught in her throat, despite her anger. 'Imagine that, Robert. That upstart you call your wife throwing me out of the house I grew up in, and you backing her decision.' She unlocked the door and gazed at him, full of fight now she was better. 'Where is she? I've got something to say to her.'

'Agnes is still in London. I was worried sick about you. You knew where the spare key was kept; why didn't you come home? You know I wouldn't have turned you away, despite what I said. Damnit, Kenna, I was drunk, and I promised Jeanne I'd look after you, see you settled.'

'I was too frightened to come home after Agnes threatened me with a knife. Then I was taken ill. I had to sleep in someone's shed, then a mouldy old house that was falling down . . . and I caught a cold which turned into pneumonia. The doctor said I'm lucky to be alive.'

'I enquired at the poorhouse and the morgue, but didn't think of the hospital.' His voice was contrite enough to convince her he was sorry, but then, he'd always been good at fooling people. 'I'm so sorry, Kenna. I'm relieved you're back. Rory Challoner will come to claim you the day after tomorrow. If you don't want to marry him I'll find someone else.'

What was the point when it would still be a stranger? 'No, I'll wed him if he'll still have me, Robert. It's only fair, because he's waited two years to get his hands on my inheritance.'

'Aye, that may be so, but he'll only receive the accumulated interest as a lump sum. After that the pair of you will get an annual amount until you reach the age of twenty-five, when the bulk of it will be handed over. I'm so pleased you've returned. Of course he'll still have you – there's no reason why he shouldn't, is there?'

'Of course not.' She feigned a yawn. 'Don't twist me up with discussions of finance. I need to sleep.'

'Come and give me a hug, then. I don't want us to be bad friends.'

She shut the door in his face and turned the key in the lock. 'I'd rather not.'

'You don't have to lock the door.'

'Aye, Robert, I do. Everything you do is motivated by your own self-interest. You made inappropriate advances to me once before.' She managed a wry smile at her own hypocrisy, and when he began to speak, said loudly, 'I don't want to hear your excuses about that again. I'll just say that if you'd been at all interested in my welfare you wouldn't have left me on the streets and gone off to London with Agnes in the first place.'

'How was I to know you wouldn't come back? I left money in the dresser for you to buy food with.'

'You were hoping I'd die so you could have my inheritance for yourself. You got me to sign all sorts of papers when I was young. One of them was a will, I imagine. Why else would you have enquired at the morgue? So you see, I can no longer trust you.'

Impatience filled his voice. 'Of course there was a will. You left everything to your sister, remember.'

'And Jeanne made you her next of kin, as you knew she would. It would have been very convenient if I'd died, and I'm not going to take any chances.'

'You're being irrational, Kenna. Why should I want to kill you? We'll talk in the morning.'

'We're through talking, Robert. I'm going to do what you want, marry Rory Challoner. Let that be the end of our association. After that, I hope never to see you again.' Pulling off her shoes she slid under the eiderdown and didn't relax until she heard Robert shuffle off, then his door slam shut.

She pulled the eiderdown over her head and thought of Dominic, and the intimacies of love she'd shared with him. Her heart began to ache. After the kindness he'd shown her, she should have left him a note. What would he think of her when he woke, to find she had gone off without a word?

Six

Dominic had grown much too fond of Kenna, so perhaps it was better this way.

Instinct told him it wasn't as he stared at the smear of blood on the sheet. He must have scratched her in his hurry, or perhaps she'd scratched him. He smiled to himself. She'd certainly been passionate. Then again, perhaps she'd begun to menstruate.

'Damn her,' he muttered and, picking up her crumpled chemise he stared down at it, remembering her body, so warm, pliant and giving, then recalled how it felt to be inside her, sharing her passion and joined in love with a sharp jolt of desire.

Love?

'Yes, *love*,' he growled, and wondered how the hell he had managed to fall in love with someone like Kenna Mackenzie.

That morning when he'd woken and reached out for her only to find her side of the bed empty, a yawning pit of loneliness had opened up inside him. Without even looking he'd known that she'd gone. This morning – this *terrible* morning – Dominic had forced himself to realize the truth: that despite his reservations over Kenna Mackenzie's unsuitability, he *was* in love with her and willing to give her the benefit of the doubt. If he'd married her and taken her with him to Hampshire nobody would have been any the wiser about her background anyway.

'A parting tumble under the sheets was all my good intentions were worth,' he said out loud, kicking himself for his lapse into self-pity. All right, so he hadn't offered her marriage last night, but as good as. Only a fool would reject his offer of a comfortable home and three square meals a day, then return to a life that would bring nothing but degradation.

Dominic was the first to admit that his pride had taken a beating. Kenna was well educated and presentable, even though down on her luck. He thought she might not have been on the streets for very long, since she hadn't been all that experienced at pleasuring a man, and he knew she was clean.

As for her tale of woe, he still felt uneasy about it. Despite her plausibility he hadn't considered the possibility that her story was anything more than something her imagination had conjured up to impress him with. He'd always been aware of the regard she held him in and had enjoyed being her knight in shining armour.

'Ah, vanity, vanity,' he murmured.

He brought the chemise up to his face and inhaled her scent. Perhaps she'd told him the truth. Perhaps there was something to the story she'd offered him. He hadn't bothered to remember the details, had just let them filter through his natural scepticism and wash over him.

He sighed, examining himself in the mirror in the grey morning light. His eyes saw a dark-haired, lovesick fool who needed a shave. He'd taken Kenna's gratitude for granted, had seen her as fair game and had used her for his own ends. Now he'd lost her.

But had he lost her? Perhaps she'd woken during the night and simply removed herself to her own bed.

He nearly tripped over his feet in his rush to get to her room. The bed was rumpled, probably to put Mairi off the scent. He threw open the wardrobe doors. The interior smelled fusty. Rows of Harriet's gowns hung there. He stared at them, recognizing the one he'd stripped from Kenna Mackenzie's body the evening before – an action Harriet would have objected strongly to. The chest of drawers contained neatly folded garments. It was as if she'd never been here. He was puzzled that Kenna hadn't taken some of the clothing with her.

She couldn't have gone far though. He smiled to himself. He'd stay on an extra couple of days and try to find her.

Now Kenna had made up her mind to wed she couldn't wait to leave Edinburgh. Neither could Robert, it seemed, for he made no attempt to provide food except for some bread, milk, cheese and butter, plus the oats already in the larder. They ate dinner early, at a nearby restaurant in Princess Street.

She asked for her allowance and was rewarded with the necessary coinage with bad grace. Robert was restless, prowling about the place and muttering to himself.

When February ticked over into March, Kenna packed her trunk. With the changeover came a blustery wind driving bands of cold rain before it. But Dominic's skill had completely healed her lungs, and although she was not yet up to her previous weight she felt healthy and strong.

Rory Challoner arrived for her at midday on the second of March. He barely glanced at her with his icy blue eyes before pushing past her and shaking hands with Robert, who said, somewhat sourly, 'You're a day late, Challoner. I thought you weren't coming.'

'Aye, it snowed and I missed the train. But I gave you my word, and that should be a good enough indication of my intention. Let's get this business over with. The girl looks skinny. Is she ill?'

'She's been suffering from a cold on the chest, but she's over it now. Kenna, wait in the kitchen,' Robert ordered. 'You can make us some tea.'

'I'd rather have a dram of that whisky sitting on your desk. It'll help keep out the cold.'

After a while Kenna heard shouting coming from the study and went into the hall to listen at the door.

'The only reason I'm taking the girl off your hands is because of her inheritance. It's the money I need, not a woman.'

'Aye, I know, but one goes with the other and I've got to be assured that Kenna will be respected.'

'What d'you think I am, mon?' Rory shouted. 'She'll be treated the same as any other wife. You didnae tell me her money wouldn't be available until she was twenty-five, though.'

'Her father made the provisions.'

'I didnae hear you tell me that before, mon.'

'For Christ's sake, Challoner, I explained that you'd get the interest and an annual sum until the bulk of her fortune can legally be placed in your hands. If you take my advice, you'll leave it invested after that, because once it's spent, it's gone.'

'When she's my wife I'll decide what's tae be done with it. Call the female in. I want to take a proper look at her before I decide.'

'Kenna,' Robert bawled.

She opened the door and entered the study, hands on hips, her eyes blazing. She told the arrogant uplander, 'Let's get one thing straight, Rory Challoner. As far as men go you're no bargain. Look me over if you wish, but as far as I'm concerned you and your mouldy estate can go to merry hell, and stay there.'

A wary look came to Robert's face. 'Kenna, you promised you'd do as I told you.'

Promises to Robert were made to be broken, and she'd just been warming up. 'Aye, I know, but not if it means being insulted by some hairy-faced, mule-mannered uplander with a bog for a brain. I won't marry any man who doesn't have any respect for me.'

'Will you not, then?' Rory said calmly.

Kenna's hands went to her hips. 'I most certainly won't, you . . . you *mule*!'

A laugh tore from Rory's throat, then another, but his eyes butted hard against hers with a warning that she'd gone far enough. She pressed her lips together.

'I'll take her. But mind you, Robert Gilmore, I'll nae wed the wench until the first interest payment is grasped firmly in my fist.'

Kenna snorted. 'Anyone would think you were doing me a favour instead of the other way around.'

'With a waspish temper like yours, aye, I reckon I am. The trouble with city women is they think too much of themselves with their airs and graces. You need a good slap across your skinny backside.' Leaving Kenna spluttering with repressed anger he turned to Robert. 'You can cover the cost of the journey while I'm here.'

'I'll refund the train fare. As for the interest, that will take another month. I've got to go down to London to convert it into cash, and then it'll be transferred to the Merchant Bank in Edinburgh.' Robert opened a box, counted out some coins and stacked them in a neat pile. He also slid a sheet of paper across the desk. 'Here's your receipt for the interest. All you need to do is take it to the bank in four weeks' time and sign for it.'

Rory's eye's widened when he saw the amount, and he seemed impressed when he nodded. 'Aye, well, it doesn't seem too bad. We'll be wed as soon as this is honoured.'

Kenna stamped her foot. 'The pair of you haven't listened to one word I've said.'

Rory turned. 'I've been listening – and for two years I've waited, like you asked. Now you tell me I'm a bog-brained mule. Well, mebbe I am. But at least I keep my word, else I would nae be here. Let's hear the truth. D'you want to wed me or not, woman?'

'Of course she does,' Robert said.

Kenna glared at him. 'No, I don't want to wed him, but I will, because I haven't got any other choice, have I?' A regret labelled Dominic drifted into her mind.

'Well, at least we have something in common, lassie, and we both know where the other stands,' Rory said with a sigh.

'Then can you at least agree to stop arguing?' Robert said, all charm.

'Aye, I suppose so,' Kenna said ungraciously.

Rory cleared his throat and shuffled his feet in assent.

Robert gazed from one to the other, a smile on his face. 'Good, then let's get on with it. Kenna's luggage is in the hall. I'll go and find a cab while you get your coat and bonnet on, Kenna.'

Rory eyed the trunk and made an attempt at humour. 'You might think I'm a mule, woman, but do you really expect me to carry that bluidy trunk all the way to Glenchallon?'

Anxiety filled her. 'It's everything I own and I don't want to leave it behind. It contains mementoes of my dead sister and parents We can hire a carter when we get off the train, can't we? I've got some money to pay for it.'

He gave a huff of laughter as his eyes slid to hers, brimming with amusement. 'Aye, girl, we won't leave it behind since it's important to you. As for the carter . . . I reckon we'll find one, at that.'

She gave him an uncertain smile, not knowing whether he was teasing her or not. 'Thank you.'

Robert's smile left his face as soon as the cab turned a corner. He hadn't counted on Rory Challoner being a day late and he didn't have much time.

Hurriedly, he packed anything of value into a couple of travelling trunks he brought down from the attic. He gave the house one last check through. His chest of drawers was empty. He threw the rest of the food into the backyard for the rats to eat, after mixing it with what remained of the poison. He threw the packet on top. His suitcase already packed, Robert had ten minutes to spare before the cab came for him.

It took him to a solicitor's office, then waited while he exchanged the house deeds and keys for a sum of money. Robert counted it, then placed it inside a satchel and made out a receipt before handing the solicitor the sum agreed on. The pair smiled and shook hands.

A little while later the cab deposited Robert at the docks, where a clipper out of Boston was loading passengers and luggage for the return journey. He joined the queue going aboard and when he reached the officer on duty, said, 'Bart Parnell.'

The officer on duty gazed at the passenger list. 'Have you got your medical clearance certificate and ticket, Mr Parnell?'

'Aye,' he said, thinking he must get used to his new name as quickly as possible, as he handed them over. It had been easy to assume another's identity, the certification of a dead client who'd been born in the same year as himself. He'd just happened to be a lawyer who'd had nobody to leave his personal fortune to except the church he'd belonged to. The institution had been interested in the property and money, but had ignored the personal aspect that had gone into making the man.

Robert had rummaged through the house first, helping himself to a wallet, identity papers and a family tree. There had been the monogrammed watch, amongst other bits and pieces, which would help to support his new identity.

The officer scrutinized the documents then gazed at him,

his glance assessing. 'A one-way ticket. You're staying in America, then?'

'Aye, there's nothing to keep me in Scotland since my wife died, and we always dreamed of moving to Boston together when she was alive. I hope to set up a law practice, then find myself a good woman and settle down.'

'Perhaps we can talk some more on the journey. Some of the officers run a little poker game in the saloon. You're welcome to join us. Small stakes, of course. It would be bad for business if we relieved the passengers of too much cash. You know, it's possible that I may be able to furnish you with an introduction or two in Boston in return for a good game, if you're interested, Mr Parnell.'

The man's meaning couldn't have been clearer. Robert smiled and held out his hand. It would be handy to have contacts to start with. 'I'm interested. And your name is . . .?'

The man took Robert's hand in a firm grip. 'Second officer Jethro Kester at your service.'

'Thank you, Mr Kester. I'll bear in mind what you've said.'

'Welcome aboard then, Mr Parnell. You've cut it a bit fine, since we sail on the tide in approximately half an hour.'

Robert shrugged. 'Sorry, I was held up. A woman.' He felt a twinge of guilt at what he'd done to Kenna. She'd been the best of the Mackenzies, and he'd always had a soft spot for her, despite what she'd thought of him. Still, by the time the uplander had discovered there was nothing in the bank for him, he'd have probably got under her skirt. He didn't look like the type who'd wait until there was a ring on her finger. But then, what man was?

Jethro smiled. 'A man must have his needs catered for. I hope you have a comfortable journey. Your trunks will be stowed in the hold.' He clicked his fingers at a waiting seaman. 'Show Mr Parnell to his cabin, Saunders.'

Dominic had prowled all over Edinburgh, but to no avail. Uneasily, his mind kept wandering back to the tale Kenna had told him about her brother-in-law's wife throwing her out.

He shook his head as, defeated, he let himself into the house.

Mairi was sitting in the kitchen, drinking cocoa. 'Ye canna find the lassie, then?'

'No. I was a fool, Mairi. I should have listened to her.'

'Aye, well, what's done is done. Likely as not she's gone back to her relatives and they've taken her in. Kin is kin, and blood is thicker than water, after all.'

Except Kenna wasn't tied by blood to her brother-in-law. *Blood* . . . the word niggled uneasily in his mind as he remembered the blood on the sheet. With it came the thought of his wedding night, of Harriet, ignorant of what was expected of her and nearly hysterical over the smear of blood on the sheet the next morning.

Colour flooded his cheeks as the light dawned. Kenna was not, and never had been, the girl he'd imagined. He'd taken her innocence, then insulted her afterwards by suggesting she should become his mistress.

He had a sudden sharp memory, one of a girl begging a man to allow her to go home, of her being rebuffed. She'd had large, wounded eyes the colour of amber, and had run from him into a lane because he'd frightened her. That hadn't been the action of a street girl.

What a fool he'd been! Out loud he murmured, 'I made a mistake, you know, Mairi. Kenna wasn't a street girl, at all.'

'Aye, but I never thought she was, and I wondered when you'd come to that conclusion myself. But there was no telling you.' She patted him on the shoulder. 'You know, that young woman thought the world of you, Doctor Sterne.'

Heavily, he said, 'And I'll wear that on my conscience for the rest of my life, because I realized it too late. Are you sure she didn't tell you where that brother-in-law of hers lived?'

'Robert, she said his name was. And his wife was called Agnes. That's all she said to me, except that he was a lawyer of some sort. Whatever he was, he wasn't a suitable guardian if he threw her out to fend for herself. And if I ever meet him, I'll tell him what I think of him.'

Dominic couldn't keep a faint grin from coming to his face. No doubt she would, for Mairi had grown fond of Kenna. 'I'll leave you some money and a card with my

Bournemouth address. If you discover where she is let me know. And if you happen to run into her on the street, tell her . . .'

'Och, I'll know exactly what to tell her –' Mairi tut-tutted – 'that I've been trying to find you a good woman and when you find one for yourself you ignore all my hints and let her slip off your hook.' She shook her head. 'Let's hope she doesn't marry that uplander. Serves ye right if she does. You'd better get off to bed now, Doctor, you have to catch that train early tomorrow, and it's a long journey you've to make with the child. She'll be as lively as a lop with all the new sights and sounds to look at, too.'

'What about you, Mairi?'

'Don't you go worrying about me,' she said gruffly. 'You've enough on your plate, and I'll be up before you with a guid breakfast to fill your stomachs. I'll be coming to see you settled on the train, picnic hamper in hand and the dog in his wicker cage.'

'You're a good woman, you know, Mairi.'

Her face reflected the pleasure his words gave her, but tears sprang to her eyes when she said, 'Get away with you.'

Seven

The train journey was tedious, but at least they had the compartment to themselves.

Kenna's uncommunicative companion hunched into the corner and was soon asleep. She dozed on and off herself after they left the city and the train began to meander through the countryside. The terrain became hilly. It was pretty country, she thought, in her wakeful moments.

Rory awoke when the train whistle blew. His fierce blue gaze settled on her. 'Did ye nae pack us something to eat, lass?'

'I didn't have time.'

'We'll just have to go hungry then.' He gazed out of the window, his glance taking in his surrounds. 'We should be there in a wee while.'

A wee while turned into three-quarters of an hour before the train clanked to a halt. Innerleithen Station was a small building with a platform, and was a short walk from a river. The engine stood beside the platform panting like a dog while Rory unloaded Kenna's luggage. He waved his arm at the driver, who waved back, then the train whistle blew and the engine blew steam and clanked into motion. There was nobody in sight.

'Is there a refreshment room?'

'Does it look as though there is? Wait here with your trunk. I'll go into the village and see if I can buy something tae eat. If you want to relieve yourself go behind that bush. There's nobody around tae see ye.'

He came back in fifteen minutes with a feast – a can of milk, bread, cheese, two boiled eggs and some potato scones, all wrapped in a blue-checked cloth. He handed her a portion of bread and cheese. 'Eat that, you can wash it down wi' the milk. Be quick about it, mind. I want to get home and we've fifteen miles to travel.' He placed the eggs and scones in her basket.

She gasped, even though she thought he must be joking. 'Fifteen miles!'

'Aye. We should get five in before it gets dark. The rest we'll do tomorrow.'

The air smelled sweet after the train. 'What's the river called?'

'The Tweed,' he grunted. 'It supports most of the woollen mills in the area.' Hefting the trunk on his shoulder he began to stride off up a steep track. Hurriedly, Kenna gulped down the milk and set off after him.

It was not long before she was out of breath. She sat on a rock to recover from the steep climb, calling out, 'Wait.'

He didn't need to state his irritation; it was clearly expressed on his face. 'Ye canna be tired already, we've hardly started.'

'I'm sorry. I've been ill and it's left me weak. The doctor said I need to rest to recover my strength, and that will take time. I'll be all right in a minute, I promise. Just let me catch my breath.'

He stared into the hills while she did, her trunk still balanced on his shoulder, his legs braced slightly apart. He was a well-muscled man. She felt guilty for making him wait, and attempted to converse with him. 'I thought there would be a carter. I never imagined your home would be fifteen miles from the station. I'm sorry to put you to so much trouble. I'm not used to the country.'

He turned to gaze reflectively at her and she couldn't tell whether he was annoyed or not as he said easily, 'Aye, I know you're not. As for the trunk, you called me a mule and I can carry the trunk just as easily.'

'Are you going to remind me of that for the rest of my life?'

A smile spread across his face. 'Aye, I might. Nobody's called me a mule before. You have a fine temper on you, Kenna. Better you stop talking now and save your breath for walking. Are you able to go on now, or do you intend to be a burden to me?'

'I can manage,' she said huffily, and followed after him downhill. She trudged up the next slope with the wind at her back giving her a welcome push. Again, she was forced to rest, and that set a pattern for the rest of the day.

She was aware that the hilly countryside around her was beautiful as the shadows of the afternoon lengthened across the ground. But it was scarred by lead mines, which had stripped the surrounds bare of foliage.

When the sun sank the sky took on a misty purple hue, and the shapes of trees blackened against the horizon. The air became chilly. Kenna stumbled over a stone and fell flat on her face. She couldn't get up.

'Wait,' she called as the fitful moon went behind a stretch of cloud and Rory disappeared from view. A few seconds later he came back and hauled her to her feet. Taking a scarf from his neck he tied one end around her wrist and the other to his belt. 'This will help you to keep up. The mist will soon close in on us. There's a croft down by the burn where we can shelter. It's nae much further.'

Indeed, she could hear the churn of the water over its rocky bed. The mist was already forming dense patches in the dales. As for herself, she was nearly boneless with fatigue. Thank goodness Rory knew his way, she thought, as they headed downhill into a stand of trees. She stumbled wearily past him when he slowed and would have walked into the burn if he hadn't jerked on the scarf.

'There should be a crossing, somewhere. Give me your basket, then wait here until I come back.'

'You will come back for me, won't you?'

'Are you deaf, girl? I just said I would.'

When he left she felt as though she was the only person alive in a world that drifted eerily around her. The air was moist, and although she tried not to think of Dominic, she couldn't help herself. Tears tumbled from her eyes at the thought of never seeing him again.

There was a jerk on the scarf that made her jump. 'There's a crossing made of stones, but the water's covering them. I've been over with the luggage, and I'm going to carry ye across on my back. Don't struggle, even if I stumble, otherwise ye'll unbalance me. Do ye ken?'

'Aye. What if we fall in?'

'Try and keep your feet on the bottom, and grab anything solid you can find. But the water's fast-flowing at the moment and likely it will sweep you away. The water gets shallower further down. Ye'll have to try and keep your head out of the water until you can touch the bottom, otherwise ye'll drown.'

Fear filled her. 'I promise I won't struggle.'

They went along the bank a little way. He crouched, so she could scramble on to his back. Her arms went around his neck and her legs around his hips. He was reassuringly solid and sure-footed.

'Loosen your hold around my neck a wee bit. Good,' he grunted, when she did as she was told, and took a few steps to adjust to her weight. 'Here we go. It's only a few steps, now.'

The few steps took several heart-stopping minutes. Kenna held her breath every moment of the way and the churning sound of the water below her seemed to take on a new menace. Rory was careful, taking one stride forward to the next stone, then bringing the other foot over to stand there for a few seconds before attempting the next one.

Kenna suddenly realized she couldn't see the burn beneath them, and if she couldn't then neither could Rory, unless he had the vision of an owl. The tension in him communicated itself to her through his rigid muscles, and on the occasions when his foot slipped, she gave a small squeak and found it hard not to tighten her grip on him.

Then the air left his body in a relieved sigh, and she found herself standing on the opposite bank. Trunk once more on his shoulder, he placed the basket on her arm, took possession of the trailing scarf and set out through the thickening mist, with her stumbling over the stones and tussocks like a cow at the end of a rope, so she felt like mooing.

She held back her giggle at the thought; she didn't think her future husband had much of a sense of humour at the moment.

He came to a halt in front of a tumbledown croft and kicked the door open.

'Couldn't you have just turned the knob and opened it?' she said, when the door banged back against the wall and hung on one hinge.

He looked surprised. 'My hands were full. Besides, the place is falling down already.'

Soon she was jerked forward once again. When they were inside she dragged the scarf from her wrist and let it fall. The sense she'd developed while she'd been living on the street reached out into the unfamiliar darkness, but there seemed to be no danger in the dark waiting to pounce. She relaxed.

Soon, Rory had put a light to the stump of a candle he'd found. He went outside again to gather firewood.

Kenna looked around her. The place was filthy. It contained only a wooden bed, a chair and a rickety table. She'd slept in worse places. Soon, the firelight flickered on the walls. Rory collected water from the burn in the metal milk can, then handed it to her to drink from.

The water hit her stomach with a chill. 'I'm hungry. Can we eat the eggs and potato cakes?'

'We need them for breakfast. Try to get some rest.'

'On that dirty bed?'

'Be grateful for small mercies. At least ye have a roof over your head for the night. If ye want a hotel, go back to Edinburgh.'

Kenna felt edgy and argumentative as she stretched out on the hard surface. 'You're not the most well-mannered man I've ever met.'

'I am as I am. Take me or leave me.'

'To be honest, I'd rather leave you.'

He gave her a level look. 'Likewise. I don't think you're the type of lassie who will fit easily into my life.'

'Then let's cancel the arrangement before we make each other's lives a misery.'

His voice gruffened. 'I'm beginning to wish I'd dropped you into the bluidy burn. Shut your mouth, woman, will ye? Go to sleep, for I'll not put up wi' your carping for much longer.'

Kenna was too exhausted to do anything else, but her anger was a choking, molten lump in her throat. Why had she allowed Robert to talk her into this? She removed her boots, wincing when she revealed a crop of blisters. Tearing a strip of fabric from her petticoat she wrapped it carefully about her sore feet, then stretched out on the bed.

Rory sat in the chair by the fire, his back to her, and surrounded by an air of brooding.

The candle flickered and they had absolutely nothing to say to each other.

The constant music of the burn was strangely comforting though, as were the scrabbles and squeaks of mice.

During the night Kenna dreamed she felt Dominic's arms around her, and his warmth as he pulled her into the shelter of his body. She sighed and relaxed against him, murmuring his name.

Morning, and Kenna found herself alone in the dirty, tumble-down croft. There was no sign of the Dominic of her dreams. There was also no sign of Rory, even though she called out his name. It must have been Rory who'd held her, but she'd given little thought to where he'd sleep when she'd taken the bed, and at least he'd kept her warm. The fire had been built up during the night, but it had collapsed into a heap of glowing ash.

She cursed when she saw that the food in her basket had been devoured by the rodents. The potato cakes were gone, and sharp little teeth had cracked through the egg shells to get at the contents.

Outside, the mist had thinned. It was layered at waist height, and stirred about her as she headed for a stand of trees, where she could see to her comfort. On the way back she came across some mushrooms and stopped to pick them. When she reached the croft she walked around the building and found a tin pail in an outhouse. She filled it with water from the burn, pulling up some watercress that grew along the bank at the same time. At least they'd have some vegetables to eat.

Going outside again she collected some firewood. Carefully, she coaxed the ashes in the fireplace into life and set the pail on top. When it was warm, she jammed the back of the chair under the doorknob.

Washing the stale sweat from her body, she dried herself on the remains of her petticoat then took a comfortable old skirt and bodice from her trunk. When she was dressed she wrapped herself in her shawl. Taking some salve from her trunk she smeared it on her blisters and wrapped her feet tightly in a clean strip of linen before easing her boots back on. She threw the bloodied rags on the fire, then brushed her hair out and braided it.

The fire had burned down to ashes again. She was just wondering where Rory had got to when the door was thrust open and the chair went flying. The can he carried in one hand was half-filled with milk. His glance went to the mushrooms and watercress as he set it down, and he smiled in approval at her.

A couple of brown trout dangled from his other hand. Without saying a word he set the milk on the table then scraped a bed in the ashes with the toe of his boot. Stuffing the mushrooms inside the fish, he laid them side by side and covered them with ashes again. He stood. 'Breakfast will only be a few minutes. Drink some milk if ye're hungry.'

'Yes, I am. Thank you. Where did you get the milk from?'

'From a goat. She had a sucker at her teat, and did nae want to part wi' it, mind.' His clothes and hair were damp. He shrugged when he saw her eyeing him. 'The goat butted me into the burn when I was tickling for the second trout.'

Kenna couldn't help but laugh, and he grinned. 'I needed a bath, and I'll soon dry off when we start walking.'

Kenna felt the need to apologize. 'I'm sorry I caused you trouble yesterday. I didn't mean to nag.'

'Aye, well, we were both tired. We'll get used to each other's ways in time.'

Kenna had never experienced anything quite so delicious as the fish they ate. When the second one had cooled sufficiently she wrapped it in watercress, then placed it carefully in the blue-checked cloth. She put the parcel into her basket to keep for their dinner.

'Ready?' Rory said, and she nodded.

One hill followed another, but at least the snow only topped the highest peaks, which were often hidden by cloud. The wind was capricious, sometimes an icy blast that set her skirt swirling, sometimes a keening moan over the patches of bare rocks and at other times a gentle sigh in the undergrowth. Rory seemed to be oblivious to either cold or drifting rain, and was untiring. Not so Kenna. Her blistered feet began to throb, so in the end she was hobbling along, wincing with every step.

They'd left the track earlier, had eaten the second fish and watercress as they walked and were now following the burn. She thought he hadn't noticed her distress, but after they reached the next valley, he turned. Ahead of them was a steep hill, thickly covered with conifers.

He indicated a group of flat rocks on the edge of the burn. 'We'll rest here, so I can tend to your feet.'

She sank to the ground with relief. Rory lowered the trunk to the ground then removed her boots. He sucked in a breath when he saw the bloodied strips of linen. 'That must hurt like hell. Ye should've told me, girl.'

'I didn't want to hold us up and become that burden you told me you didn't want. There's some salve in my trunk.'

He pursed his lips but said nothing, just carried her to a stone next to the bubbling water and seated her so her feet were immersed. It was freezing, but blissfully soothing, but after a while her feet were numb. Her petticoat was getting shorter and shorter, she thought, as he awkwardly patted her feet dry with it. He spread the salve along the linen strips and bound her feet with them.

'Wait there,' he said and, leaving her to pull on her boots, he walked away with her trunk. He returned without it ten minutes later. 'I've hidden it from sight. I'll come back for it.'

The shadows were beginning to lengthen. 'Is your land much further?'

'We're on my land. The house is two miles past the trees, and down into the glen. I was hoping we'd be there by now.' He stopped before the rock she was seated on, his back to her. 'Get on, lass, I'll carry ye the rest of the way.'

She felt guilty that her slowness had held them up, but didn't bother arguing. She even began to like him when he said, 'It's my fault your feet are sore, I should have expected a city lass to have tender feet. I'm surprised you got this far. You're a game one.'

'I'm not as frail as you imagine. I'm not used to walking such long distances, that's all. You could have warned me.'

'Aye, weel, it didnae cross my mind, since I'm used tae walking everywhere.'

They were soon in the trees. There it was cool and the light was shaded in various patterns of shadows by the overhead canopy. The undergrowth was dense, and there seemed to be no defined path. Kenna soon lost her sense of direction, but Rory trudged confidently on, his breath becoming heavier as they reached the peak. Then they were going downhill, the forest growing lighter and lighter until they emerged from the trees.

Below them, in the distance, was a small loch, shining silver in the grey evening light. There was a house set in a clearing on one side. Beyond, another stand of trees dipped down to the edge of the water. A straggle of smaller buildings drew the eyes to a bigger house set back a little way from the loch in front of a hill.

Rory set her down. 'Welcome to Glenchallon, Kenna.'

She nodded. The isolation of the place dismayed her, but she tried not to let it show.

He placed his fingers in his mouth and gave a piercing whistle.

There came the sound of frenzied barking, then two dogs detached themselves from the house and came streaking up the slope, their tails streaming behind them. The dogs came upon them at speed and leaped upon their master with delight, twisting and turning and giving small yips and yelps of welcome.

Then it was her turn. She was sniffed all over. 'This is Kenna Mackenzie,' he told them. 'She's my guest, and ye'll treat her wi' respect.'

One of them thrust his nose into her hand and she fondled it, while the other tried to push his shorter nose into her other hand.

'Amos and Willy,' he said, then hefted her on to his back again.

The nearer they got to the house, the bigger and shabbier it seemed to become. There were slates missing from the roof and the windows were dirty. 'Don't you have any servants?' she said.

He laughed. 'Aye. I have Maggie Harris, for what she's worth . . . and there she is.'

The woman was well past middle-age, her back slightly stooped. Her eyes were a lively but washed-out blue. There was a feeling of energy bristling around her.

'Ye're home then, Master Rory.'

'Aye, it seems so.'

'Has the wee girl hurt herself?'

'The walk was too far for her and her feet are blistered.'

'Ye should have come up through the village. It's shorter.'

'So McTavish can poke his nose into Glenchallon business? He wants tae know the history of everything that goes past his store. Anyone would think he was the estate gatekeeper.'

'Och, it's a fool ye are, Rory Challoner. Ye can put the lassie down now. I daresay you're both hungry.'

Although she found the woman's casually familiar manner irritating, Kenna nodded.

'Weel, come away into the kitchen wi' me. There's a pot of chicken broth warming on the stove and some oatcakes to dip into it.'

As Kenna limped painfully after her, Maggie said, 'Has the Challoner taken ye to the altar yet?'

Kenna's stomach rumbled as she shook her head.

'Then I'll find ye a room of your own to sleep in. God knows, there's enough of them. Remember, yon laird has no rights to you till there's a ring on your finger, so make sure your door's kept locked.'

'I would'na take liberties with the lassie before marriage,' Rory protested. 'Besides, she's still a stranger tae me.'

Maggie grinned when she noticed Kenna's shocked expression. 'Aye, that's what all you men say. But it's spring and a lassie has to be canny about such things. You keep your door locked, girl.'

'Och, get awi' with your gab, Maggie. Ye'll give Miss Mackenzie the wrong impression. Besides . . . she needs fattening up a bit.'

Kenna glowered at him. 'I'm not a cow you've bought, and I find this conversation to be indelicate.'

'Now don't start nagging all over again. Maggie was only being friendly. I spent guid money advertising for the woman I needed for Glenchallon.'

'And how many replies did you get?'

'A few,' he said evasively.

He gave Maggie a black look when she chuckled and said, 'Only one.'

'Robert Gilmore assured me ye were sound of wind and limb. So far that hasn't proved to be the truth.'

'I've been ill. I told you. Everyone catches a cold now and again.'

'Aye, and I'm making allowances for that. But I'm holding back the wedding until the other part of the contract has been filled.'

'Are ye now, *Laird*? I might have something to say about that, myself. I might decide not to wed you after all.'

He stared hard at her. 'We have a contract.'

'Your contract is with Robert Gilmore, and he canna be trusted. The only reason I'm here with you now is because his wife threw me on the street without a penny to my name. Then he wore me down and gave me no choice. Robert Gilmore cheated my father and sister to get his hands on our money. Don't think he'll part with it that easily.'

Rory was unbelieving. 'Gilmore told me ye'd try to blacken his name. And he gave me some cash on account to show his guid intent. We shook hands on it. No wonder he wanted you off his hands. Och, I'm not going to stand here arguing, and neither will I stand for any of your nonsense. I'm off to fetch your trunk before the dark closes in. Where are those damned dogs? Willy! Amos!' he shouted.

Kenna watched him go, her eyes narrowed. 'Only a fool would trust Robert,' she whispered after him.

'Ye could nae have been straighter with him, Kenna Mackenzie. He's always been one to learn the hard way, and to blame others for his mistakes. All I can say is God help ye if yer right.'

'What do you mean?'

'He's got a temper on him, that's what I mean.'

'Aye, well so have I.'

Maggie gave her a black look. 'Sit down and eat your

broth, now. Then I'll have a look at those feet of yours. The very idea, making ye walk over the hills. If ye'd come up the track through the village, likely you could have fetched yerselves a ride on a cart.'

'He didn't know my feet were blistered.'

'More fool you for not telling him then, for you got what you deserved.'

Dominic's family had welcomed himself and Evelyn back with open arms. At present he was residing in the family home with his mother. It was a rambling house of comfortable proportions, with a garden built for children to have adventures in, one of four other similar houses.

He'd been here for two weeks now. He stood inside the French doors in the comfortably elegant drawing room, watching Evelyn being chased by Hamish and the young maid called Hennie, who'd been assigned to her, around the flowerbeds.

'I knew Evelyn would like it here,' he said to his mother, who had joined him. 'She adores having a family. I hadn't imagined she was quite so gregarious until I saw her with her cousins.'

'It's certainly a healthy environment for a child with the sea not far away and no manufactory industry to spoil the fresh air and beauty of the chines. Evelyn's a lovely little girl, Dominic. I'm sorry Harriet didn't live to see her grow up. Evelyn needs siblings of her own. Have you any plans for the future?'

'Plans? You know my plans, since I've discussed them with you. I have an option to buy one of Westover Villas.'

'You can afford it?'

'Easily. You forget that I inherited from Harriet.'

His mother smiled. 'Then you'll know exactly what I'm talking about. My dear, Evelyn would benefit greatly from having a mother, and you'll need a wife to run your household when you settle into the practice. Evelyn was telling me about someone called Miss Mackalenzie. She seems to be very fond of her, and she seems to think the woman will come and visit her here.'

'Kenna Mackenzie.' A faint smile touched his lips, but his

heart sank at the thought of never seeing her again. 'Kenna is hardly more than a girl. I do wish that she would visit, but Edinburgh is a long way to come from, and she doesn't know where we live.'

'Does the young lady mean something to you, Dominic?'

'Kenna gave Hamish to Evelyn.' He hesitated, then turned to gaze at his mother, saying candidly, 'Actually, she means everything to me. I did a foolish thing. I misjudged Kenna and convinced myself she wasn't good enough to be my wife, even though I was in love with her. I insulted her, and I realized her worth too late.'

'In what way did you insult her?'

'I suggested she become my mistress. Then when I woke it was to find that she had fled.'

His mother sucked in a breath. 'Oh, Dominic.'

'I'm sorry, I didn't mean to shock you, Mother. There's more. Kenna's young, only twenty. She was a guest in my home and I manipulated her feelings to serve my own ends – and that after she'd placed herself in my care. What do you think of your son now, Mother?'

'I'm appalled. I think that was absolutely unforgivable of you. You were always the most well-behaved and reliable of my children – always the one who knew where you were going and how to get there. But while I'm horrified that you've hurt this girl, you've also recognized that your own feelings are entirely human, so you've hurt yourself in the process.'

'I know I have. I feel absolutely bereft without her.'

'Then you must find her, Dominic. Will she have you, now, d'you think?'

'I think Kenna cares enough to forgive me. But I hurt her badly, and she left without word. I don't even know where she lives.'

'Has she no family?'

'No. She said her parents died when she was a child. Her sister had passed away six months previously and her brother-in-law and his new wife had thrown her on to the street.'

'Does this girl . . . Kenna, know that you care for her?'

'I didn't tell her. I saved her life and healed her body but I didn't listen to what she was telling me. I just basked in her admiration like a conquering hero, then took advantage of her.'

She gazed at him with a chuckle, saying with some surprise, 'How like your father you are. You know, you're being much too hard on yourself. No wonder you've been so preoccupied since you've been here. With your connections in Edinburgh, surely you can find her? You could leave Evelyn with me, now she's used to me.'

'How would I start?'

'You know her name, and you know she had a sister who died recently. And she had a mother and father. Somebody must have known them, and their deaths must be on record.'

'D'you realize how many Mackenzies there are in Edinburgh?' And he remembered something else – something that brought a frown to his face and a sense of urgency into his mind. 'She mentioned that her brother-in-law had arranged a marriage for her. What if she's now wed another?'

'My dear Dominic, if you truly love this girl you will stop making excuses and go and find her. Leave no stone unturned. If she's wed another . . . well, then you must wish her well and walk away from her. You won't win her hand by standing here talking to me about it.'

'I'll travel up to London tomorrow, and will pick up a train to Edinburgh from Euston Station.'

Evelyn was brought in by Hennie, her face newly washed, her hair brushed and her cheeks flushed from the exercise.

'You may tell cook she can serve tea now, Hennie,' Charlotte told the maid.

There was big grin on Evelyn's face. 'Hamish chased a rabbit and it went down a hole. Can I go and visit my cousins tomorrow, Papa?'

'I'm afraid not. I have to go back to Edinburgh tomorrow.'

Evelyn's face fell and she went to lean against Charlotte Sterne's knee. 'But I don't want to go back home. I want to stay here with my grandmamma. I like it here. And I love my cousins.'

'Oh, we're not going back there to live, my love. I have some business to attend to in Edinburgh. I might be away for a week or two. Grandmamma will look after you while I'm gone, if that's all right with you?'

Charlotte said, 'I'll take you to visit your cousins, dear.

The stable lad can drive us over, then he can take your father on to the coach station so he can be taken to Ringwood in time to catch the Southampton train.'

Scrambling on to her grandmother's lap, Evelyn hugged her, then gazed Dominic's way, her face reflecting her thoughts. 'Are you going to bring back Kenna Mackalenzie? I'm sad without her. So is Hamish.'

'I can't promise, but I certainly hope so.'

'I'll draw her a picture of us at Grandmamma's house and you can give it to her when you see her. She'll like that.'

'She most certainly will.'

Later, when Dominic folded Evelyn's offering and placed it in his travelling bag, he recalled the locket Mairi had given into his safekeeping – the one that had belonged to Kenna. His desk was downstairs in the hall, still crated, waiting to be moved to its final home, which wouldn't be long since he'd more or less decided on the Westover Road villa. Although it was larger and far grander an address than he needed, both he and Evelyn liked the house, and it was within walking distance of the homes of his family.

Fetching a crowbar, he prised the front off the crate and opened the drawer. The locket had slid to the back. He closed his fingers around it, smiling as he brought it out. He flicked it open with his thumb. Kenna's father's name came instantly to mind when he saw the miniature of the man. Andrew Mackenzie. He'd been a lawyer, she'd said. His eyes flicked to the woman, who wore a faint smile exactly like Kenna's. How alike mother and daughter were, and he'd closed his mind to that likeness before. What a fool he'd been. Why hadn't he listened to her – believed her?

He gazed at the two likenesses a long time, then snapped the locket shut and slid it into his pocket.

Eight

Kenna opened her eyes to an unfamiliar water stain on the ceiling, then moved on to a painting so dirty that she couldn't make out what the subject was. For a moment she wondered where she was, then she remembered.

She'd had a bad night, woken by unfamiliar creaks and groans, and she sighed as she noticed the cobwebs in the corners of the room and the dust coating the furniture. The bedstead rattled as she sat up, and the lumps in the mattress felt like molehills.

Lowering her feet to the floor she encountered bare floorboards, then winced as she hobbled on her sore feet to the window, where bands of rain skimmed across an expanse of wild sky. The wind churned the surface of the loch into broth and moaned around the house. Draughts butted impatiently against her bedroom door, rattling it, as if someone was trying to get in.

She was hungry, but something told her it was long past breakfast time. There was a bell pull, but it wasn't worth pulling, since Maggie had made it perfectly clear she would not get any special treatment and would have to shift for herself. Not that Kenna would have demanded any service. To Kenna's mind the woman had been overly familiar and overbearing for a servant, even an old retainer. If she became mistress of this house, that would stop.

If? Why was she thinking this way, when the words that would make her the Challoner's wife were a forgone conclusion to those who knew? Except for herself, who couldn't quite believe she'd agreed to the marriage when she loved another man and had given her body to him.

She put the thought aside while she dressed. It didn't take her long to don a warm and comfortable skirt and bodice, which seemed more suitable wear for the uplands than her city clothes did.

She found a staircase, the walls lined by dark portraits of fierce-looking, bewhiskered gentleman, some in hats with feathers, and some proudly holding dead animals or fondling the ears of a dog. They were interspersed with the decapitated heads of unfortunate stags with sorrowful eyes, each with a fine spread of antlers.

She followed the staircase down, noting the peeling paint, the damp patches, cracked walls, and most of all the dirt and mould that had accumulated in the corners. The place smelled of dogs, mice and damp. Surely Rory Challoner didn't expect her inheritance to stretch far enough to restore this ancient brute of a house?

Downstairs, two kettles steamed gently on the top of the range. At least the kitchen was clean. She opened the larder looking for the tea and coffee, and was in the act of opening a tin when Maggie challenged from behind her, 'And what are you doing in my larder, girl?'

Kenna turned guiltily, as if she'd be rummaging through the woman's purse. 'I'm looking for some tea.'

Maggie took the tin from her and set it back on the shelf. 'We dinna have any tea.'

'Coffee, then.'

'We dinna have coffee either. If you're thirsty there's water in the pump.' She shut the larder door with a thump and folded her arms over her chest. 'Ye'll have to get up earlier if you want breakfast, lassie.'

Kenna wasn't about to allow Maggie the upper hand. 'Exactly what is your position in this household, Mrs . . . uh, Harris?'

'I'm the housekeeper, and this is my kitchen.'

'What you mean is that this is the kitchen you work in as a servant. I find your tone to be insolent, and I'd prefer it if you addressed me as Miss Mackenzie from now on.'

Maggie's face reddened. 'Weel see about that. Don't think you can come in here and tell me what to do. I've known the Challoner since he were born, and your city ways don't frighten me.'

'Likewise, your country ways. And I don't care how long

you've known the laird, that doesn't make you his mother,' she said caustically, and the woman's eyes narrowed. 'As for breakfast, I saw some eggs and bread in the larder.'

'I thought I made it clear I was nae going to wait on ye hand and foot?'

Kenna sighed at the obdurate look on the woman's face. She hadn't wanted to raise her voice, but it was needed. 'I'm not asking you to, and I'm not going to fight for every damned thing I need. Let's not argue about this. Move aside.'

'I'm nae arguing, just telling you how it is.'

'Do as she says, Maggie,' Rory said from the doorway. 'The girl's had little to eat over the past two days and needs her breakfast.'

'But I was keeping those eggs for yerself.'

'Do as you're told, woman.'

'Aye, I will, when you start paying me the wages you owe me.'

'Ye've got a roof over yer head and food in your belly, haven't you? You can always find yerself another job if you don't like it here.'

Her hand went to her hips.

'For God sake, move, Maggie!' he roared, his face darkening with anger, and both of them jumped. 'I'm sick of listening to this squabbling. Let the lass get herself some breakfast and a jug of tea, and from now on you keep a civil tongue in yer head. I'm off to catch some fish.' He stomped off, leaving a sullen silence behind him.

A few seconds later Maggie heaved a self-pitying sigh. 'The tea kettle's on the stove. Add some water to it after you've had yours, so it'll last all day.' Moving to the door she had the last word. 'And don't forget to clean up after yerself, *Miss Mackenzie*.'

After she'd eaten Kenna found a bucket, scrubbing brush and some soap. Although she was unfamiliar with the domestic arrangements of the house she filled the pail with cold water from the pump. The rest of the day she went back and forth, emptying the filthy water and replacing it with clean as she scrubbed her room out. There was no sign of Maggie, but Kenna doubted if she'd get any help from her, anyway.

An application of suds revealed the picture on the wall, leaving the water black. It was covered in soot. How odd that it had got so filthy. The subject was a young woman seated on a wall in the sun, a dog at her feet and her arms filled with heather. Kenna didn't know whether she liked it or not. The woman's face was beautiful. A torrent of dark curls tumbled down her back. Beseeching blue eyes gazed straight from the portrait into her own, and the woman's expression was filled with an incredible sadness that tugged at Kenna's heart.

In a cupboard she found some beeswax, which, although cracked and dry, became pliable when she held the tin over a candle. The work was tiring, but she enjoyed the warm glow of the wood as its beauty emerged from under the dirt. When she'd finished, her hands were sore. She determined to clean the adjoining sitting room and make it her own.

Dinner consisted of fish with potatoes and onions, followed by rhubarb tart, the fruit so sour that Kenna could barely swallow it. It was eaten in silence. Kenna helped Maggie tidy up, but received no word of thanks. Rory went off with the dogs afterwards. Going to bed, Kenna fell into an exhausted sleep.

The next morning she arrived downstairs in good time for a breakfast of oatmeal. She barely received a glance from either of them.

'Would you tell me where the laundry room is, please?' she politely asked Maggie, before the grievances, along with the unpleasant atmosphere of the previous day, were resumed. 'I need to do some washing.'

'Aye, 'tis through that passage yonder, and at the back. There's a copper, but ye'll need to chop some wood to light a fire under it. The lines are out the back. The midden is at the end of the garden.'

Which wasn't a subject for the breakfast table. 'Is there a bathing room?'

'I use the loch, though 'tis cold enough to crine a man at times,' Rory said, and laughed.

'It would take more than the loch to shrivel you,' Maggie retorted.

'Aye,' he said comfortably, and his blue eyes came up to her face, so Kenna knew exactly what was in his mind. Even though he was a rugged and attractive man to look at, she had no urge to engage in the intimacy that marriage would bring, especially before a ring was on her finger. The thought that he regarded her in such a way brought a faint flush to her face.

Then she thought of Dominic and experienced such a depth of anguish that she nearly cried out with the longing in her to see him. She'd considered that she'd be able to put Dominic aside once he'd gone from her life, but that had proved to be impossible. The possibility that she might never see him again filled her with deep despair, and she wondered what he was doing at that moment. She recalled his kind, angular face so vividly that she could have leaned forward and kissed his mouth.

'You can take a bath in the laundry if ye like, there's a tin tub there and it saves running up and down the stairs with kettles of hot water,' Maggie said, a slight whine in her voice. 'With only myself employed here, 'tis another task I don't need. God knows, I do my best tae keep on top of the work.'

'I realize that, Maggie. But with two of us sharing it your task should become easier, not harder. I've never had a maid picking up after me, so I don't expect special treatment.'

'Aye, weel . . . if you keep out from under my feet in the kitchen and shift for yerself I daresay we can let bygones be bygones.'

'There,' Rory said, offering Kenna an encouraging smile when he should have been putting Maggie in her place. 'What could be fairer than that? Has my grandfather been down fer his breakfast yet, Maggie?'

'He came down early, still in his nightcap. He's gone back to bed, said he had a cold in his water and I was to take his breakfast up to him. I told him about the . . . *Miss Mackenzie*, here. He was angry because you'd gone to fetch her without telling him. He said you're a damned fool to bring a city girl here, especially a Mackenzie, and you should marry a local lassie.'

'Aye, but I need Kenna's money. Did ye tell him that?'

'He knows it. He said that no amount of money will put this place to rights, and I agree with him. The place moaned and groaned as if it was in its death throes last night. Fair gave me the willies, it did.'

'Och, what does he know, or you, come to that? Glenchallon has been standing here for ever. He'd be saying something different if he was the laird and the place was his. It's as solid as a rock, I tell ye. It just leaks a bit here and there.'

'The foundations are in water, and last winter when it rained it came up through the cellar door and flooded the hall. And the roof timbers are rotten where the rain comes in the roof. And the hill at the back has become saturated through with water since the auld laird had the pines cut down and sold for timber. There's nae a root left to hold back that hill. One of these days it will slide on top of us, ye mark my words. And the cracks in the walls are getting wider.'

'Aye, weel, I'll replant the hill as soon as I have some money to hand. The pines will soon suck up the water. Some mortar in the cracks will fix them. And you've forgotten to say that the floorboards are rotten in places.' His smile faded. 'The pair of ye are all gloom and doom. What does the auld miser expect? If he'd loosen his hand on his own purse strings it might help us a little.'

'He left some coins to buy him his whisky.' Maggie jerked her thumb in Kenna's direction. 'He said he wants to meet her.'

'Does he now? I'm not having him poison her mind. He'll have to wait till I'm ready.'

Annoyed at the pair of them talking about her as though she wasn't there, Kenna interrupted them. 'Your grandfather lives here? You didn't say.'

'Did I not? Aye, he's my grandfather on my mother's side –' he exchanged a glance with Maggie and shrugged – 'for what it's worth. Magnus is a miserable auld sod who hasn't got a guid word for anybody. Keep away from him.'

Which made Kenna all the more eager to meet him. But not today; she wanted to finish cleaning her rooms. 'I'll make his acquaintance when I decide to, not when you decide I will.'

His mouth fell open. 'You're a feisty one, aren't you,

Kenna Mackenzie? Please yerself, then, but don't say I didnae warn you.'

'I take it ye'll be going to the village store?' Maggie said to Rory with a sly grin.

Immediately, his manner became defensive. 'Aye, what of it? And keep a civil tongue in yer head, now.'

'I was going to suggest that if Miss Mackenzie is going to clean everything in sight, and take a bath every day, then we need some more scrubbing soap.'

'I'd like some scented soap for my bath. Lavender, if they have it.'

'Would ye now? I hope you've got the money to pay for it, then. My purse doesn't run to fancy stuff.'

Kenna flushed. 'Aye, I have, and I'm not asking you to.'

'We need some sugar. And you need to pay the dairyman's bill if we're to be left any more milk,' Maggie said.

'For God's sake, can't he wait a few more days while I collect the tenants' rents?'

'He reckons he's waited long enough. There's a list of what's needed on the dresser. Ye might have to sweet talk Fiona McTavish. But ye'd know how to go about that, wouldn't yer?'

'Och, shut your mouth, woman.' And he glared at her ferociously.

The constant bickering was beginning to get on Kenna's nerves. Swallowing the sticky oatmeal and washing it down with some stewed tea, she went upstairs and took a couple of coins from her allowance. Handing them to Rory when she came back down, she said, 'That should cover the cost of my soap.'

His eyes speculated on her for a minute, then he shrugged, and nodded.

She watched him go off, noting the direction he took in case she needed to go to the village shop herself one day.

Rory enjoyed the fine morning as he stepped out, whistling to himself.

It was demeaning being laird of such a fine estate, and he without a horse between his thighs to take him to collect his rent or a coin he could call his own inside his pocket. He jingled the coins he did have, thinking that his grandfather and Kenna Mackenzie both had cash to spare.

How the old man got the money for his whisky had always been a puzzle to Rory. He must have a cache stashed somewhere in the house, but Rory had never been able to find it. As for Kenna, perhaps he should ask her to pay for her keep until they were wed.

Nae, but that would make him feel like a beggar. It would be enough when he got the interest from her inheritance, though he wasn't looking forward to leaving Glenchallon again to collect it. And he'd have to walk all the way to Edinburgh unless he could get the price of a train ticket out of the girl.

The interior of the shop was dim after the sunlit day. Fiona had a sour look on her face. He hoped she wasn't going to be difficult. He'd had enough of squabbling women for one day, and had a rare need for comfort on him.

'And what d'you want, Rory Challoner?'

He laid the list on the table and smiled at her. 'That, and anything else you have to offer.'

'I haven't seen you for a month,' she said sulkily. 'Someone said you'd gone off to the city on business.'

'Aye, but I'm back now, and I missed you, Fiona.' Locking the door he drew her close against him and gave her a kiss. 'You're a bonny piece, and I've got something nice fer you.'

Her eyes hooded and she slid one hand down between them. 'Aye, Rory, I can feel it. That's all you think I'm good for, isn't it, lying on my back?'

'Nae, lass, but I've been saving this up for a month for ye, so let's be having you before the customers start arriving.'

'D'you think I'm some whore to drop my drawers the minute you walk through the door?'

He grinned. 'Wheesht! Fiona, you don't wear any breeks.' When she tried to push him away he tightened his hold. 'Do you love another, then, Fiona?'

'Nae, Rory, but sometimes I think you don't love me.'

He kissed a spot just behind her ear and a little shudder went through her. 'Of course I do.'

'Truly?'

'Truly. Haven't I proved it often enough?' She needed to

be sweet talked. He kissed her mouth, and, inching her skirt up over her buttocks at the back, stroked her smooth skin and observed, 'You have a couple of bonny handfuls of arse.'

She giggled. 'You can stop that, Rory Challoner.'

He lifted her against him, and her legs came up around his waist. By the time he got into the back room and got himself inside her he was desperate. 'Damn, I didnae mean to do that,' he said as he almost immediately jerked his release into her moist centre.

'Oh, it daesna matter, ye're always in a rush first off, and ye do better second time around,' she whispered against his ear, and proceed to undo her bodice. Her exposed breasts were white and quivering. His mouth closed around the brown nubs and he gently sucked them. 'Not too hard, they're a bit sore,' she said.

Fifteen minutes later when he tried to withdraw, her legs went up around his waist in a vicelike grip, while her hands pulled against his behind, keeping him there inside her, where her muscles pulsated around him. She was surprisingly strong, irresistible.

'Fiona, I—'

'I said it daesna matter, ye ken,' she murmured again.

'Aye, it does matter. I don't want to plant a bairn inside ye.'

'Ye're not listening, Rory. I've missed my second course, so I reckon ye already have,' she said against his ear. 'Ye're going to become a father, Rory Challoner, so ye'll have to make an honest woman out of me now. What d'you say to that?'

Gazing at her, and not knowing whether to laugh or cry, Rory cursed soundly before he quickly finished the business at hand, for somebody was impatiently rattling the door handle.

While Fiona quickly tidied her skirt and went through to the shop, Rory nipped out the back door to relieve himself in the bushes, then made his way round the front and entered the shop, brushing from his clothes the bits of hessian lint the sacks had left there.

'Good morning, Laird,' Fiona said, her eyes round and innocent, and her voice as sweet as sugar, so he grinned to himself.

'I didnae see you on the road, Laird,' Jessie Peel said.

'That's because I cut over yon hill.'

'I didnae see you on yon hill, either.'

'Yer eyes must be failing you, Mrs Peel. But I saw ye, all right, dancing down the road, ye were, and kicking up yer heels to show off those fancy garters ye're wearing.'

The auld woman cackled with laughter. 'Och, ye're full of blether.'

'What can I get for ye, Jessie?' Fiona asked her.

'I haven't decided yet. You can serve the Challoner first.'

Nosy old biddy, Rory thought as he handed over his list, tickling Fiona's palm as he slid it into her hand. He felt warm-hearted towards her, and watched the sway of her hips as she went about her business. As she smoothed her apron down over her stomach their eyes met and she gave a small, secretive smile.

His wee son was tucked away inside her, he thought with pride, then his heart sank. He couldn't wed Fiona because he was promised to Kenna Mackenzie. 'Ye'd better add a bottle of whisky for the old man, and do you have any soap?'

'Ye've already got some in your order.'

'Aye, but I mean the fancy stuff city women wash in. Lavender, if ye've got it.'

She looked doubtful for a moment, then smiled. 'Aye, there's some Castile soap somewhere. I got it in for Christmas, but nobody bought it because it was foreign, and it's made from olive oil.'

Climbing up the ladder and affording him a glimpse of her ankles at the same time, Fiona handed down a small box with three white soap tablets nestled in it. A dusty purple ribbon was tied around the lid.

'Is it lavender scented?'

'Aye . . . smell it?'

He held it to his nose and inhaled. A faint smell of scent filled his nostrils. He smiled and replaced the lid. 'It's a right nice smell, at that. I reckon she'll like it.'

'Reckon who will like it?'

Rory shrugged. He didn't want her to know about Kenna yet, she'd only kick up a fuss. 'Maggie, of course.'

'Is it her birthday then?'

Jess cackled. 'Maggie would be sixty-five, if she's a day. What does an auld woman like her want with scented soap?'

'Why do women usually want soap? To wash in, of course. Put it on my account, Fiona.'

Fiona lowered her voice, 'Pa said—'

'Och, you tell McTavish I'll be collecting the rents tomorrow. I'll call in to pay it then.'

'I'll tell Pa to expect you, then. Ye'll be wanting to talk to him about that business you've got with him, will you not?'

'Aye, I suppose I do, but there's nae rush and it can wait a few weeks until I've got the details sorted out in my head. D'ye ken that, Fiona?'

'Aye, I ken.'

He avoided her eyes and left. Detouring to the dairy he grudgingly paid the milk account with the coins his grandfather and Kenna had given him, then set off back up the hill towards Glenchallon. Rory pondered his problem. All he'd done was buy himself a week or so of time. What the hell was he to do now? He desperately needed Kenna's money, but his heart, and other bits, were definitely with Fiona – and he'd more or less told her he'd wed her.

His mouth quirked into a grin. Perhaps he could marry Kenna for her fortune, kill her to inherit, then wed Fiona.

His smile faded and his eyes sharpened. Was it such a wild idea, after all? Accidents happened all the time and there were several ways he could think of to get rid of her. She could drown in the loch to start with . . . or she could fall down the stairs and break her neck. God knew, the stairs were rotten enough. But he'd already showed Kenna which ones to avoid. But then, she might go walking and blunder into one of the peat pools in the bog, or be trampled by a couple of rutting stags. Then again, a tree branch might fall on her.

'Aye, and one might fall on you if she gets wind of what you're thinking,' he told himself with a chuckle, for she was a girl with spirit, and now he'd got used to seeing her skinny body he found some things attractive about her, like her small waist and the flare of her hips. Still, he amused himself thinking of other ways of disposing of the woman on the way home.

As he walked around the back of the house he came across her. She was trying to split a log with an axe which lacked an edge. She hadn't got very far with her task. He stood and watched her. She had a determined look on her face as she attacked the log, and was using all her strength. Then she missed the log altogether, and the axe got stuck in the wooden block she was using.

She planted her feet on the block and applied some pull to the handle, snarling at it, 'Come out, you stubborn creature!' It jerked free suddenly. Staggering backwards, she lost her footing and sprawled on the cobbles, the axe just missing her head as it flew from her hands. 'Stupid damned axe!' she shouted at it.

She was determined, he'd give her that, Rory thought, and her useless city ways made him laugh. He chuckled and held out his free hand to pull her up, abandoning all thoughts of killing her when he saw the way her breasts jutted against her bodice. 'I'll sharpen the axe for ye after I've put this stuff in the kitchen. Ye don't have to use force, ye know. Just let the axe head drop on to the log and it'll split. I'll show you how tae do it.'

'Thank you, Laird,' she said caustically after he made good his promise and handed the axe back to her. 'I don't know how I'd manage without your help.'

'Aye, but ye can't help having city ways, I suppose.'

She gazed at him for a moment or two with a disbelieving look in her eyes, then she began to laugh, and when he asked her what she was laughing at she laughed even louder. Disconcerted, because he didn't know what she found so funny, he left her and went stomping off indoors, wondering if she was mad.

Kenna watched Rory go, her merriment fading. She shouldn't have laughed. He was right; she couldn't help having city ways, any more than he couldn't help being an uplander. There was nothing wrong with either.

She'd be the first to admit that the landscape here was spectacular, but she'd always be an outsider to him, and to all his friends and tenants, no doubt. If she bore him children, they'd belong to him and to Glenchallon, since the place would be ingrained in their hearts from the minute they were born. That would be the bond that would keep her tied in an unhappy union with a man she neither loved nor understood.

If she held any affection for Rory Challoner she'd be happy with the life he could offer her here. But he only wanted her money, and just now she'd give anything to be back in Edinburgh, in her own bedroom.

But, that too was a lie. Above all, she'd rather be in Hampshire with Dominic and Evelyn, for that was where her heart really was.

Nine

It felt as though Dominic had never been away from Edinburgh. It was drizzling with rain when he alighted from the train, and several degrees colder than Hampshire had been. He took a room at the Waverly Hotel in Princes Street, which was situated close enough to the station to walk to. He spent the evening thinking of the best way to go about finding Kenna.

The next morning he made his way to the law courts, handed over his card and asked the enquiry clerk behind the desk if they had any record of a lawyer called Andrew Mackenzie. 'He had two daughters, and I believe he died a few years ago.'

'I'll enquire, Doctor Sterne,' the young man behind the desk said with a smile. 'Would you be seated?'

It took several minutes before he came back. 'Mr Tam Fellowes was a friend of Mr Mackenzie, and remembers him well. He can give you five minutes, if you'd follow me, sir.'

Fellowes was sharp-eyed and affable, and Dominic immediately felt at ease with him. 'Call me Tam,' he said when they'd shaken hands and exchanged pleasantries. 'May I ask why you need the information?'

'I have a brooch that belonged to Andrew Mackenzie's daughter. It would hold sentimental value for her.' He showed him the trinket.

'Ah, yes, that's Andrew and his wife. Teresa, her name was.' He gave a faint smile. 'We spent some enjoyable evenings together. Jeanne wouldn't have much use for the brooch now, she died last year, you know. Such a shame. She was married to her father's clerk.'

'Robert something?'

'Aye, Robert Gilmore his name was. He practised law for

a while, though not very successfully. Andrew didn't take to the chap at first, said he was lacking in integrity, but that didn't stop him from taking Gilmore on as a partner. *Noblesse oblige*, I suppose. Andrew died of some stomach complaint shortly afterwards. A pity. He was good at what he did and his skills in court added considerably to his wealth. The firm went downhill after he died. There were rumours, you know.'

'What sort of rumours?'

He shrugged. 'One or two of Gilmore's acquaintances were a bit dubious . . . and there was talk that his qualification wasn't quite what it should be. I haven't seen the man around the courts for quite a while.'

'Did you know he'd married again recently?'

'No . . . no, I didn't. Not that he ever talked much about his business. It's possible that he's left the district since there were rumours that he had plans to go abroad.' Tam Fellowes gave him a quizzical smile. 'What's this really about? I can't imagine anyone going to all this trouble over a brooch.'

'No, you're right, Tam, and the brooch belonged to the younger daughter, Kenna. She came into my life just when I was on the brink of leaving. She'd been treated badly by Robert and the new Mrs Gilmore. To cut a long story short, I began to care for Kenna, but she disappeared before I could declare myself, leaving no address. I still hold her close in my affections.'

'Ah, an affair of the heart. As much as us men try to deny it, it strikes us all at times, robs us of our good sense. Yes, I do remember Kenna, though she was a great deal younger than her sister. A lively child, pert and pretty, and she had a good mind on her. She must be about twenty by now. I suppose she'll still be living in the family home. I was the executor of Andrew's will, you know. She inherited half of everything, and was left quite well off.'

'What about her brother-in-law, Robert Gilmore?'

'He was entitled to his wife's half of the estate after she died, and was appointed as trustee of Kenna's portion. She would have been too young to take charge of it, you see.'

'Thank you, Tam. You've been very helpful. I was wondering if you could furnish me with an address for this Robert Gilmore?'

He did, adding, 'Come over to my house to dinner tomorrow evening and let me know how you get on. In the meantime I'll see what else I can find out.'

Dominic took his leave of the man and headed for Ainsley Place. The door was opened by a woman in her early thirties. There was a sound of hammering coming from inside. Dominic doffed his hat and handed over his card. 'My name is Doctor Dominic Sterne. I'm looking for Robert Gilmore, who is a lawyer. I believe he lives here.'

She smiled. 'I'm afraid not, Doctor Sterne. We bought the house and furnishings from Robert Gilmore some time ago and have recently moved here from Glasgow. My husband is George Stuart, and I'm Anna Stuart.'

'I see. I'm sorry to bother you, Mrs Stuart. I wonder, would you have any idea where Gilmore went?'

'No, but my husband might. Is it important?'

'To find Mr Gilmore? Not in itself. I'm really looking for his sister-in-law, Kenna Mackenzie. I have something that belongs to her. I thought Mr Gilmore might know where she was.'

'Oh, I see.' She stepped to one side. 'Do come through, Doctor Sterne. George is hanging pictures while the children are busy at school. I was just about to call him down for some refreshment. He might be able to help you. Would you care to join us?'

Her husband was a nondescript man of average build. He came down, a portrait of a woman held in front of him. He heaved a sigh as he lowered it to the floor. The nameplate stated Teresa Mackenzie, but Dominic would have known it was Kenna's mother without it, for the resemblance was unmistakable. Just seeing her made his heart sing.

'That can go, Anna,' he said.

'Would you allow me to make you an offer for it? The lady in the portrait is the mother of the girl I'm looking for. I'm sure she'd like to have it when I find her.'

'Och, man, you can take it with you. I've got no room for someone else's kin, I've got too many of my own to cope with.' He extended a hand. 'George Stuart. I don't think I can help you with any information. We've not long moved to Edinburgh.'

Anna brought out a splendid dark fruit cake. 'Ye'll have

some with your coffee, now, won't you, Doctor? I made it myself.'

'And a grand cook she is too, there's no one who can bake a fruit cake like my Anna.'

They'd nearly finished their coffee when George suddenly smiled. 'I know who might be able to help ye find the previous owner of this place. The lawyer who handled the house sale. Malcolm Owen was his name. We have his address on the correspondence.'

Anna smiled at Dominic as she saw him out. 'This lass you're looking for . . . do you love her?'

So, she'd seen right through him. He smiled, and nodded.

'Then I hope ye'll find her, for you're a nice man.'

Dominic went back to his hotel with his stomach full of cake, the portrait of Teresa Mackenzie under his arm and the address of yet another lawyer in his pocket.

He set the portrait against the wall and gazed at it, sighing as he murmured, 'I'm in love with your daughter and intend to wed her if she'll have me. I'd be much obliged if you could help me find her.'

Teresa Mackenzie's painted amber eyes gazed into his, and she continued to smile benignly at him from her frame.

The next morning Dominic took a cab to the older part of Edinburgh and found himself in a dingy office not far from the docks.

There was something that appeared not quite trustworthy about Malcolm Owen. Usually Dominic's intuition was supported by fact before he acted on it. This time, he decided it was too strong to ignore.

'Robert Gilmore?' the small, balding man stated quickly, his eyes darting away. 'I can't say I've ever heard of him.'

'Odd,' Dominic said. 'I understand you handled the sale of a house in Ainsley Place recently. The seller was Robert Gilmore, the purchaser, George Stuart.'

Owen blustered. 'Did I? One does so much clerking in this profession that it's hard to recall names. What of it?'

Dominic offered him the bare minimum. 'I need to get in touch with Robert Gilmore and wondered if you had a forwarding address.'

'Are you a law enforcement officer?'

A policeman? 'Of course not. You have my card, Mr Owen.'

'Yes, of course.' His eyes washed over it, then he picked up a paper knife and traced the point over his blotting paper. 'I'm afraid I can't give you an address, Doctor, um –' he glanced at Dominic's card again, his hand trembling – 'Sterne. As you would afford your patients the assurance of privacy, so I must do the same with my clients. Good-day to you, sir.'

Dominic had hardly made it to the door when the man asked tentatively, 'May I ask what this enquiry is in relation to, Doctor Sterne? Nothing dishonest, I hope?'

Why would he jump to such a conclusion? When coupled with his earlier question, it aroused suspicion. This man had something on his conscience he was trying to hide, and he knew more than he was saying. His nervousness had made him jumpy.

Dominic made no indication that he suspected all was not right. 'No, Mr Owen, it's not. I'm trying to get in touch with a young woman who was his ward, since I have something which belongs to her.' Apart from my heart, he thought wryly.

Owen's jowls quivered along with the relief displayed in his expression, and he mopped a handkerchief over his sweating brow.

A strange reaction. Gazing through narrowed eyes at him, Dominic said, 'Are you unwell, Mr Owen? You seem to have a fever.'

'It's a warm day. Thank you for calling. If I think of anything that might be useful to you I'll send word over to your hotel.'

Inclining his head, Dominic walked from the building into a day that was anything but warm. He drew in a deep breath.

Robert was long overdue and Agnes had begun to run out of money.

She didn't intend hanging about London by herself any longer. Sensing all was not quite as it should be, Agnes picked the lock on Robert's travelling trunk and found nothing of value in it, just a few items of clothing. The sly bastard had done what he'd told that sister-in-law of his he'd do. He'd deserted her. Well, if he thought he'd get rid of her by abandoning her in London he could think again. She liked being a respectable married woman, and she intended to stay that way. And if Robert bloody Gilmore tried to deny he was married to her she'd kick up a fuss.

After all, it had been she who'd helped him to get hold of Kenna Mackenzie's cash. She'd forged Kenna's signature on all sorts of legal papers to transfer it to his first wife's name.

Jeanne Gilmore's death certificate had stated that she'd died from a malignant growth in the stomach. But the doddering old fart who'd signed it had hardly been able to see well enough to write his own name. Agnes suspected Robert had used arsenic, for she'd come across a container hidden behind a false back in the kitchen cupboard just before they'd left for London. Not that she'd told him she'd found it. She'd left it there as evidence, in case she ever needed it.

To supplement her funds she'd allowed herself to be picked up by a prowling gentleman in a carriage outside the theatre in Convent Garden the night before. Though she'd been obliged to close her mind to what he'd demanded of her, he hadn't quibbled about payment. It wasn't the first time she'd done that sort of thing when she'd been short of cash, but she'd been faithful to Robert since her marriage and wasn't happy about being obliged to return to it. Still, needs must when the devil drives, she told herself by way of excuse as she packed her bag.

She sneaked out of the hotel in the early hours, creeping through the kitchen and into the back alley. The night porter was snoring loudly in his chair in the foyer, supposedly guarding the front entrance.

Making her way to Euston through the dark streets Agnes waited until the railway office opened, then bought a ticket back to Edinburgh on a train which departed at nine twenty-five.

The train sped through the countryside, making short stops at various stations here and there for the passengers to refresh themselves. It was a tedious journey and she heaved a sigh of relief thirteen hours later when they pulled into Waverly Station. Smiling grimly, she thought to herself that Robert was in for a big surprise.

Night had fallen and she spent some precious money on a cab to Ainsley Place, where she quietly let herself inside the house, which smelled differently to what she remembered – of beeswax polish and freshly baked bread. The smell made her stomach growl from hunger.

Agnes didn't bother being quiet as she lit a candle from a night light. She gazed at the brass candlestick and couldn't remember seeing it before. And he'd moved the furniture, she thought, cursing as she tripped over a stool.

She made her way to the kitchen where she found the bread which had been left on a rack to cool. She took a pot of butter and a stone jar full of strawberry conserve from the pantry. *My . . . Kenna has been industrious*, she thought. She was probably trying to get back into Robert's good books.

Her mood lightened. That's why Robert hadn't returned to London. He'd found his sister-in-law and, as usual, she was proving to be difficult.

After eating she swigged down the crumbs with some milk from a brown, earthenware jug, another thing she'd never seen before.

She'd just set it down when the door swung open with a creak. She turned, to find herself staring into the eyes of a stranger.

'Who the hell are you?' she said.

Ten

Rory didn't go out of his way to make Kenna welcome at Glenchallon, neither did Maggie take much interest in her.

She turned up on time for her meals, which consisted mostly of fish or venison, or she went without. She stayed out of Maggie's way as much as she could and minded her own business.

Rory was hardly ever around. He seemed to spend time in the hills surrounding the house, but she didn't know how he occupied his time. When she ran into him he avoided her eyes and was uncommunicative, her attempts at conversation bringing a few grunts. By the end of the first week she was bored – and tired, for the tortured sounds coming from the house woke her from her sleep every night, making her heart pound.

'Is there a piano?' she asked Maggie one afternoon.

'Aye. Upstairs in the library.'

Her eyes widened. 'There's a library?'

'Didn't I just say so? Up the stairs, take the corridor to the left and second door along.

The auld Challoner put it there because his wife played it when she was alive, and it reminded him of her. He couldn't bear to look at it.'

'He must have loved her.'

Maggie snorted fiercely. 'He could nae stand the sight of her. He said she was insane.'

'And was she?'

'Aye. She thought the house was haunted and its spirits spoke to her at night. She was a frail wee thing who should have stayed in the city, for she was frightened of her own shadow and took her own life eventually. She slept in the room that you use. Isla Challoner's portrait is there on the wall. It was painted shortly after they were wed.'

Prickles of unease raced along Kenna's spine and she stared at Maggie, eyes wide,

Maggie grinned. 'You don't have to worry, she didn't die in that room.'

'How did she . . . *die*?'

'She was expecting a child. Six months gone she was and she threw herself from the window on to the flagstones below. Made a mess of herself.'

'Oh, the poor woman.'

'Poor woman?' Maggie snorted. 'May the devil take Isla's soul, for it's what she deserved. It was a wicked act to kill herself with the child inside her, and her leaving a five-year-old son without a mother to love him.'

A role which Maggie had obviously assumed. That explained why Rory put up with the crabby old woman.

As she turned to leave, Maggie said, 'If ye're going to the library you can take the old man his tea tray. Better tell him ye're going to use it, else he might think it's Isla come back and have a heart attack. His rooms are next door. Don't mind his ramblings. Sometimes he's as eccentric and unstable as his daughter was.'

'What's his name?'

'Magnus Fergusson.'

Kenna found her way easily enough. The door was open. When she knocked a voice as deep as a gravel pit said, 'Come in. Put the tea on the table.'

There were several tables, most of them covered in tubes of paint, bottles of turpentine and other tools and utensils used for the art of painting. Magnus stood before an easel in front of the window. He was tall, thin and stooped and his hair flowed down over his shoulders from under a red velvet hat.

'Which table? They're all occupied.'

His brush stopped in mid-air and he painfully turned to stare at her. His eyes were a piercing blue, his face a web of wrinkles. He scrutinized her steadily, shock apparent in his eyes, saying nothing.

She held his gaze when his eyes came up to her face, then smiled. 'This tray is heavy, Mr Fergusson.'

'Of course, I didn't think.' He swept books from a table next to an armchair. He moved back when she moved forward to relieve herself of her burden and pointed to a stool. 'Sit there in the light so I can see your face. Why have you come? I didn't invite you.'

'I came to play the piano, and brought your tray up with me.'

'It needs tuning. Sit! I won't bite you.'

Seated, she felt more vulnerable and shrank back when he reached out to her. He withdrew his hand. 'They told you I was mad, didn't they?'

His voice reminded her of Dominic's. 'You have an English accent,' she said, her surprise evident.

'My parents were Scots. I was raised in London by my uncle, who was an English baron. He had me trained to be an architect. But you didn't answer my question.'

'It's not one I want to answer really. You tell me, sir. *Are* you insane?'

'Certainly not . . . at least, not today.' His smile was almost a grimace. 'Are you?'

She chuckled. 'I don't know. What does insane look and sound like?'

'A good point. But I must tell you that you must be crazy to stay at Glenchallon. The place could fall down any moment.' He took her chin in his hand and examined her face. 'There's a resemblance, you know. That's what I was afraid of.'

'A resemblance to whom?'

'My daughter, Isla.'

A chill ran through her. 'Rory's mother?'

He nodded, then picked up a sketching block and took the armchair. 'Stay and have tea with me while I sketch you.'

'There's only one cup on the tray.'

'Use the glass on the table for me, it's only had whisky in it. Besides, the piano needs tuning. I can tune it in the morning if you like. Then you can play it.'

'You can tune a piano? You're a man of many talents.'

'You don't have to flatter me, you know. I used to teach music and painting.'

'You said you were an architect,' she pointed out.

'I said I was trained to be one; that doesn't mean I practised it. I preferred art and music. That's how I met my wife, Katherine, I was her tutor. We ran away together, married for love. Her parents wouldn't forgive us, so they cut her off. She died from consumption.'

'I'm sorry, that must have been hard for her, and for you.'

'It was. She gave me Isla, who was so much like her. There's an air about a girl on the brink of womanhood, something so tender, innocent and vulnerable that men want to take possession of it. But sometimes, they forget to cherish as they conquer. The consequence is the destruction of the very quality that attracted them in the first place.'

'Is that why Isla looked so sad?'

'What do you know about Isla?' he said fiercely.

'Her portrait hangs on the wall in my room. I've just cleaned the soot from the surface. Her eyes show her suffering, and I can feel her distress.'

'Isla's husband smeared it with soot so he wasn't reminded of his guilt when he saw it. I painted that picture a few months after she'd married. She begged me to take her away to London, but I couldn't. I'd given her to her husband and he wouldn't agree. Instead, I stayed here, so she'd have someone who cared for her and I watched her husband suck the life from her.'

He picked up a stick of charcoal and his hand flew over the paper as he sketched, the expression in his eyes retrospective, and a tender little smile playing about his mouth. Kenna placed the tea next to him. After a while he exhausted his energy. Throwing the paper aside, he stood, grunting with the effort, then shuffled on worn slippers to the window, where he stared out at the rain for several minutes.

He seemed to have forgotten her, but when she rose, intending to leave, he said, without turning round, 'The light's not good enough for painting at this time of day. What's your name, girl?'

'Kenna Mackenzie.'

He passed a trembling hand over his forehead. 'Ah yes, I remember. Well, Kenna, we shall be friends, I think. Tomorrow you can come and play pianoforte for me if you wish. Same time.'

Kenna had found the old man to be more learned and

interesting than she'd expected. 'I'll look forward to it, Mr Fergusson,' and she wondered if he'd remember to tune the instrument – or indeed, if he had the skill to.

'Isla didn't kill herself,' he said quietly. 'She was pushed. The piano hasn't been played since.'

Startled, Kenna gazed at the old man's crooked back. Maggie had said Isla had killed herself, and that would have been a great shock to him. 'Who pushed her?'

He didn't answer. 'Ten years later to the day her husband fell down the stairs and broke his neck. He was drunk. Isla's death put a curse on Glenchallon. Her spirit is still here, living in torment and waiting to be set free.'

Goosebumps raced through her body.

'Close the door behind you when you leave, it helps keep the draughts out,' he said.

Rory questioned her at dinner.

'You visited my grandfather today, then.'

'Aye, I took his tea up.'

'What did he say?'

'Say?'

Rory sighed. 'Yes, say. You had a conversation with him, did you not?'

'Of course. Mr Fergusson seemed very lucid.'

'What did he talk about?'

Maggie pause in her eating and gazed fixedly at Kenna.

'He did some sketches of me and said the light was bad. And he told me he'd trained to be an architect when he was young.'

Maggie nodded. 'That's the truth.'

'And, what else?' Rory said.

'He invited me to take tea with him tomorrow. He's going to tune the piano so I can play for him.'

'That was Isla's piano. I'm surprised he'd let you use it.'

'Why?'

'He doesn't usually take to strangers. Did he talk much about . . . her?'

Something about Rory's voice urged Kenna to caution. 'He hardly mentioned her, except to say she had put a curse on the house. And he said I reminded him of her.'

Rory stared at her for a long moment, as if trying to see what his grandfather had seen. He had the same piercing look in his eyes as his grandfather, but where Magnus Fergusson's eyes displayed a deep-seated intelligence in their depths, Rory's bristled with the belligerence of his questioning.

'My mother threw herself out the window. She killed herself,' he said, exchanging a glance with Maggie, who smiled at him and patted his hand.

'Yes, so Maggie told me. That must have been hard on you. I'm sorry.'

He shrugged. 'I canna remember her. Tell me if the old man says anything.'

'About what?'

'How do I know? Anything. His money . . . his will, or if he owns any property anywhere.'

'But why should I when it's his private business?'

'Because his business will be my business when he dies.'

'Then why don't you ask him yourself?'

'Because he won't tell me. He just starts ranting.'

'Your grandfather is an astute man. He'll see right through it. I like him and I'll lose his companionship.'

'Then if you're not going to be helpful you might as well find something more useful to occupy yourself with. You could help Maggie work in the garden.'

'That's my garden, and I don't want anyone else meddling in it,' Maggie snapped, as though she was having a privilege taken away instead of being offered some help. It's not for growing pretty flowers in.'

'Well, there's always mending to do.'

'I can repair the household linen, as I've always done.' This accompanied by a sour look from Maggie.

Rory shrugged, saying in a studied, casual manner that told Kenna he'd had it on his mind for some time, 'Well, you know best, Maggie, but if she can't do anything useful she'll have to contribute something towards the household expenses.' This addressed to Maggie again.

'If you're talking about my allowance, that's my business, not Maggie's. And I'd like to remind you that I'm not your servant.'

His eyes slid back to her. 'Aye, but if you can afford fancy soap for yourself you can afford to contribute towards the food. I've got an account to pay at the local shop, and the tenants' rents don't stretch far enough.'

'How much is it?'

'That's for me to know.'

'You'll get the interest from my inheritance in three weeks,' she pointed out. Even though she was growing increasingly dubious as to the materialization of such an outcome, it was useful to remind him of why she was here. She didn't mention her fears though, because she needed to make alternative plans – and those plans didn't include handing over all she had, only an amount that was fair.

'Aye, but I haven't collected it yet, and I'll have to feed you for the next three weeks before I do. And I'll need money to go and collect it. I'll expect you to hand over your allowance later.'

All Rory Challoner thought about was money. Well, he could expect all he liked. She would not hand over all of her allowance. Since she needed some sewing needles and cotton, she decided she'd pay the bill at the village store instead. That way, she'd know it was paid and that she'd contributed something. Besides, it was a nice morning and she could do with a walk.

'I can keep household and estate accounts, so could help out with the bookkeeping,' she offered. After all, she'd have to do it when they were wed. *If they were wed*, she amended, because the situation she found herself in suddenly didn't seem quite real to her, and she couldn't see herself becoming the wife of Rory Challoner.

'Household and estate accounts?' He scratched his untidy head. 'I can't say I remember any books.'

Maggie claimed the task 'And besides, I keep a tally of household expenses and I don't want a stranger meddling in it.'

Kenna ignored her and kept her eyes on Rory. 'Then how do you know what's being paid out, and to whom? And what about the rents? Surely you have a rent and receipt books, and keep a record of what you spend on repairs?'

'The old laird kept books,' Maggie said. 'He had to, so

he knew how much he owed to whom. They'd be in the estate office. The trouble is, you close your mind to things, Master Rory.'

'Perhaps that's because you're answering the questions for him,' Kenna pointed out. But the woman wouldn't be told.

'Aye, mebbe, but one day somebody will walk in here and claim the estate. Not that the house is worth anything, the condition it's in. We'd be better off living in the lodge.'

Annoyed, Rory shot to his feet and glared at them both. 'Shut up, the pair of you. How I run the estate is nobody's business but mine, and the bookwork can wait. As for repairs, I'm not useless, I do them myself – what else d'you think I'm doing when I'm out all day? It saves money. Has Grandfather been down, Maggie?'

'His rheumatism is still playing up, he said. Does he think he's the only one who suffers? He just likes to see me run around after him. He can wait a while for his oatmeal and tea this morning. I've other things to do.'

'I'll take it up to him myself. I need to have a word or two with him.'

When Rory left the kitchen Maggie took a bill from the dresser drawer and held it out to Kenna. 'Here, if you're thinking of paying the account. Heed my advice: keep your own money well hidden.'

The account was bigger than she'd expected. Kenna went up to her room. Taking some coins from her purse she looked around for a safe place to hide the rest of it. Nowhere too obvious. Her glance lit on the fireplace, with its elaborate black iron grate and tiled surround. The fire cradle was piled high with pine cones, thickly coated in dust. She shoved the purse into the ash tray underneath, and slid it back into position.

As she was leaving she heard Rory shout from upstairs, 'Don't you talk about my mother and father to her again! It's none of her business.'

There was a crash, and the reply from Magnus Fergusson was a dismissal of such succinct vulgarity that Kenna didn't know whether to grin or to blush at admitting to herself that she knew the meaning of such a word, especially when spoken in such perfectly accented English.

She ran down the stairs when a door slammed shut,

surprising Maggie, who was at the bottom. The woman gave her a grin. 'He'll never get the better of Magnus Fergusson.'

Rory came down brushing porridge from his jacket, his face like thunder as he glared at them. 'What are you two staring at?' Pushing through them with some force he headed out through the door and slammed it behind him, almost squashing the dogs, who just managed to slide through the gap before it latched. A chunk of plaster fell from the ceiling above the stairwell and shattered into a powder that spread across the tiled entrance hall.

Giving a sigh, Maggie went off to fetch a broom, muttering, 'I'll be glad when the place falls down.'

An event which was imminent, according to Magnus. When Kenna went outside Rory was stomping off up the hill towards the forest. She suddenly felt sorry for him. It was obvious he loved his home. Just as obvious was the fact that the house was falling down around his ears and he lacked the funds to stop the rot.

The house needed demolishing before it fell down, Maggie was right about that. But Rory was stubborn to the point of stupidity. And he was a rude, unmitigated bore. She'd liked him better on the journey up, when he'd been his own man, comfortable with his heritage. He had too much pride and not enough skill to keep an estate like this on a businesslike basis, especially since he'd inherited a large debt.

His image in her mind was replaced by one of Dominic and Evelyn. She bitterly regretted going off without telling them, and her fingers strayed to the golden band she wore on her wrist with their names inscribed inside. She'd read more into the gift than Dominic had intended. Evelyn's idea, he'd said, and who else would have described it as magic? It had been intended as a gesture of friendship, nothing more.

Allowing him the intimacy they'd both craved had been a mistake that had placed him in an awkward position. It had meant more to her than it had to him because the act of loving they'd shared had confirmed his initial opinion of her. Decent women did not become intimate with men they were not married to. Perhaps Dominic had been relieved that she'd solved the problem by walking away. As for her, she'd walked from one problem into a bigger one.

The more she saw of Rory Challoner the less she wanted to wed him. If Robert decided to part with all of her inheritance it still wouldn't be enough to tempt her. But if her brother-in-law's intentions turned out to be honest, and if Rory did happen to get his hands on her money – she'd never be able to get it back.

The countryside was spectacular, something she hadn't fully appreciated when she'd arrived, for she'd been too tired. The track she was on sloped gently down through tracts of heather-covered heathland interspersed by stands of pines and oaks. The track meandered off into the distance before disappearing into the haze of mistiness in the valley bottom, that had not yet dispersed. Beyond, in the far distance, the tops of hills were painted with snow.

She stopped, drawing into her body a deep breath of air perfumed with pine. A peregrine hovered on high. The breeze was cool, even though the sun shone. But the morning had an air of brightness that was brittle, and it told her it would rain later.

How could she feel so trapped in a landscape so beautiful and vast? Then she realized it wasn't she who was trapped – at least, not yet – but Rory Challoner.

The village shop was a good two miles. Kenna's blisters had mostly healed over the last few days so the walk was a comfortable one.

A bell on a string jingled as she opened the door. She walked into a dim interior that had a general pungency of smell that couldn't be separated into individual ones. It took a few seconds for her eyes to adjust. When they did, Kenna discovered four people gazing at her in complete astonishment.

'Good morning,' she said into the silence.

At the back of the shop a man was poised with a sack of flour on his shoulder. He grunted as he placed it carefully on the floor in a little puff of white dust. Behind a counter that resembled a slab of toffee, the hand of a handsome, comfortably-built woman froze on a packet of salt.

It was a few seconds before the man moved forward, brushing his hands down the sides of his apron. His eyes were cautious, his smile wary. 'I'm Donald McTavish. How can I help you, lass?'

Kenna indicated the other two women, obviously customers. 'They were before me.'

'My daughter, Fiona, is seeing to them. And you are . . .?'

'Kenna Mackenzie.'

'A Mackenzie, is it? I've never set my eyes on you before, lass. You must be a stranger to these parts.'

She tried not to grin at the observation, for their reaction to her had made that glaringly obvious. 'Aye, I am. I'd like a reel of white cotton thread and a packet of sewing needles, if you have them.'

'Aye, we have them.' He disappeared behind the counter and brought them out from a drawer. 'Is there anything else you need?'

She handed over the account. 'I'll pay this while I'm here. If you'd kindly give me a receipt.'

While the shopkeeper's eyes widened, those of his daughter narrowed. She said, 'You're visiting up at Glenchallon, are you? A relative of Maggie's, perhaps?'

'No, I'm not related to Maggie. I'm the laird's . . . *guest*.' She counted out the required amount of money and placed it on the counter. 'Receipt it if you would please, Mr McTavish.'

The astonished man wrote 'paid' across the account, signed and dated it, then, as if he thought the money might disappear before his eyes, he quickly scooped it from the counter into a drawer underneath.

Before she left Kenna asked them, 'Is there any way I can post a letter from here?'

'Aye. My father takes them into town to the post office every Thursday, and he brings any incoming letters back for people to pick up. Would you like your name added to the list?'

'I'm not expecting any mail at the moment, but yes, that would be kind of you.'

'Where are you from, lass?' one of the customers said.

'Edinburgh.'

'Staying long?' the other one asked, her eyes alight with curiosity.

Kenna stifled a grin. 'I haven't decided yet.' Tucking the receipt into her pocket, Kenna placed the goods in her basket, said good day, and left. Because it was uphill on the way back she took it a little slower, and to catch her breath she seated herself on the wall of a stone bridge spanning a small burn.

Footsteps pounded up after her and from around the bend came the girl from the shop. She came to a sudden halt, red-faced with the effort and breathing heavily. 'Are you seeing Mr Fergusson?'

Kenna nodded. 'I'm visiting him this afternoon.'

Fiona held out a parcel. 'Will you give this to him? It's the tubes of paint he ordered. Don't tell the Challoner. He daesna like the old man to waste his money.'

Placing the parcel in her basket Kenna smiled at Fiona. Everyone wanted to know everyone else's business around here, and without telling them their own. 'I won't tell him.' Then, curious, she said, 'I'm surprised Mr Fergusson can walk this far to place an order.'

'The milk carter brings the order and money down if he wants anything. My pa buys anything Mr Fergusson wants when he goes into Galashiels with the cart on Thursdays. And the milk carter usually takes the goods up tae him.' Abruptly, she said, 'Have you known Rory long? Did you meet him in Edinburgh?'

Something about Fiona's manner warned Kenna not to be too open with her. 'I've known him only short while. He's acquainted with my brother-in-law, who's in London at the moment with his new wife. He's a lawyer and the laird had some business to transact with him.'

'I see. He did get a legal letter a while back. I suppose he's looking after you until they come back. I wondered, will you be staying at Glenchallon long?' The woman was prickling with things unsaid, and her face was anxious.

Kenna picked her words carefully. 'The possibility of my stay being a long one is beginning to look doubtful. You appear agitated. Is there something you want to say to me?'

'Why should you think I'm agitated?' Fiona said defensively, then the fight seemed to go from her. 'Rory and I . . . you know . . . we're a couple. We'll be wed before too long if all goes well. I just wanted you to know that.' Her hands smoothed over her apron, betraying the likely reason for that wedding. 'I'd be obliged if you didn't tell anyone. I haven't told my pa yet. And please don't tell Rory I told you. He daesna want anyone to know, not for a month or so, anyway.'

The laird possessed a rat-like cunning, Kenna thought, under no illusions that Rory would try for both marriage and a mistress, and treat them equally badly. Anger towards the man he was filled her, but not by the flicker of an eyelid did Kenna reveal her true feelings. 'I won't tell anyone. I hope you'll be happy.'

Fiona's smile reached into her dark eyes, making her appear younger and more animated. It was as if the danger Kenna represented had suddenly evaporated. Fiona McTavish was a nice woman, one just a little past her prime in the marriage stakes. She was in an awkward position, and desperate for the proper solution to her problem. 'I'll be a good wife to him.'

The woman was too trusting if she thought marriage to Rory would be that easy, but Kenna was not going to be the one to shatter her illusions. And she wasn't going to stand in her way either, for Fiona could be the answer to her own problem.

'How are you getting on with Maggie?' Fiona chatted, now she'd rid her mind of her worry. 'She's nae too bad if you keep on her right side.'

Kenna's smile was a wry twist. 'As I've learned. I'd better go now. It was nice talking to you, Miss McTavish. I'll bring down a letter to post in the morning. What time does your father leave?'

'About six o'clock. Put it in the basket on the kitchen table next to the milk jug. The milk carter will collect it and bring it down. It'll save you the walk. And call me Fiona, everyone does.'

'Thank you then, Fiona. You can call me Kenna.'

'Aye, that would be nice and friendly indeed,' Fiona said, and headed off down the hill. She stopped at the bend and waved happily.

It won't be nice and friendly for long, Kenna thought, her mind now completely made up. She would write to tell Robert she was returning home as soon as she could make the arrangements.

There was no sign of either Maggie or Rory when Kenna got back to Glenchallon. She took her purchases up to her room, then came back down.

There was a pan of broth keeping warm on the hob, and fresh bread on the table under a cloth. Kenna helped herself to a thick slice. The broth was thick with barley and diced vegetables, the gravy rich and strong with the taste of venison. Her appetite was back with a vengeance after the walk.

Maggie came in just as she was wiping the bread around the bowl. She nodded approvingly. 'That will put some meat on your bones. You can take the old man his broth up when you've finished yours. It will save my legs.'

Kenna bit back a retort. She'd be gone soon, so it didn't matter.

Eleven

The last note left Magnus Fergusson's violin to shimmer into the distance like the sound of crystal pinged by a fingernail. For a moment or two his creased face absorbed the silence in its wake, then he gave a faint smile, opened his eyes and laid the instrument gently back in its case. His bent fingers caressed the wood. 'I haven't played for a while. My fingers are stiff.'

Kenna put the lid down over the keys of the piano. He'd listened to her play through some exercises, then had selected easy pieces for them to play together. Purcell's *Lilliburlero, Air in D Minor*, then Chopin's *Etude number 3*. 'I haven't played the piano for a while, either. I enjoyed it, though. I'm sorry about the false notes.'

'It wasn't your fault. I'm afraid I overestimated my own skill and the instrument wouldn't tune properly. The damp has got at it, and my hearing isn't as good as it used to be. A pity. I should have looked after it better, but there was nobody but myself to play it and I prefer the violin for myself. You play competently.'

She laughed and made a face at him. 'My piano teacher used to say that, and she used to smile in exactly the same way.'

'And what way is that, young lady?'

'With a slight air of superiority, as if she wanted to add, "Well enough for drawing room entertainment, at least."'

He chuckled. 'Isn't that what most ladies aspire to do?'

'Aye, you're right, but if music teachers are so much better, why are they teaching music for a living instead of being feted on some concert stage?'

'My dear, Kenna, you're too hard on music teachers. Most of us know when competence becomes genius, and the latter happens only rarely, even amongst ourselves. But even Mozart taught music. And Chopin would have starved in his garret if he hadn't taken in pupils.'

'And which composer do you compare yourself to, Mr Fergusson?'

He looked amused as he indicated the stool. 'You're too astute, and too provocative to be comfortable with. I'd forgotten how potent drawing room chat can be. I'm out of the habit of being sociable and all my illusions have been stripped away. Now I'm an old nuisance who complains when he's upset and roars when he's angry.'

'A pity you think of yourself that way. I quite like you despite your being a nuisance.'

'You do?' He gave a short bark of laughter. 'I'm touched. Nobody has liked me for a long time – but then, I'm not your nuisance, I'm somebody else's.'

'I'm beginning to learn how that feels, myself.' She ignored the stool and went to gaze out of the window, which was nearly the height of the room and had a wall supporting it beneath to thigh height. Standing there felt like being on a ledge looking over a chasm. A two-inch wide crack started from the ceiling, ran around the window frame in both directions, and joined up as one under the window sill. It disappeared down behind the floorboards like a jagged streak of lightning. A faint draft came up through the floor beneath.

Above her, the corner of the ceiling had fallen away. Her hand placed on the wall seemed to attract the quivering tensions in the house as it struggled against its demise.

Sadness filled her, for the people who'd occupied its spaces and had sheltered beneath its roof in the past, and for Rory, who didn't know how to let go and was paying for his ancestors' pride with this burden of a house to weigh him down.

There was a storm coming in. Purple and black clouds roiled in magnificent menace. The room had lost much of its light, and a sharp gust of wind spattered sleet against the window. The temperature had dropped sharply and the loch was now a churn of white, as if the grey surface was alive with jumping fish. A bird flew in to land on the surface, its feathers ruffling up from behind it like an Elizabethan ruff.

It turned to face the wind, settling into the water with its head hunched into its body.

A sharp poignant memory of Dominic filled her mind, so she lost her breath in the rush of longing to see him again. She wished she'd never come here. Once again she felt trapped in the drama of the landscape. The coming storm had filled her with energy as if the flickers of lightning on the horizon had made her restless.

The voice seemed to come out of nowhere, a sibilant whisper that made her start. *Leave Glenchallon.*

She spun around, her body pricked by an unexpected coldness. A grey film of age reflected from the eyes of Magnus, so they seemed blank. Then he moved his head slightly and they cleared.

'You heard her, didn't you?'

'I heard nothing,' she lied, wondering if he could detect the quaver in her voice. 'I must go, I need to write a letter. Thank you for the music, Mr Fergusson. I enjoyed it.'

'So did I. You looked like Isla sitting there at the piano. I'd be happier if you called me Magnus, you know.'

'I'd like to, Magnus. I'll come and see you tomorrow.'

'Perhaps.' There was a gust of wind. The door creaked as a draught swung it open on its hinges, as if someone was inviting her to depart. Outside, the hall was as dark as a pit. 'Tell Maggie I'll come down for dinner,' he said.

Kenna's feet were reluctant to carry her down the stairs, to the room that had once belonged to Isla. She kept hold of the banister as a guide, her feet feeling cautiously for each step, and being careful of those she knew were weak.

A step behind her creaked. She paused, listening. For a moment or two she heard nothing except the thundering pulse in her ear, but as it quieted there was a scuffing sound, then a breath expelled.

'Who is it?' she said. 'Who's there?'

A quiet chuckle raised the hair on her neck. As if that didn't frighten her there was a flash of lightning. For a moment she saw a figure standing there on the staircase. A peal of thunder hid her squeal of fright.

'Who are you?' she shouted with as much bravado as she could muster.

With the next flash she saw the figure disappear through the wall.

Thoroughly unnerved, she turned and fled down the stairs towards the light coming through the small window set high in the wall over the door. She'd go to the kitchen. Even Maggie's caustic company would be better than her own at present.

As she reached what she thought to be the bottom of the banister, she remembered the railing curved away from the bottom two steps. She tried to correct her stride, failed, tripped, and flew down the last two steps. Her momentum took her sliding across the hall into a table standing against the wall. There, she sprawled on her face, the wind knocked from her. The table rocked back and forth, then tipped. Kenna remembered in great detail the heavy bronze that usually stood there – a kilted man leaning on his stick, his dogs vying for his attention. A lifeless stag was laid at his feet, its magnificent head with its spread of antlers lolling to one side.

She covered her head with her hands, curling defensively as the table crashed down. The bronze missed her by a fraction, landing with a solid thud. She received a glancing blow on the shoulder from the table somersaulting over the top. She burst into tears, mostly from relief.

A door opened. 'What the hell's going on?'

'I saw a ghost, then fell down the stairs and knocked the table over.'

Rory began to laugh. 'A ghost, was it? Did he say who he was?'

'It was a woman. It's not funny, I might have been injured.'

'Aye.' Rory pulled the table from her body and came to squat beside her. 'I should have asked you, not laughed. Are you all right, lass?'

'I think so.' She sat up, feeling foolish. 'I really *did* see a ghost. It walked through the wall.'

'About three-quarters of the way up, near the landing?'

'Aye. Have you seen it too?'

'There's a sliding door in the panelling, Behind it is a set of servants' stairs leading to the kitchen. It was probably Maggie you saw.'

Embarrassed when she saw the laughter in his face, Kenna refrained from mentioning the voice she'd heard in his grandfather's room.

Restoring the bronze to its rightful place and gazing at the floor, Rory said soberly, 'It's lucky that didn't hit you. It's cracked a tile and one of the antlers has snapped off and embedded itself into the floor, barely an inch from where your head was.

He pulled her to her feet and gazed at her, gently moving a stray strand of hair away from her damp eyes. 'Are you sure you're all right?'

'I have a bruise on the shoulder, that's all.' She shuddered when he drew the antler from the floor. It was sharp and pointed. 'Can it be repaired?'

He shrugged. 'Why are you weeping?'

'I was scared. I don't like this house. It's sad and I feel trapped by it.'

He pulled a handkerchief from his pocket and dabbed the tears from her eyes. She jumped when thunder rolled overhead and he pulled her close, his unexpected sensitivity surprising her. She wished it was Dominic's arms around her. 'You're just homesick. You'll soon get used to it, and to the storms.'

Kenna didn't want to get used to either, and she didn't want this contact with him, their bodies so close that she could smell his sweat and feel the hard, muscular power of him. She said, almost in a panic at the thought of any intimacy with him, 'I'm all right. Let me go.'

His eyes gazed into hers. 'We should get used to each other, not wait until we're wed. I have feelings.' And she knew what those feelings were as his mouth fought for possession of hers, for he was hard and surging against her.

Her own feelings were those of repugnance. She managed to turned her head away from him and, using all her strength, pushed at him, spitting out with all the fury that was in her, 'Keep away from me.'

'So that's how it's to be?' he sneered. 'Well, as long as you give me a bairn every couple of years that's all I'll want from you.'

'Except for my money,' she said bitterly.

'Except for your money,' he agreed. 'Though I'm beginning to wonder if you're worth the effort.'

Kenna thought of Fiona, a nice young woman who carried Rory's child, unless she was mistaken. Fiona's child should inherit the estate, not be forced to look on – a bastard born on the wrong side of the blanket. She experienced a twinge of regret that she didn't have Dominic's child inside her, despite her spinster status.

'Believe me, I'm definitely not worth the effort, Rory,' she said. 'And neither is this house. I shouldn't have come. I want to go back to Edinburgh.'

'Stop your whimpering,' he said. 'Don't forget I've got your guardian's signature on a piece of paper.'

She laughed. 'So you have, and that's all you have at the moment, a piece of paper. Robert was in a hurry to get rid of me. It wouldn't surprise me to learn he'd leased the house and stayed on in London. He's a complicated and *dishonest* man, you know. There was something he was keeping to himself and you shouldn't have trusted him.'

Bunching her bodice in his fist he drew her forward and shook her. 'Complicated or nae, if that money isn't there I'll give him a good thrashing, even if I have to travel to London town to shake the cash out of his pockets. Then I'll come back here and thrash you.'

It was growing darker by the minute. Hail began to clatter on the roof and against the windows. A film of muddy water crept across the floor, and scores of drips and trickles fell out of the void above. A gust of wind blew the front door open with a smash. Rory swore, and while he hurried forward to close it, Kenna headed towards the kitchen.

The light from a couple of oil lamps was a welcome sight. 'Is there anything I can do to help?' she said to Maggie, who was up to her elbows in flour.

'I can manage.'

It was the reply Kenna had expected. 'Aye, I daresay you can, but there's water on the hall floor and I thought I might be able to clean it up.'

She began to grumble. 'Nothing can be done about it. It comes out of the hill at the back and fills the cellars. And it's nae use placing buckets under the leaks. There are too many of them. You'd be running back and forth all night emptying them. But there's nae telling the Challoner. He closes his eyes to things he doesn't want to see or think about. The water will find its own level and will drain away in its own good time, like it always does. How was yon grandfather?'

'Magnus enjoyed having company, I think.'

She raised an eyebrow. 'Magnus already, is it? Aye, the auld body *is* lonely, though when the melancholy mood is upon him he doesn't bear living with. I heard the music when I went upstairs, him playing that fiddle of his. It's been a long time.' She punched her fist into the dough she was making, sending puffs of flour into the air. 'It was a right pretty sound. It reminded me of when Isla was still alive. Close they were . . . father and daughter. Too close for the auld Challoner's liking. He didn't like the influence Magnus had over her.'

Kenna had been close to her own father. Her heart had nearly broken in two when he'd died. And when Jeanne had gone, Robert had made her feel like a stranger in her own home, for he'd shut her out of his own grief, as if he was the only one suffering and Kenna didn't have any of her own.

Now Andrew Mackenzie was reunited with her mother and Jeanne, and she was left behind with nobody to love – except a man she would probably never set eyes on again. 'I was close to my father, too. He died a few years ago. I miss him a lot.'

Maggie's eyes butted up against hers, unsympathetic. 'I don't miss mine. He was a miserable old sod who took the strap to myself and my mother every Sunday after church. My mother ran away and ended up in a poorhouse. He wouldn't take her back and she died there.' Maggie sighed and indicated a heap of potatoes. 'If ye want something to do ye can peel those tatties. It'll save me a job. Make sure you take all the eyes out, but keep the peelings. I boil them up with some bran for the hens. Did you pay the bill at the general store this morning?'

'Aye.' Kenna found the receipt in her pocket and gave it to the woman, then picked up a sharp knife and started to peel.

'McTavish signed it himself, that's good. He won't be able to dispute it, then,' Maggie said with some satisfaction.

Kenna tested the water to see how Maggie would react. 'I met his daughter, Fiona. She was friendly and seems like a nice young woman.'

'The Challoner didn't want ye to go to the store, ye ken.'

'Oh, why not?'

'Because the villagers go there and cause mischief with their tattle and he doesn't like them knowing his business. Ye'd have come as a surprise to them, and they'd have asked questions.'

'But isn't that what you intended when you gave me the account to pay, Maggie?'

Her expression became sly. 'What did ye tell bonny Fiona?'

'The truth. That I was a guest here.'

Maggie's blue eyes came up to hers, sharp with enquiry. 'And what did Fiona McTavish have to say about that?'

Kenna smiled at her. The residents of Glenchallon were overly concerned about who said what, and about whom. 'What Fiona said to me must remain confidential between us. But I think we understood each other.'

Maggie's eyes showed an unexpected approval at her answer. 'You're a canny one, Kenna Mackenzie, I'll give ye that. And sensible for a city-born lassie.'

Kenna accepted the compliment without comment. The less that was said to Maggie about anything, the better. But Maggie seemed to be playing a game of her own. 'By the way, Mr Fergusson said to tell you that he'll be coming down for dinner.'

'He must be feeling a bit better.' Annoyance made Maggie's face disagreeable. 'Playing that music would have made him remember the past. He'll want to be addressed as Lord Fergusson.'

'He has a title?'

'Aye, he's a baron. The title came down from his uncle – though no money or property as far as we know. We haven't been able to find where he keeps his papers, including his will.'

None of which was Maggie's business, Kenna thought.

'Yon Magnus likes to play the aristocrat now and again.

He'll want to eat in the dining room, and will expect you and the Challoner to dress for dinner. I'm making a venison pie, that's his favourite, at least. I'd better light the fire and give the table and siller a bit of a polish. The water won't reach in there, on account that there's a step up into that room.'

'I can do that.'

'It's my job to. But all right, since I didn't count on extra work being thrust on my shoulders this late in the day. Ye'll need some light, so take some spirit for the lamps.'

'Do we have any wine to decant?'

'Aye, there's a bottle of burgundy the auld sod gave me for Christmas. He knows I dislike red wine, which is why he gave it to me. He's mean spirited like that. Serves him right that he has to drink it himself.'

The rattle of hail suddenly stopped, leaving an unnerving silence filled with drips in its wake. Several creaks were followed by a loud crack.

Kenna exchanged a glance with Maggie, who shrugged. 'Likely the ice has built up in the gutters and one of them has fallen.'

'It sounded like glass.'

'It wouldn't be the first time a window has cracked for no reason. Weel then,' she said impatiently, 'ye haven't got all day, so ye'd better get on with it. I suppose I'll have to eat alone after I've served you. Magnus Fergusson likes to keep people in their places. Not that he's much to go on himself, title or nae.'

'Magnus Fergusson is a fine man.'

'Aye, weel, if you say so. Out of the way now, girl. I need to get to the oven.'

Kenna, who'd taken to wearing her comfortable skirt, bodice and shawl, looked forward to the chance to dress up a little.

But when the time came, Kenna was the first to admit it seemed rather incongruous, the three of them dining at a long table with candles flickering in silver candelabra while water dripped around them. It was as if they were characters acting in a play.

Rory looked handsome in a tartan kilt of a dark greeny-blue. He was deferential towards his grandfather and polite to her. Kenna wore her best blue gown with her mother's pearls at her throat. Maggie served them with good grace and addressed the old man as Lord Fergusson.

Afterwards, he sent Maggie scurrying to fetch his fiddle and played some Scottish airs composed by Neil Gow that set Rory smiling and her own her feet tapping. He ended his concert with a lament.

It seemed to Kenna that Magnus was reliving what had gone before, rather than what could be. There was sadness in the room when the last plaintive note died away. Tears welled in Kenna's eyes. 'That was beautiful,' she whispered.

His gnarled old hand reached out to cover hers. 'I wrote it for my daughter, Isla, Rory's mother. It's the anniversary of her passing. You remind me so much of her, Kenna. Stay away from the windows, if you would. There's death in the wind.'

Rory's smile faded as he looked from one to the other, the expression in his eyes wary. But he said nothing.

George Stuart unexpectedly presented himself at Dominic's hotel room when Dominic was dressing for his appointment to dine with Tam Fellowes at his club.

Dominic set George down with a double malt he'd ordered for himself, and the man sipped it appreciatively while Dominic shrugged into a frock coat with buttoned cuffs.

'I see you don't follow the fashion of wearing a moustache with your side whiskers,' observed George, who sported a prolific set with a definite dash.

'I prefer to be clean shaven.' Knotting his tie to his satisfaction Dominic then arranged a handkerchief in his top pocket and seated himself on the bed next to his top hat, gloves and cane. 'I'm sorry to keep you waiting.'

'The whisky was worth the savouring of it, and I came at an awkward time. I didn't know whether to bother you with this or not, Doctor Sterne, but Anne insisted. She thought it might be of help in finding your young lady.'

Dominic hoped so.

'We were disturbed a couple of nights ago by a young woman who let herself into the house with a key. She gave my Anna quite a fright, and—'

'What did she look like? Who was she? Was it Kenna?' Dominic asked eagerly.

'The young woman had dark hair and dark eyes, but she didn't resemble the portrait you took away with you. She was an attractive young woman, but in a bold sort of way. Not the type a professional gentleman such as yourself would fall in love with, or care to marry even if you did.'

Love wasn't discriminatory. Dominic tried not to grimace as he remembered his own prejudices regarding Kenna, which had been based on her initial appearance and an assumption on his part. He was ashamed of the way he'd manipulated her tender feelings to steal her innocence, and would never judge a person by outward appearances again.

'The young woman would nae give her name, but she picked up a knife and became abusive and agitated. The language she used when we told her we'd bought the house came straight from the gutter.' George's mouth pursed with disapproval. 'I was forced to grab up the poker, and threatened to inform the police if she didn't leave. She picked up her travelling bag and ran from the house, shouting out that she'd make him pay for what he'd done to her.'

'Make who pay?'

'That, I cannot say, Doctor Sterne. But I've had the locks changed, so we won't be getting any more unwanted visitors unless we open the door to them.' George swallowed the last sip of whisky and stood. 'I must be away now, Doctor Sterne. I'm sorry to have been a bother.'

'It's me who's been a bother. I can't apologize enough for what you're going through. It's likely that the woman is connected to Robert Gilmore.'

'Aye, that's what Anne thinks. Myself, I wouldn't presume to advise you of that. But you know what women are like when it comes to matchmaking, and Anne's convinced your young lady will turn up. As for the rest, it's no bother at all. Usually we live a quiet family life. Now we're greatly piqued by the intrigue of your personal business, and we're looking forward to a satisfactory conclusion to this. I believe that might be construed as natural curiosity – or nosiness if you'd prefer.'

'Then I'll keep you informed.' Dominic laughed, then slipped a note from his money clip and held it out to George.

'Please buy your Anna a posy of flowers on the way home as a small gesture of thanks from me, bless her romantic heart. You have a treasure there, George.'

'And she certainly lets me know it.'

'I'm most grateful for any information, however unlikely it might sound. This may be connected if the woman used a key to gain entrance. What was she doing when you discovered her?'

'She was seated at the kitchen table helping herself to our food. She seemed genuinely shocked to see us there. Nothing was missing, so the motive wasn't burglary.'

'I do hope you won't send Kenna away if she turns up on your doorstep.'

Smiling now, George said, 'I think we'll know your young lady when we see her. And if she needs a place to stay we'll certainly accommodate her until we can contact you.'

'Thank you, I'd really appreciate it.' They shook hands and George was gone.

Dominic's eyes narrowed thoughtfully. Two people had walked into the Ainsley Place house in the same week, himself and a woman. That was too much of a coincidence.

Had the woman been Agnes Gilmore? If so, what of Robert? He seemed to have disappeared without a trace. The whole affair was beginning to stink.

Tam Fellowes agreed with him.

They'd dined well on succulent roast lamb with all the trimmings and had followed it up with a jam pudding in a sea of custard and an excellent cheese board accompanied by liquor and Turkish coffee.

The room, which smelt pleasantly of tobacco smoke, leather and liquor, buzzed with the muted hum of male voices, into which the occasional bark of laughter intruded. Dominic felt totally relaxed in the company of this man.

Leaning back in his leather armchair the lawyer contemplated Dominic as he warmed a brandy between his hands. 'It does sound likely that the woman was Agnes Gilmore. That makes me think that Robert Gilmore has fled. What's more, he's cut all his ties. He sold the business some time ago. Then his wife conveniently dies and he marries his mistress over the anvil. Then, if you're right about the woman being Agnes Gilmore, he sells the house, using a solicitor of dubious reputation to do the conveyancing. He then arranges a marriage of convenience for his ward, who is supposedly a wealthy young woman. He then abandons his wife and disappears without trace. What does that say to you?'

'That he's got something to hide.'

'Exactly.'

Fear leaped through Dominic, leaving him with a sickness in his heart. 'You don't think he's hurt Kenna in any way, do you?'

'It's possible. Remember, though; Robert Gilmore was her guardian. If he were to inherit Kenna's funds he would have needed proof of her death. And that would raise questions so soon after her sister passing away. Rather, he may have fraudulently forged her signature to transfer her funds. It's possible that his wife helped him in that. He's probably married Kenna off on a promise of funds. You should be prepared for the possibility that she's another man's wife.'

Not until I hear it from her own lips. 'The sister . . . Jeanne, wasn't it? Do you think Gilmore may have had a hand in her death?'

'It's possible.'

The two stared at each other, then Dominic shrugged. 'Aren't we letting our imaginations run away with our good sense? I don't think we should inform the authorities of our suspicions on the strength of hypothesis.'

'Not yet, of course. We can't go accusing someone of murder, not without evidence. But I doubt very much if Gilmore is still in Edinburgh, or even in the British Isles. It's quite possible he's changed his identity to cover his tracks. I'll ask my clerk to find out if Gilmore handled any deceased estates in the year before he sold his business. That would give him an alternative identity to assume.'

'There must be hundreds.'

'Aye, but I'm looking for a man of about his age – someone with no kin who can dispute Robert Gilmore's claim to the identity.'

'I feel so helpless. All I really want to do is discover where Kenna is, and attempt to put things right between us.'

'I know, but the law isn't your area of expertise and one

thing often leads to another. We should put this matter into the hands of someone who is an expert. I have an acquaintance who runs a private detection agency,' said Tam. 'He's thorough, and expensive, but he only charges on results. Although I can't guarantee his availability, he might be able to recommend someone. Perhaps he can find this Agnes Gilmore – who seems to be the key to the whole thing. I imagine she'd know the plans Robert made for Kenna.'

'And you think she'd tell us?'

Tam grinned widely. 'If what we suspect turns out to be true, then she'll be a woman scorned, remember.'

'So she will.' But so was Kenna, Dominic reminded himself. How much he'd hurt her was yet to be revealed, and with each day that passed came the feeling that the woman he loved was slipping away from him.

Twelve

It rained heavily for three days. The hall at Glenchallon was ankle deep in water, which loosened many of the tiles. The water flowed through the corridors into the downstairs rooms, with the exception of the dining room.

Rory filled sacks with sand and built a knee-high barrier in front of the kitchen door to keep as much water out as he could. That had the effect of keeping it penned in but as it deepened it began to run over the door step and under the door. Water dripped from everywhere and ran down the walls. Chunks of plaster fell from the walls without warning and the house took on an unhealthy, mouldy odour.

'I've never seen it this bad,' Maggie kept repeating.

Magnus retreated to his room and Maggie complained about her aching joints. Rory became morose and hardly spoke. Kenna did what she could, running up and down the stairs with food for the old man, who was now as miserable as his grandson.

Nothing would stem the tide, and the noises the house made were alarming. After a while Kenna pointed out the obvious to Rory. 'Why don't you smash a channel through the step so the water will run out through the front door?'

He glared at her. 'And have the burn flowing right through the house?'

'It's already doing that, as far as I can see. A channel will allow it to flow out faster. Why can't this be discussed sensibly?'

'I don't want your advice, that's why. What does a city girl know?'

'Enough to be able to reason things out. If you won't listen to me, listen to your grandfather.'

'It's obvious you've been listening to him,' he grumbled.

'I can see how bad things are for myself. Is the lodge in better condition?'

'Aye, it is.'

'Couldn't we move in there until the rain stops and this place dries out?'

'The lodge is used for storage. Besides, the rain won't last for ever.'

'But surely we could clear some space—'

'No! Didn't you hear what I said, woman? Keep your bluidy nose out of my affairs. They don't concern you.'

She felt like smacking his face. He was stupidly stubborn. Like King Canute, he was trying to hold back the inevitable tide of water. He would fail just as badly. Kenna wished the rain would stop so she could make good her escape. Her temper, which had been on the edge for some time, sent out a short, sharp flare of rebellion.

'Then do me the same favour. Keep your nose out of my affairs in return. I'm sick of being questioned over everything I do and everyone I talk to.'

'Ye'll do as you're told.'

'No, Rory – no I won't. To hell with you.' Turning her back on him she stomped off through the muddy water, her skirt held aloft, and sending ripples out to lap against the walls.

Later, she was invited to tea with Magnus. The fire struggled to ignite the saturated coal and smoke sputtered up into the maw of the chimney.

He seemed to have shrunk, and resembled a miserable bunch of grey rags sitting in his armchair. His fingernails were bluish claws curving into the shredded leather armrests of his chair like an eagle latched into its prey. His lips had a bluish tinge too.

'You don't look well. Do you feel all right? I could fetch a doctor.'

'The weather makes me ache, and there's not enough light to paint,' he groused. 'Besides, this old body is past repair. Will you play the piano for me?'

'As long as you don't complain. The piano won't like the damp.'

'The piano is like everything in this house. It's reached

the end of its life. Today would be a good day to die, I think. Don't stay here at Glenchallon, girl, else it'll rob you of your soul. I should have left after Isla died.' His chin sunk on to his chest and he mumbled pathetically, 'I'm waiting for her to come and fetch me. She told me she's lonely without me.'

Kenna played a few short Chopin pieces, the notes plunking tunelessly. She abandoned it when Magnus began to snore. The rug had slipped from his knees. Was that how she'd end up, old and neglected and full of regrets – waiting for death to claim her? Feeling a deep compassion for him she placed the rug back over him before she left for her own room.

Something was different. What? Her eyes skimmed over it. Things were disturbed. One of her slippers was turned on its side; the lid to her jewellery box was open, not that she had very much – a ring and a string of pearls that Jeanne had given to her, which had once belonged to their mother. She'd lost the miniatures of her parents, and thought the drunk who'd robbed her of Dominic's cloak and hip flask must have taken the brooch from her pocket, where it had been pinned for safekeeping.

'Dominic, come what may I'll always love you,' she said, her voice almost a caress, and her fingers strayed to her most precious keepsake, the gold bracelet. At the same time her glance fell on the chest of drawers. The top drawer was open a crack. She went over to it. Her undergarments had been tossed about.

There was the creak of a floorboard behind her and she turned to see Rory standing there. Although the door was open to the corridor outside she had the feeling he'd been hiding behind the door. 'Have you been through my things?'

'Aye,' he said. 'I was looking for the money ye promised me.'

It was an effort to stop her glance turning towards the fire grate. 'And did you find any?'

'No, I didn't, except for a shilling or two on the dresser. Where is it?'

'I paid the bill at the village shop with it.'

He stared at her, unbelieving. 'Ye did what?'

'I think you heard me clearly enough.'

'Ye went into the village shop and deliberately made a fool of me by paying the account?'

She wasn't going to take the entire blame. 'I was going to the village shop and Maggie suggested that I pay it. So I did.' She shrugged. 'It was a little more than I expected, but I can't see why that would have made you look a fool.'

'Who did ye pay the money to?'

'Mr McTavish signed the account. He was rather a pleasant man.'

'Aye, he would be if he was getting money out of you. Was there anyone else in the shop?'

'A couple of customers,' she said vaguely.

'What did you tell them?'

'What was there to tell? We passed the time of day and I said I was your guest. I told you earlier, Rory, I won't be subjected to these inquisitions. The fact that I'm residing in your house doesn't give you the right to search through my room for money. I demand that you allow me some privacy, and if anything is missing I'll report it to the authorities.'

'I'm the law on this estate, so ye needn't waste yer time writing a report.'

'Then you can return my two shillings. I've contributed more than enough to the household accounts, and you don't want people to think you're dishonest.'

Taking the coins from his pocket he threw them on the bed with bad grace. 'You've a mean turn of mind sometimes, Kenna Mackenzie. Who's this Dominic you were talking about? You said you'd always love him.'

She saw no reason to be less than honest. 'Aye, I'll always love Dominic. He's a doctor who saved my life when I was sick. He returned to England.'

'What was he to you?'

'I've just told you. He was my doctor . . . and a good friend to me when I desperately needed one.'

Rory shrugged. 'He's of nae account then.'

Dominic was of every account to her. 'How can a friend be of no account? Have you never been in love?'

His jaw worked for a moment, then he said, 'Aye, could be that I have.'

'What was her name?'

His face reddened as he mumbled something intelligible.

She couldn't resist it. 'Oh, I've just remembered. I also met Fiona McTavish. She followed after me to tell me about the arrangement for sending letters. We had quite a chat.'

Alarm filled his eyes. 'What did Fiona tell you?'

She deliberately misunderstood him. 'That there was a box near the gate for letters, or I could prop one against the milk jug, she said. Oh, and her father took them into Galashiels to the sorting office on Thursdays. That's when he goes in with his cart.'

'Nae, that's not what I meant. What did she say about me, and Glenchallon? Did the pair of ye gossip about my business?'

She managed a puzzled expression as she cooed, 'And why should we talk about you? It was our own business we talked about. Female talk. Fiona is a nice woman, I think she and I could be good friends.'

He avoided her eyes. 'Aye, perhaps after we're wed. In the meantime I'd be obliged if you didn't encourage her friendship. The less her father knows of my business the better.' He added hastily, 'I'm asking, nae telling, you ken.'

'As I don't know any of your business how can I discuss it with her? As for my own business, that's for me to know.'

So he intended for Fiona to be the loser, Kenna thought after he'd gone. Not if she could help it, for that would make her a loser too.

The rain had cleared up. But the water still oozed up through the cellar door and crept out into the hall and the surrounds. Now, it had taken on the appearance and consistency of slimy grey cream.

'I've never seen the like before,' Maggie said worriedly, standing there looking at it.

They tucked up their skirts, and barefooted, used some spades from the shed to push the mud towards the door. There, what wouldn't be shovelled over the stone step, collided with the barrier and stealthily subsided back into itself. After an hour of solid work there wasn't a noticeable reduction in the mud.

'There's something sinister about it,' Kenna said, almost

to herself, straightening up and trying the stretch the cramp from her back muscles. 'This is a waste of time.'

Maggie came to stand close to her and shivered. 'This mud is almost alive, and I'm worn out.'

An ominous muffled cracking sound came from the depths of the house. The two women exchanged a glance. The house was dying hard, Kenna thought. She said, 'Where's the Challoner? He should be helping with this.'

'He went off last night. He's hunting, I expect. I'll ask the old man about the mud when I take his breakfast up. He knows about such things.'

'One of us should clean the lodge and take some stores there, in case they're needed. And perhaps we should pack a bag apiece, with a change of clothing and anything personal or valuable we want to keep?'

'The Challoner won't like it.'

'I don't care whether he likes it or not, and he's not here to ask. He might want to stay in his bed if the place falls down around his ears, but I don't intend to. And neither do I want to drown in mud. I'll see to the lodge. Is there a key?'

'The door's not locked. Folks are honest around here, and it's not fair you suggesting otherwise,' Maggie said sullenly. 'And if you don't mind me saying, you're taking a bit much on yourself ordering me around. You're not mistress of this house yet.'

Must we always be locked in combat? Kenna thought wearily. 'I do mind you saying that because I suggested nothing of the sort and you're just determined to pick. Please yourself what you want to do.'

She gathered some of her things together and had just set out for the lodge when a shout came from Maggie. She turned to find the woman running furiously towards her, away from the house.

'What is it now?' Kenna said, waiting for her to catch up.

Maggie, ashen-faced and puffing for breath, gasped out, 'It's the auld man . . . he's deid . . . sitting in his chair . . . his eyes wide open.' She placed a hand on her heart. 'He's placed the portraits he's painted over the years all about the room. There's his wife, Katherine. Rory's father, and the Challoner himself. And he's gazing at a picture of that daughter of his, her that was Isla Fergusson, and he's smiling at her. It gave me the willies!' Throwing her apron over her head, Maggie burst into tears.

Kenna trudged back to the house and sloshed through the mud to the stairs, with Maggie behind her.

Upstairs in the old man's room, Kenna saw Rory strongly in Isla Challoner's portrait, but there was a resemblance to them all through the piercing blue eyes. Magnus would have expended a lot of effort dragging all the canvasses around the room, and his worn-out heart must have failed. It was as if he'd dragged his family around him because he'd known his time had come.

As Maggie had said, Magnus was gazing directly at the portrait of the daughter he'd loved. It seemed as though she was looking at him, and that would have brought him great comfort just before he'd died. He'd not been dead long, for there was still some warmth to him.

Kenna closed the old man's eyes, and when Maggie had recovered from her shock, they carried him to his bed between them. There, his smile sank over his remaining teeth. They washed him and dressed him in his best suit before his body stiffened, Maggie trembling all the while. Kenna brushed his sparse covering of silver hair.

'Is there a doctor to declare death? And an undertaker to supply a coffin?'

'They'll have to come out from Galashiels. I'll go and ask Donald McTavish to go and inform them of the death. It'll cost a couple of shillings for his time, though.'

'It's a long walk to the store. I'll go if you like.'

'Nae, lass. I'm not going to be left alone with the auld man's corpse.'

'But he's dead. He can't hurt you, Maggie.'

'Aye, that's what *you* say, but I wouldn't put it past him to come back to life and kill me stone dead.' She hurried to the window and opened it wide to the miserable weather. 'There, that will allow his soul to escape. Perhaps his daughter will go with him and we'll be rid of them both. They didn't fit in here. Bad luck, the pair of them were.'

They buried Magnus Fergusson next to his daughter and her husband in the cemetery of the local kirk.

Kenna drew the eyes of everyone. Rory was nervous. When Donald McTavish played a lament on his bagpipes Kenna couldn't prevent a tear or two from falling from her eyes, but it was because the music affected her rather than grief for the old man, since she'd hardly known him.

Fiona and Rory studiously avoided the other's eyes, though he stepped forward to support her when she nearly collapsed, alarm on his face.

After she'd recovered her father said to her, 'That's the second time you've fainted this week, and you've been sick a couple of times. I'll have to get the doctor out to you.'

'No,' she said with some alarm. 'It's nothing, everything will be all right. You shouldn't say such things in front of everybody, they'll get the wrong idea.'

When Rory shook hands with the priest and strode off towards his home with a long, loping strides, Fiona's father's eyes sharpened reflectively on his retreating back. He turned to Kenna. 'Will you be staying at Glenchallon much longer, Miss Mackenzie?'

Both Fiona and Maggie had started to walk away and were well out of earshot now. Kenna shook her head. 'I hope to leave the area soon, and wondered if you could find room for myself and a travelling trunk on your cart?'

'Does yon laird know?'

'No, Mr McTavish, he doesn't know yet. It's better that way, I think. Don't you?'

'Aye, girl. If what I suspect is true it's better all round, since the laird will need to be persuaded to face up to his responsibilities, and having you as a guest will make it more difficult for him. I canna take you tomorrow, but will next Thursday suit?'

She slid the letter she'd written to Robert from her pocket. 'Yes, it will. I'd be obliged if you didn't mention this to anyone in the meantime. I'll tell him on the morning of my departure. It will save a good many arguments. Would you please take this letter to the post office? I don't know whether or not he'll be back from London, but it's to inform my guardian that I'll be returning home.'

McTavish nodded and slid the letter into the pocket of his apron.

Thirteen

It was Thursday, the day after the funeral. Rory had wrestled Fiona on to the sacks and was just about to have his way with her when the door through to the residence crashed open. Fiona gave a little cry when she saw her father standing there, his face like thunder. Quickly, she pushed Rory aside and jumped to her feet, her skirts falling to cover her nakedness.

'So this is what ye get up to when my back's turned, you shameless hussy!'

Scrambling to his feet, Rory desperately pulled his breeks up over his backside. 'Ye dinna understand, Donald.'

'Do I nae, then? When a man is bare-arsed under a woman's skirt and his caber is springing out of his breeks and ready to toss, I understand perfectly. Ye should be ashamed of yourself, wi' your grandfather still warm in his coffin. Get awi' up to your room, girl. I'm of a mind to lay my belt across your back.'

'You will nae give me a beating. I'm a woman grown, not a child.'

Rory, his courage restored now his testicles were safely tucked away, said, 'It was comfort I was after, Donald. Things went a bit too far, but nothing happened between us.'

Fiona gave him a glare and her hands went to her hips. He groaned when she said, 'Aye, it might nae have happened . . . not today, anyway. But what about the bairn inside me, Rory Challoner? That didn't get there by itself.'

Donald gazed from one to the other. 'I suspected as much.'

'Aye, but that doesn't mean it was me who put it there,' Rory said desperately as he saw all he'd planned for suddenly slipping away.

Fiona burst into tears. 'You lied to me, Rory. You promised to wed me.'

Awkwardly, he patted her on the back. 'Nae, Fiona. I didn't propose marriage to you. It was you who mentioned it.'

'But you said you loved me.'

'Aye, I do. But that doesn't mean I'm going tae wed you. I canna, since I'm promised to another.'

'Promised? Tae whom?' Fiona screeched.

'Tae that nice young lass who came in to pay his bill the other day, nae doubt,' Donald said. 'That's what that lawyer's letter was all about, and why he went off to the city. To fetch himself a wealthy bride. Och, he's just like his father was, a man who sponges off others as well as being a liar and a fornicator.'

'Ye must have opened the lawyer's letter and read it tae have known my business,' Rory said furiously, not that anyone took any notice.

Fiona's hands went to her hips. 'Why didn't Kenna tell me? Ooh, the sly vixen! When I get hold of her I'll wipe that superior city smile from her face!'

Donald said sharply, 'Leave the young lass out of this. It's nae her fault, it's yon laird's.'

Rory didn't see why he should shoulder all the blame, and said, 'It's Fiona's as well. She must be thirty years auld, for God's sake. She's on the shelf, Donald, and desperate. She set out to trap me into marriage.'

An outraged yelp came from Fiona. 'You're nae a gentleman, that's for sure. Pa's right, you're a cheat and a liar.'

'I'm nae either of those things,' Rory shouted at them. 'Ye don't understand. I'm the laird of Glenchallon and I'm doing the best I can to save my estate from ruin.'

'And I'm going to do my best tae save my daughter from ruin, Laird of Glenchallon. I'm going to fetch my gun and I'm going to load it with shot. Then I'm going tae shoot your bluidy Challoner balls into smithereens. Make up your mind tae it. This bairn you've foisted on my lass will be the first and the last one you'll ever father if you don't put a ring on my Fiona's finger.'

When Donald turned away, Rory turned in the other direction and made a run for the shop door. Fiona managed to catch him before he unlocked it and hurled several potatoes at him, each one bouncing off his shoulders.

As he burst through the door cursing, he had to run the gauntlet of several astonished people waiting to get in.

'Fiona must be in training for the Highland games,' someone remarked as a barrage of potatoes followed after him. The people in the queue chuckled.

Donald appeared, brought his shotgun up to his shoulder and fired. Rory picked up speed.

Donald looked around him at the avid eyes of the onlookers, stating with some satisfaction, 'That will teach the bugger to take liberties with my daughter.'

'In trouble, is she?' someone enquired.

'She's nae in trouble – at least, nothing that a ring on her finger won't fix.'

'Pa, it's none of their business, and you're shaming me,' Fiona said from behind him. She was blushing furiously, her temper discarded in favour of self-pity.

'You've shamed yourself, girl. You're lucky I haven't taken the strap to your backside, since your mother will be turning in her grave – but that daesna mean I won't. Now, get on with serving the customers, I'm already late for Galashiels. And the next time that low cur comes sniffing after you it would be best for him if his visit was straight and above board.'

'He'll never marry me now,' Fiona said dolefully.

Donald rarely smiled, but he did now. 'I wouldn't be too sure of that.'

The day was overcast, but dry. Maggie had gone upstairs to clean out Magnus Fergusson's room, she'd said. Kenna thought she was using Rory's absence as an opportunity to search for any money that had been hidden.

The atmosphere of the house was oppressive. Kenna decided to investigate the hidden stairs down to the kitchen and make herself a drink when she got there. The panel slid quietly to one side and she closed it behind her, fighting off panic as the darkness pressed in on her. Her eyes quickly adjusted to the faint light coming from the various gaps and cracks, and she felt better. There was one just above her. It must have led to the old man's quarters, for she could plainly hear Maggie muttering to herself. 'There's bound to be a will somewhere. And cash. The auld fart always had money to hand.'

Kenna's eyes sharpened. Had Maggie's been the voice she'd heard telling her to leave Glenchallon? Sickness filled her heart. Magnus Fergusson had heard voices, and they had convinced him he was mad. What mischief had Maggie been up to, and why? And did Rory know about it? Kenna felt her way down the stairs and emerged through a door into the scullery.

The urge to get out of the house was irresistible.

Climbing the hill to the edge of the trees, she seated herself on a fallen log with her back against a tree to think, drawing her shawl around her shoulders. The storm had played havoc with what pines remained, tearing branches from the trunks and leaving in its wake pale, splintered gashes and scars in the serrated bark. The air was aromatic with pine oil, the sap already oozing to fill and seal the smaller wounds.

From where she sat there was a fine view over Glenchallon and the surrounding countryside, even the cemetery where Rory's ancestors were laid to rest under lichen-covered stones. Although she'd only known him a short time, Kenna felt as though Magnus Fergusson had been her only genuine friend here. His death had saddened her, for he'd been a fine man, one she'd liked to have known better.

Glenchallon House looked solid from where she sat – a deceptive ruin that was rotten to the core. Smoke was belching from a couple of the chimneys, giving a cosy, homely look to it. The sun reflected in leaping orange gleams from the old man's bedroom window. The peace was a gift to savour. She closed her eyes, listening to the bird song.

She must have fallen asleep, for the snap of a twig brought her back to awareness. She opened her eyes to find that the afternoon shadows had lengthened. Her nose twitched, for she could smell smoke in the air. Sometimes, the heather on the heath was burned to get rid of the old twiggy growth and encourage tender new shoots. The smoke drifted for miles. Her attention was captured by a movement so small that it could have been the twitching of a mouse's whiskers. Her eyes shifted sideways.

There, half-concealed by a shrub, was a red hind. How beautiful and glossy she was. Kenna's slight intake of breath must have alerted the beast to her presence, for their eyes met and held for a few moments. Then the hind was gone, and so quickly that Kenna only saw the bob of her tail as she sprang away and disappeared.

She remembered the carcass Rory had hung in the kitchen two days previously, and shuddered. Even so, she could appreciate the skill that had gone into catching such a wary prey. They needed to eat and Rory was superb at keeping the table supplied with meat and fish.

She hadn't yet investigated the lodge and was overtaken by curiosity. Rising, she followed the tree line to where it sloped downwards. The door opened silently on oiled hinges at a push from her hand.

As Rory had said, it was used for storage. But a space in the sitting room had been cleared. There was a portrait on the wall, Rory's father by the look of it. He had a rather discontented expression on his face, similar to the one Rory sometimes wore. Otherwise Rory didn't resemble him much, except for the mouth.

'I come and talk tae him sometimes,' Rory said from behind her.

She jumped. 'I'm sorry, I didn't know you were here. I didn't mean to disturb you.'

'You didn't disturb me. My father didn't get on with Magnus Fergusson.'

Had anyone at Glenchallon ever got along with each other? she wondered. She sensed a need in him to talk. 'You miss your grandfather, don't you?'

'Aye, I do. I loved him, even though he wasn't really my grandfather – though he wasn't aware of it and I never told him.'

She stared at him. 'What are you talking about? Of course he was your real grandfather!'

He shrugged. 'Isla wasn't my mother. Maggie is.'

'Maggie!' Kenna couldn't believe the woman was his mother. 'But how? That's the most ridiculous thing I've ever heard. Who told you such a thing?'

'Maggie did, when I was a child. She said it was a secret,

and she made me swear on the bible that I wouldn't discuss it with anyone. And I used tae hear Isla whispering in my ear when I was asleep. "*I don't love you, Rory, you're Maggie's wee laddie*." I used to think I had the madness inside me, too. Now it doesn't matter because everyone except Maggie is dead.'

What a wicked old woman she'd been. 'If this tale is the truth, your mother would have been carrying a child at the same time as Maggie. Someone from outside would have noticed. They'd have wondered what had happened to one of the infants.'

'Isla's child died. Maggie said that being with child didn't show on her because she was plump. I was born a few days earlier in this very lodge. My father and Maggie used to meet here. I was placed in the dead bairn's cradle and the other was buried in the garden. It was a boy, too, and we looked alike, so Isla didn't even know the difference. Maggie looks after the grave. She grows flowers on it.'

It would be cruel to laugh when he was being so serious. 'Didn't you see those portraits in your grandfather's room, all lined up? You're the very image of your mother, Isla, and your grandfather. You all have the same eyes and noses, and a similar shape of face. You have your father's mouth, though. You shouldn't believe Maggie. It was she who made those ghostly voices, so Magnus thought he was going mad. I thought I'd heard Isla's ghost on the day I played the piano for Magnus. He heard it to, but I denied it when he asked me.'

He was staring at her, the shock he felt clear in his expression. 'Aye, I remember. I've heard her myself from time to time. Always in my grandfather's room . . . whispering.'

'Maggie did it from the servants' stairs. Her mind's gone, Rory. I stood in there today and listened to her ranting to herself. There's a space where the wall is cracked, right under his window. It's where the stair turns to double back on itself towards the scullery. There's a stool there, that she must have used to stand on, while she talked through the crack. I imagine she did the same to Isla, and listened to any conversations they had.'

His voice took on an edge of hysteria. 'Ye're lying . . . ye're making it up!'

'I've got no reason to lie. Ask her. I just stood there and listened to her. You could do the same. She was in your grandfather's room, talking wildly to herself. She was looking for his will and any money he'd left there. I think it could be *Maggie* who is ill. What happened to Isla? Your grandfather told me she was pushed.'

Colour drained from Rory's face and he sank on to a chair. 'Aye, and nae matter how much I try to forget I can't free my mind of it. Maggie told me that the child Isla carried would inherit Glenchallon because I was my father's bastard. I hated that baby. One day she waited until Isla was standing at the open window. Grandfather was in the other room playing his violin. Isla was standing at the window, listening. Maggie whispered to me to push her out.'

'Oh, Rory. You didn't?'

'She said it was a game, that we'd do it together and Isla would fly away over the loch taking the bairn with her. She held me in front of her and we crept up on her.'

'What happened then?' she asked when he paused, his downcast head held in his hands.

'Because it was a game, I giggled. My mother turned . . . she was smiling and held out her arms to me. Maggie pushed me forward. I fell against her stomach and she staggered backwards with her arms outstretched like wings. But she didnae fly. The back of her legs hit the window sill and she toppled. Maggie snatched me back.' Tears fell from his eyes now. 'I didnae mean tae do it. Maggie said my father would take me away and hang me by the neck from a tree if anyone found out.'

Kenna sucked in a breath.

'Maggie told me to tell everyone that my mother had jumped, and went to fetch my grandfather. I was too scared to move until the grandfather stopped playing that damned violin, right in the middle of a tune. Then he came through and led me away. I told him I hadn't pushed her. He hugged me tight and said he believed me.'

In front of Kenna was a grown man who'd lived in the shadow of a lie, and had carried the burden of his mother's death on his shoulders from childhood. She wanted to take him in her arms and comfort him, but knew he wouldn't welcome it. Nor did he deserve it. Gullibility wasn't a crime, but it was about time he grew up and took responsibility for his own actions.

'Maggie is a wicked woman. You should confront her with this,' she urged.

'Aye, I will,' he said simply. 'Do I really resemble the Fergussons?'

'Aye, you do. Come on, we'll go and take a look at them and put your mind at ease. And there's something I need to tell you, Rory. I've decided to leave Glenchallon next week. I'm returning to Edinburgh.'

His eyes sharpened. 'Aye, well, I daresay you heard what happened between myself and McTavish. I expected as much. I'll return the receipt that your brother-in-law left me, though it was a contract and I'd be entitled to keep a portion for my trouble.'

And just when she'd thought he was becoming more human. She felt like chiding him about his meanness, which seemed to be part of him, but she didn't. The man had nothing but an ancient house that was a millstone round his neck, and his pride. The most she could manage was an ironic, 'That's generous of you. I haven't heard anything about what's happened, but I'd guess it's Fiona?'

Bitterly, he said, 'Fiona's been letting me have my way with her, and is now having my bairn. I ran off like a cur with my tail between my legs. I'll never live it down.'

'Aye, you will, Rory, when you see the beautiful bairn she'll give you. You'll want to give the infant a better childhood than the one you had, and if you have a son you'll be able to teach him to hunt.'

He brightened. 'There's that, I suppose. That's if Fiona still wants me after what happened today.'

'You might have to humble yourself a bit, Rory Challoner, but that won't hurt you. You're so proud you've got thistles sprouting out of your ears as well as your behind. It's a wonder you can sit down.'

His huff of laughter warmed her ears. 'You can talk, lass. Someone should take a stick to yours, skinny though it is. You remind me of my mother – Isla, that is. Not Maggie.'

'Aye, I ken who your mother is. I reminded Magnus of

Isla, too. He was worried. He told me your mother was pushed from the window. I think he was frightened it would happen to me.'

'God rest his soul then, for he must have suspected it was me who did it all along.'

'I think he knew it was Maggie who was behind it. You were a child, five years old. You thought it was a game, but it wasn't. It was accidental on your part, remember that, Rory.'

'Aye.' He touched her face. 'Ye're a good lass.'

'Just go down to see Fiona later tonight and do the right thing. As for me, I'm leaving because we were marrying for the wrong reason. Fiona does loves you. You should wed her.'

'Aye, I would . . . but there's the house to consider.'

'You can't afford to consider it. I know you love Glenchallon but it's past repair. There's too much sadness in it and the house is dying. Don't make it a barrier between yourself and happiness. You must put the coming child first.'

'Aye, I should.' A frown touched his brows, drawing them together. 'But they'll put Maggie in gaol if she's found out, and I can't have that.'

'That's up to you, Rory. You owe her nothing except her wages.'

The floor beneath them gave a faint tremor, so slight that she thought she might have imagined it. But Rory had felt it too. 'What was that?'

They went outside and towards the house. There was something different about it.

Alarm punched at her. 'Look at the hill, at the side of the house!'

One side of it had slid, leaving a gash gouged out of the side. As they watched it slipped a bit more and the gash widened.

It was as though Glenchallon had waited until the old man had gone, for what Magnus predicted was coming true.

Rory shrugged. 'The hill has slipped before and it'll happen again. One day I'll replant the trees.'

One day? Couldn't he see how serious this was? 'Maggie's inside the house!' she shouted, as a chimney stack toppled sideways. Picking up her skirt, she began to run like a rabbit, jumping over the tussocks as if her feet had springs on them.

Rory overtook her.

As they neared the house they saw flames leaping from the fractured chimney. The air was full of smoke that filtered ash and sparks through the roof tiles. Rory cursed. He loped off towards the door, burst through it and took the stairs two at a time, with Kenna scrambling after him. They both stopped short, Kenna trying to catch her breath.

Muttering to herself, Maggie was slashing at the portraits Magnus had left there, and feeding them into a fire which spilled into the room and roared ferociously up the chimney.

'You daft auld cow,' Rory yelled at her. 'You've set the chimney afire, and the bluidy house with it!'

'I'll fetch some water.' Running downstairs, Kenna went out to the pump. She filled a pail with water and sludged back through the sticky, shifting mud and up the staircase again. The fire had taken a good hold of the floorboards. Rory was beating at it with a worn rug, scattering sparks everywhere. Flames licked through the ceiling where it met the chimney. The effect produced by the dowsing of her pail of water was a hiss and a small cloud of steam.

'Leave it, Kenna,' Rory said. 'Fetch your things and get out as quick as you can. Run down to the village for help.'

Snatching up all she could in one frenzied dash, Kenna dumped it by the gate on the way, except for her purse, which she tied around her waist. She pounded the two miles downhill to the shop, even knowing it was a wasted effort. She was out of breath when she threw open the shop door, and gasped out, 'Glenchallon is on fire. The laird needs help.'

Within minutes several men were hurrying up the slope, for already they'd smelled the smoke wafting down into the valley, and were sniffing the air like hounds.

Fiona brought Kenna a glass of water while she caught her breath. 'How bad is the fire?'

'Magnus Fergusson's room. Maggie tried to burn the portraits of Rory's folks. The fire would have spread by now for it was already in the roof. That place is full of cracks and draughts and the room full of oils and turpentine Magnus used for his painting.'

'I hope the whole place goes up,' Fiona said, then more

sharply, 'Why didn't ye tell me ye were promised to Rory? I must have sounded like a fool tae you.'

'You didn't, Fiona. Instinct told you I might be a threat and you tried to warn me off. The trouble was, you didn't know I'd been given no choice in the matter – and I didn't know about you until that moment, so it was a shock to both of us. As it is, he's all yours. I made up my mind at that moment that I wouldn't wed him. I've asked your pa to take me down to Galashiels on his cart next week. I'm going back to Edinburgh.'

Fiona smiled with relief. 'Rory's not much of a catch, really. He's full of plans but he's nae clever enough to figure out how to carry them out.'

'He's never had a father to guide him. He's got some nice ways, I suppose. But he certainly needs a good kick in the pants now and again. He might change if he's given the chance. He intends to make amends, from what I can gather.'

'Aye, well, hasn't he always been full of good intentions?' She sighed. 'Ye can't help who you fall in love with and for all his faults, I do love him.'

'As anyone can see.'

'You know, my pa owns over half of the Glenchallon estate. The McTavish family has been buying up portions of it for years, though Rory daesna know it yet. He'll give it back to Rory if we wed, a sort of dowry.' She crooked her arm through Kenna's. 'Come on, I'll lock up the shop. Let's go and watch Glenchallon burn down.'

The fire was well established when they got there. There was a chain of men passing buckets along the line, but it didn't seem to do any good. They scattered in all directions when the roof collapsed and sparks began to shoot into the sky.

'Can you see the Challoner?' Fiona said worriedly.

Rory was facing Maggie across the stairs. Both were streaked with smoke and sweat, while the fire crackled, swirled and roared around them. There was no stopping it.

'You lied to me all these years, Maggie.'

'Aye, but your father didn't give me another glance when Isla came into his life – he got the fever in him, his blood running hot for her like a rutting stag. She wasn't robust, but he didn't give a damn. He possessed her, and he pestered her and made sure she knew he was her master. When my own babe slipped dead from my womb, he didnae care. So I made you mine instead, and I made sure there wasn't another child from Isla and your father.'

'You killed my mother.'

'Nay, lad. It was you who pushed her out of the window.'

'You filled my head full of lies, and ye pushed me into her. You're a wicked auld woman who ruined the lives of my family and stole my childhood from me. And ye won't get away with this, Maggie.'

The heat from the burning staircase could be felt through the soles of his boots and the air had an explosive dryness to it. Behind him and below him were flames. Sparks rained down on them, burning his skin. Maggie's hair was smoking.

'We have to get out of here,' he muttered.

Maggie slid open the panel to the servants stairs and disappeared down it. He shuddered as choking smoke billowed out of the panelling. Tongues of fire reached down from the floor above. He held a handkerchief over his mouth, but before he could follow after Maggie the staircase collapsed sideways and he was pitched over the banister rail. The fall would have killed him except for one thing – the mud cushioned his fall. It also prevented the burning debris that rained down after him from burning his skin too badly. Rory moved with the mud, trying to keep his balance as it oozed towards the open door, taking him with it. He sucked in deep breaths of sweet air when he got outside and crawled away from the building.

'There's the Challoner . . . there he is!'

Rory was plucked from the mire by strong arms and carried over to a log where somebody placed a flask to his mouth. He took a long swallow to clear the smoke from his throat and gazed at the home of his ancestors through red-rimmed eyes. The place had turned into a roaring inferno.

Windows shattered and the upper floor collapsed with a roar into a shower of sparks. The men fell silent as the place burned, then one of them pointed at the mud and shouted, 'What the devil is that?'

It was the mud coming off the hill behind, and making its way out through the front doors. It quenched some of the flames and sent up clouds of steam as it oozed steadily down towards the loch.

Smoke-stained and weary, the men gathered together around Rory. His dogs pushed them aside and sat one at each leg to gaze adoringly up at him.

'Has anyone seen Maggie?' somebody thought to ask.

'She went down the servants stair tae the kitchen. Didn't she get out?' Rory said. He turned to where Fiona stood with Kenna, but it was Kenna's eyes he sought first. He nodded, and with a quick flash of understanding Kenna knew that Rory was a man freed from his past.

In case anyone misconstrued that look Fiona stepped forward to make her claim on him clear to all. 'Miss Mackenzie can stay with me until it's time for her to go back to Edinburgh – if you're agreeable, Father? I daresay the Challoner will want tae use the lodge, because there won't be much left of the house to save.'

'Aye, he'll want to do that, nae doubt,' McTavish said. 'And you're welcome tae come down for a bite to eat with us, Laird. I daresay a wee dram wouldn't go astray, either, while we sort things out.'

'I'll see tae those burns on your arms. They need some salve and bandages.'

'Och, it's nothing. Stop fussing, Fiona,' Rory said with a modest shrug.

Voice gruff and tears trembling on her lashes, Fiona told him, 'You'll do as you're told, Rory Challoner. We can't have it getting infected. Are you listening to me now?'

'Yes, Fiona,' he said, and grinned at her.

They left Glenchallon burning and walked down to the McTavish residence, where Fiona clucked and fussed over her man's burns while she tended them with salves and bandages. Kenna grinned, for the Challoner lapped up the attention, as if he'd been starved of it.

Later, while the two women cooked, the men sat in the parlour with a bottle of whisky between them. Whatever was arranged between them must have pleased Rory, for he was in a good mood despite the loss of his home – or because of it, perhaps, since the decision had been taken from his hands.

The evening was the most relaxed that Kenna had known since she'd been there, despite the ominous red glow in the sky and the smell of smoke. Fiona waited on her father and her laird with an air of propriety and the two became more inebriated by the minute. She was pink-faced, brisk and determined now her future was settled. Eventually, Rory was bedded down on the parlour couch and Kenna shared Fiona's bed.

In the morning the village folk came from far and wide to do what they could, or to just stand and stare, and comment. It had rained overnight, cooling the fire but adding to the mud, which had spread discolouration far out into the loch. Acrid smoke drifted up to become part of the dark stain on the sky.

The Glenchallon kitchen was smoke-blackened, but open to the sky. It was there that Maggie's body was found, half in and half out of the door to the stairway. She was black with soot and her hair was singed but she was otherwise untouched.

'I expect the smoke killed her. At least she didn't burn, she can be thankful for that,' said Fiona unsympathetically as two men wrapped the servant in a sheet to be taken down to the kirk for examination and burial.

It was odd how a tragedy such as this brought folk together, Kenna thought. But although the villagers paid their respects, their sympathy stayed with the living. Their way of thinking seemed slightly uncharitable.

'Maggie has ruled the roost up at Glenchallon for far too long,' somebody muttered. 'I swear she thought she owned the place.'

'Aye, and I wouldn't have put it past her tae have deliberately set fire to the place, either.'

Fiona and Kenna helped to make the lodge more habitable. A chain of women brought water from the burn at a point where it foamed cleanly over rocks into the loch. They chased out the spiders, filled the barrels, washed the crockery and placed food offerings on the larder shelves – a flitch of bacon, a batch of pasties. Soon, bed linen was flapping on the line in a strong breeze.

The poultry came out of hiding, and led by the family of fearless geese, pecked their way around the loch to where the women were gathered. Clucking and stretching their necks nervously they allowed themselves to be herded into the back garden of the lodge, which was juicy with snails, slugs and tender spring shoots. There, they settled.

A few days later Maggie's burial took place. She was lowered into the ground and a prayer said over her while the earth was shovelled on top and a stone erected.

Rory addressed the mourners, his taut features giving an indication of how he'd appear in old age. His tension showed – he was a man carrying out a duty. Behind his fine eyes was a man trapped in his traditions, with no way out. It was as if he'd just realized the extent of the responsibility he carried on his shoulders.

'Maggie has been a faithful servant to myself and my family since before I can remember,' he said. 'She'd have been pleased by your attendance and respect. On this solemn occasion I'd like to take the opportunity to thank you all for your help in my time of need, and the generosity you've displayed towards myself and my guest from Edinburgh, Miss Kenna Mackenzie. I hope she'll take away some happy memories of her stay here, despite the circumstances, and take heart in knowing that Glenchallon will rise from the ashes one day.' But she could have sworn that he gave her a slight wink.

Donald McTavish raised an eyebrow as he exchanged a glance with his daughter. Then tucked his bagpipe under his arm and played the same wheezy lament he'd played for Magnus Fergusson a few days earlier.

Kenna smiled to herself as she looked at the headstone. '*Maggie Harris. Faithful Servant.*' Rory had finally put Maggie in her place. And about time, she thought. Perhaps he could now earn the respect due to his position.

Rory Challoner was Fiona's problem now, and Kenna was glad of it. She had her own battle to fight – one she intended to win. As soon as she got back to Edinburgh she would confront Robert Gilmore, then seek legal advice.

But her hopes of a fast escape were dashed when Fiona slipped an arm around her waist and said, 'You *will* be staying for the wedding, won't you, Kenna?'

Fourteen

Over the past month Robert Gilmore had carefully created the *persona grata* of Bart Parnell in his own image. He'd changed his appearance by growing a dapper beard.

While on board he'd drunk very little, in case his guard had slipped. Wisely, he'd attended Sunday worship in the salon as well as frequenting the card games, where he'd lost, or won just enough to be credible. There was nothing much he could do about his accent, but many people from Edinburgh talked in exactly the same manner.

He'd recognized the cues put out by Jethro Kester and had indicated that his own views on slavery were populist. As a result he'd earned a couple of introductions to influential men who would help him settle.

All the while, Jethro Kester had been watching and assessing, though Robert hadn't figured out why. He held out his hand to the second officer just before he stepped ashore. 'Thanks for the recommendation to the boarding house.'

'You're welcome, Bart. I'll see you at dinner tomorrow.'

'Aye, I have the address. Are you sure Mrs Moorehouse won't mind an extra guest at her table at such short notice?'

'My sister enjoys entertaining. Before she was widowed she hosted for her husband, who also worked within the law. He joined my father's law practice after he married Jessica. You'll meet Judge Kester tonight.'

'I look forward to it. May I ask how your late brother-in-law died?'

'He was killed during some civil disorder – a stray shot. They never discovered who fired it.'

'A shame. Is there any offspring from the marriage?'

'Unfortunately not. Jessica is still young, though. It's

possible she'll meet someone suitable and will marry again before too long. She has expressed a desire to have a family.'

Now Jethro's assessment of him began to make sense, Robert thought later that evening. Jessica Moorehouse was not the most attractive woman he'd set eyes on. She was short, and her sturdy body was captured in a corset designed to contain rather than flatter a woman's assets. Her muddy complexion was made all the more noticeable by thick, straight eyebrows. A thin mouth and slightly hooked nose were topped by heavy-lidded grey eyes.

'Mr Parnell, how nice to meet you,' she murmured when he bent over her hand.

'My pleasure, Mrs Moorehouse.'

She gave an impatient sort of huff. 'Jethro tells me you're straight off the ship?'

'Aye, that I am. I hope to settle here.'

'You're Scottish.' A smile crossed her face. 'Your accent resembles my late husband's. He came from Somerset; do you know the county?'

'I've never been to Somerset, but I believe the countryside is beautiful there.' He found something to admire in her – a melodious voice and dainty hands that sparkled with diamonds.

He wondered how much she was worth and quickly assessed his surroundings. The house on Beacon Hill commanded a fine view. It was comfortably furnished, if a little too ostentatiously for his own taste. The chandeliers were crystal, the furnishings of excellent quality. The place spoke of new money and lacked the patina of graceful ageing, something that only time and history would bring. It was a show house, built to demonstrate wealth. And that wealth controlled the pecking order here, just as tightly as the class system controlled it in the British Isles.

The black footmen hardly rated a glance as they relieved the guests of their coats, cloaks and hats, though to the new immigrant they were a novelty. Had they escaped the clutches of the plantation owners of the south only to fall into a different kind of servitude in the north? At least they would be offered the pride of earning a man's wage, he supposed.

He already had a good idea of which way the wind blew

in Boston. In the past, Massachusetts had grown rich on the labour of farm women and children working in the textile mills. They were followed by the Irish and French Canadians. Boston itself had become the financial hub. The city's legal and medical professions flourished. Abolition activity was rife. Religion was embraced by the devout, and practised by those a little less so. There was an air of growth and steadiness about the place. He could almost taste the wealth in the air. Robert wanted to be part of it.

He'd noticed that the pleasant, hilly countryside was well serviced by railroads, and the harbour was full of shipping. Sure signs that a city flourished.

Robert already knew where his hosts' sympathies lay with regard to abolition, and he would listen and learn from the chat tonight.

'You have a lovely home,' he said to Jessica, and felt the urge for something similar. A man could make something of himself here, if he went about it the right way.

She placed her dainty hand on his wrist and her eyelashes fluttered. The coquette didn't suit her. 'This is a house, Mr Parnell. It needs children to turn it into a home.' Her mouth pursed. 'Theodore Moorehouse was considerably older than I . . . we had no children. He left me comfortably off. He came here with a small fortune and the desire to turn it into a considerably bigger one. When we married he took charge of my father's law offices. It's all about knowing the right people.'

And marrying the right one, he thought. Jessica's best asset was her money, which she'd been quick to flaunt. In a way he admired her for that. She knew her limitations and was pragmatic about it. She needed a man in her bed to satisfy her frustrations and give her children. These were sound reasons to wed. She was not beyond buying a husband, and he couldn't blame her for that, for to obtain her goal would not need subterfuge.

He wished Jeanne had given him a child, but she'd been difficult about the act that would bring such a thing about. She'd said it pained her.

Kenna came into his mind and a twinge of guilt attacked

him. He shrugged mentally. It was too late for regrets. By the time Rory Challoner realized he'd been duped he'd be married to her. He hoped the uplander didn't take it out on Kenna. Robert shook his head. He'd cut the strings that had bound him to the Mackenzie family now. His new life was here, and it was all falling into his lap.

When he looked at Jessica Moorehouse again she held his glance. There was an innocence to her features, and for a moment he caught a glimpse of something in her eyes – desperation perhaps, or despair. Had her husband been too old to function properly? He wondered what her dark hair would look like unbound as he said lightly, 'Were you married for long?'

'Three years. I was left well off. I hope you don't find the subject of money vulgar then, Mr Parnell?'

'Scots rarely find the subject of money vulgar, though I believe we have a reputation for preferring to accumulate it rather than part with it. Not exactly true, of course, but caution is part of our nature and we prefer good value for our money.'

She laughed. 'You should find yourself a wife with means, one who can manage your household wisely. A man who eschews solid family values goes a long way in Boston. Perhaps you should think on that.'

She'd taken the opportunity to make her meaning clear. He gave her hope. 'I'll bow before your advice and I will certainly think about it. May I escort you into the drawing room?'

'Of course you may. But wait, let me introduce you to my father, who has just removed his coat and hat. Judge Kester, this is Mr Bartholomew Parnell, who arrived in Boston today on board the *Atlantic Queen*. He's a lawyer who Jethro befriended on the voyage from Edinburgh.'

'I'm pleased to meet you, sir.'

The man was short; his head and eyebrows flaunted an abundance of grey hair. Robert saw the resemblance to his daughter in him. A pair of astute eyes met his, his hand was extended, soft palmed and with a solid gold, ruby-set ring gleaming on his little finger. 'My pleasure, sir. Have you seen that son of mine? He was supposed to join the family firm, not run away to sea and enjoy himself.'

Jethro laughed as he came striding from the drawing room to hug his father. 'You know how much I loathed studying law. Give me the sea any day. I wouldn't be able to stand being cooped up in a stuffy office. Besides, the company has offered me command of the *Esmerelda* when Captain Brown retires at the end of the year; so don't expect me to put the sea behind me any time soon.'

'Ah . . . so that's why you've invited a lawyer to dinner, to take the heat off yourself.'

Jethro threw him a friendly smile. 'I shouldn't be at all surprised. Jessica has seated Bart next to you at dinner. I'm sure you'll find him interesting.'

Jessica placed her hand possessively on Robert's arm, her nails curving into the sleeve of his jacket like little hooks. 'I shall sit on his other side. Between us we shall learn everything there is to know about Mr Parnell, Father.'

Perspiration prickled on Robert's back.

'Shall we go into the drawing room now so you can be introduced to the rest of my guests, Mr Parnell . . . or should I call you Bart?'

Feeling like an actor stumbling over his lines, Robert said, 'By all means, as long as I can call you Jessica?'

He'd never liked being manipulated. Should he encourage this, or keep Jessica at arm's length until he'd had time to take his bearings?

The thought came, unbidden and unwelcome – was this how Kenna had felt, being pushed into marriage with a man she hardly knew?

He suddenly felt like a trapped rabbit.

Kenna stitched the last tack into the hem of Fiona's gown and murmured, 'Now, let's slide it over your head. I'll start hemming it while you're away seeing the Challoner. This pale blue floral material is pretty for a spring wedding.'

'Aye, and it should do me for best afterwards. It's a grand gift. Thank you, Kenna. Your stitching is so neat compared to mine.' Anxiety settled on her face. 'I hope my father remembers the lace trim for the bodice, and the bonnet.'

'I wrote down the instructions for the haberdasher and drew a picture of how the hat should look, a little pillbox with flowers at the back. It's the latest fashion. Why should he forget?'

'He forgot to post your letter for the past two weeks.'

'Not surprising really, since a lot was going on about then, and the men have been up at Glenchallon trying to salvage what they could. He's promised to post it today. As it is, since I've decided to stay on for your wedding, my brother-in-law would have received the letter too early if it had gone off when I gave it to your father.'

As she lifted the gown over Fiona's head, Kenna noticed that Fiona's stomach had taken on a gentle prominence. She grinned. 'Don't put any more weight on before next week.'

Fiona shrugged. 'Rory's none too happy about the baby.'

'He'll get used to the idea. Besides, he should have thought of that before . . . well, you know.'

Fiona grinned broadly. 'Before I let him have his way with me? I'm thirty years old and was getting desperate. Besides, I liked it fine. It was quite a shock when ye walked through the door that day. Ye never did tell us where you met Rory.'

'Does it matter now?'

'I'm curious.'

Kenna nodded. 'Maybe, but I don't think you'll like this. I met him in my home two years ago, when I was eighteen. Arrangements had been made without my knowledge. I refused to marry him because I thought I was too young. I told him to come back when I was twenty. I didn't expect him to, but he did.'

'My God! Ye've been promised to him for two years, and he didn't say a word.' Fiona looked crushed as she fumbled with the fastenings on her skirt. 'Money, was it?'

'Aye. Somehow he got the idea that I'd bring enough into the marriage to restore Glenchallon. This way, my brother-in-law won't be able to fret over my decision. I'll simply tell him that the laird decided to marry the woman he loved. '

'Didn't you want to marry Rory?'

'My heart belongs to another, Fiona. I'd already come to the conclusion we weren't suited, and I think Rory realized he'd made a mistake. But your laird is too stubborn to admit he's wrong about anything. Sometimes, I feel like shaking some horse sense into him.'

Fiona gave a huff of laughter. 'He isn't much of a man, but he's not a bad one for all that, and I do love him.'

'There's a reason he's the way he is, Fiona. He grew up believing in a lie. I'm still not certain that he's grasped the truth but I can't break a confidence and you'll have to ask him.'

'There's no need. Rory told me last night about Maggie and about his mother. He said he didn't want there to be any secrets between us. Och, the poor man, believing all those lies, and having his mother's death on his conscience.'

'Why did Maggie do it, I wonder?'

'My father told me that Maggie was in love with Rory's father, but the old Challoner didn't even give her a second glance after he married. He was besotted with Isla.'

Not quite the impression Kenna had formed of the marriage from Magnus Fergusson. But perhaps a besotted man was more concerned with the need to slake his passion on the woman he desired. She doubted if that was on the same level as a man who loved a woman deeply and wanted to cherish and protect her.

'There was talk at the time of Isla's death that Maggie had taken a hand in it – but the talk never reached the old Challoner's ears. If it had he would have killed Maggie. He took to the bottle and neglected the estate. He paid scant attention to his poor wee motherless laddie, and fell down the stairs a few years later. The courts placed Rory under his grandfather's guardianship. That Maggie was a spiteful old cat. She couldn't have the father so she worked on the son and made him her own.'

Kenna nodded. 'When the house collapsed it removed the reason for Rory to wed for money. As soon as your wedding is over I'm going back to Edinburgh to have it out with my guardian and his wife. Perhaps I'll open a shop of my own if he'll release some of my inheritance. It will keep me busy and give me independence.'

'What about the man you love?'

'Dominic . . .?' She placed the gown to one side and a smile trembled on her lips at the thought of him, one that faded before she said, 'He's left Edinburgh and has gone back to his home in the south of England. I doubt if I'll ever see him again.'

'You should go and find him, Kenna.'

'I thought that myself once, but if he loved me he'd have told me. But he didn't. He suggested I become his mistress. He didn't think I was respectable enough to be his wife and bear his children.' She held up her hand when Fiona cried out a protest. 'No, you don't understand, Fiona. Dominic didn't say as much; but in the beginning he thought I was a street woman, and everything I did served to confirm that belief. He was a wonderfully unselfish man, but one slightly cynical because he'd seen the effect bad living has on people – and he couldn't get that first impression of me out of his head. Yet he took me into his home and saved my life. But he had a sweet young daughter to consider as well.' She smiled at the thought of Evelyn and hoped the child had settled into her new home.

'He was married?'

'A widower.'

'You went to bed with him, didn't you?'

'Aye, and I'm not sorry I did,' Kenna said fiercely. 'He wanted me and I wanted him, and I needed to repay him for restoring me to health.'

'What if he'd put a bairn inside you, like Rory did me?'

'He didn't, but I sometimes wish . . .' The smile she gave was rueful and tears came to her eyes. 'It would be wonderful to carry a child inside me that we'd created between us.'

Fiona smiled as her hands covered her stomach. Softly, she said, 'Aye, it is wonderful. Just be thankful you're not the cause of an infant being born a bastard and having to carry the stain of it through life. You're a nice girl, with lovely ways, Kenna. You're young and will find someone else to love and have children with, in time.'

The older woman's motherly concern touched something that had long been suppressed in Kenna, the need for a woman she could confide in. Her voice broke and she began to quietly weep. 'I don't want to love anyone else.'

Fiona wrapped her in a hug and held her tight as she rocked her, whispering, 'I know it hurts, but you're young; you'll get over him, I promise. Why don't you stay here with us, at least until the baby is born? You can use my room, stay with my father and help him in the shop. He'll be lonely after I've moved into the lodge.'

Kenna doubted it. Donald McTavish had worked for years to buy up bits of Glenchallon Estate. He might give it back to Rory as a wedding gift, but he'd make sure he had a say in running the place, and he'd probably run his daughter's marriage as well. Perhaps that was a good thing, since McTavish had a business head on his shoulders and would want the estate to be on a business footing by the time his first grandson was ready to inherit. Kenna had no intention of letting Donald run her life. There had already been too much interference in it.

She pulled away and scrubbed the tears from her eyes, ashamed of her weakness. She hadn't thought that being in love would make her feel so fragile. 'It's kind of you, Fiona, but I'm sick of being pushed from pillar to post. I have a home of my own. Robert Gilmore was appointed my guardian, he can't just throw me out without making proper provision for me. His attempt to marry me off has failed, so I'm going to consult a lawyer and see what my rights are. To be quite honest, I'd rather manage my own life and money.'

But even as she said it, the feeling of unease that had been building up inside her bubbled to the surface and her confidence crashed. She felt slightly sick about what lay ahead of her because she couldn't stand the thought of having to live on the streets again. Perspiration dampened her brow. 'Go on if you're going,' she said. 'Don't worry about the shop.'

'Aye, I won't do that. We're sorting out the furniture today. Rory said I'm to choose what I want to furnish the lodge with, and the rest can be stored in one of the cottages. I'm setting him to painting the walls of the living rooms and our bedroom. While he's doing that I'm going to scrub the floorboards and clean the windows. Pa's going to bring me back a rug for the parlour and a new mattress for the bed. And he said I can have the bed quilt my mother made. It's a right pretty thing.'

'I doubt if your laird will notice the pattern on the quilt.'

Colour touched Fiona's cheeks when she saw Kenna's faint

grin, and she giggled. 'Och, but you're a wicked girl, thinking of such a thing.'

'As if you're not.' Kenna placed Fiona's wickerwork basket over her arm. It contained a crusty meat pie, along with other tasty offerings for her man. Kenna pushed her towards the door and through it. Closing it firmly behind Fiona she turned back to the hem and sighed, wishing skirts didn't have such a large expanse of material in them. If anyone came into the shop the bell would alert her.

Although she liked Fiona, Kenna was tiring of her constant chatter. Her happiness was hard to endure in the face of Kenna's own broken heart over Dominic. She'd be glad when the wedding was over and she could leave Glenchallon without giving offence to her good-hearted hosts.

A week later, in the small kirk decorated with dried white heather for good luck, Fiona became Lady Challoner. Kenna felt almost envious of the happiness apparent on her face.

Rory looked handsome in a new kilt and regalia his father-in-law had provided for him.

There was a party at the lodge, which was a comfortably sized house now it had been cleared of its internal clutter. But it couldn't be compared to Glenchallon itself. Glass-paned doors led out on to the small terrace overlooking the loch, which was set with tables and chairs.

The loch was still discoloured but the mud had finished sliding and was beginning to harden. Rory had cleared a path through it and lined it with pavers, so feet couldn't sink through the hard crust. Eventually it would be shovelled away, and returned to the slope. He had plans to replant the slope with small pines when it was stable.

As for the house, the smell of burning was still strong in the air, but the half-burned timbers were stacked to one side and would be used for winter fuel. The blackened stones of Glenchallon would soon be disguised by undergrowth and would remain where they'd fallen until they were needed – perhaps not for centuries.

The village women had prepared a feast. Pies and vegetables lined the tables. A pig had been slaughtered and now rotated in sizzling, spitting splendour. When the sun went down the flares were lit and the food served. A fiddler began to play, and later, the dancing began. The drinking increased.

As midnight approached Kenna whispered to Donald McTavish that she was going home to bed.

'Aye, well, you know your own way well enough, lass. There's a good moon to give you light but make sure you stay on the path. I've left a lamp burning in the porch so you can see your way in. Goodnight, Kenna.'

Kenna left the frivolity behind, picking her way carefully. The drystone wall at the edge of the path was lit by the moonlight, which also illuminated the sweep of the countryside into the valley, where the burn threaded through the undergrowth and tumbled sweetly over the stones with a tune all of its own.

The air was cool, and sweet with spring and the rising sap. Clumps of daffodils were lambent gold. The moon sailed in the sky, lighting the clouds that sought to dim its light. Stars shone, and she closed her eyes and wished when one dislodged from its setting and flew like a radiant jewel across the sky. The enchantment of the moment made her ache.

She was almost sorry to be leaving, but beautiful as it was, this was not her place, for her heart was elsewhere.

'Dominic,' she said out loud, then louder in a shout. '*Dominic, where are you?*' Her voice echoed around the valley in layers of decreasing sound then died into a whisper.

An owl hooted. At the same time something wet touched her hand. She spun round, yelping with fright, her eyes widening, to confront one of Rory's two dogs. Her heart slowed to normal. 'What are you doing here, Willy? Did you follow me?'

Not far behind him came Amos, followed by Rory himself. He stopped a few inches away from her. 'You're the only person I've met who can tell the dogs apart.'

'It's easy. Willy has a longer nose, and Amos always clacks his teeth together before he allows himself to be petted. You should be at your wedding feast.'

He shifted awkwardly from one foot to the other. 'Fiona knows I came after you. There's something I want to say to ye, Kenna.'

'Then say it.'

'I need to say, I'm sorry.'

Tongue firmly in her cheek, she said, 'Thank you, Rory, but there's no need to apologize when I know that Glenchallon was at stake. Fiona's a good woman, and I hope you'll be happy.'

'Aye. Ye were right when you said that you and I aren't suited.'

'I know. But that doesn't mean I found you entirely awful. Sometimes you were . . . unexpected. I never thanked you for keeping me warm in that cottage on the way up here. You're a handsome, well set-up man, Rory – one who would be hard to resist if you set your mind to charming a woman.'

'Ye noticed?'

'Aye, I noticed. You're not the type of man that can be easily overlooked.'

He grinned. 'I was trying to keep myself warm by hopping on the bed and cuddling ye. I wasn't about to sleep on a rickety old chair. I don't think ye gave me much of a chance though.'

'In what way?'

'I thought ye were a sonsie girl, and I could nae believe my luck. But ye were too clever for me, and that scared me. As soon as I snuggled up to ye I wanted to get under your skirt that night. I could have made ye like me.'

'Thank goodness you were a perfect gentleman, then.'

'I was damned uncomfortable and didn't sleep a wink,' he growled. 'There's something I've always wanted to do, and seeing as we'll probably never meet again . . .' He swept her into his arms and kissed her thoroughly on the mouth. She allowed him to have this small victory.

'That's something to remember me by,' he said when he let her go.

'There's something I've always wanted to do, too,' she purred.

He chuckled until her palm flattened across his face, then his hand went to his cheek and he yelped, 'What was that for?'

'You're a married man with a bairn on the way, Rory Challoner, so don't you dare take liberties with me. You can get away back to your wife, and I hope she clouts you one across the ear.'

He laughed. 'Ye're a girl with spirit. I'd sooner have wed ye, Kenna Mackenzie, skinny arse and all. Life will be dull wi'out ye.' He turned and strode away.

'You upland devil, Rory Challoner!' she said, and picking up a handful of gravel hurled it after him.

'Ouch! You're a touchy hen,' he said, laughing as he disappeared into the darkness.

Fifteen

A few days later, Anna Stuart donned her best gown, washed her children's faces and took a cab to the Waverley Hotel, where she enquired for Dr Sterne.

He came downstairs, a smile on his face, and led her to the dining room where he ordered afternoon tea for them both. About her was an air of excitement she could barely contain.

After the children had been settled down with cake and lemonade, he said, 'To what do I owe the pleasure of your visit, Mrs Stuart?'

A smile spread across her face. Taking a letter from her reticule she laid it reverently on the table. 'This arrived for Mr Robert Gilmore. I thought you would like to see it.'

'I see. You do know it would be an offence for me to open mail addressed to another?'

'Yes, I do know, Doctor Sterne. But I do find it odd that Miss Mackenzie doesn't know the house has been sold, and her brother-in-law no longer lives at the address. And it occurred to me that you might like to return the letter to her yourself.'

His heart began to sing as he turned the letter over. There on the back, written in elegant black lettering, was his beloved's name and the address.

'Glenchallon Estate,' he murmured, 'Galashiels. Not so far, after all.' He placed the envelope against his lips and gently kissed her signature. *Miss Kenna Mackenzie. I love you*, he thought, and smiled at Anna, saying simply, 'She's still unwed.'

'When that letter was written she was still unwed,' Anna cautioned.

He felt an almost irresistible urge to tear the letter apart and read it. He slid it into a pocket against his heart.

As if Anna had read his mind, she said, 'I've heard you can use steam from a kettle spout to soften the glue, then it can be resealed without detection.'

He offered her a teasing grin. 'Mrs Stuart, I'm surprised to see that you have such larcenous tendencies. What would George make of it, I wonder?'

A faint blush touched her cheeks. 'I wouldn't do such a dishonest thing myself, of course.'

'Of course you wouldn't. Neither would I, not even if I had a steaming kettle to hand. To keep this out of temptation's way I'm going to place it safely in the hands of my lawyer before I go and find Kenna.'

An hour later Tam Fellowes held the letter over the steaming kettle spout, grinning at Dominic's shocked expression. 'Don't tell me you didn't think of doing this?'

'I won't dignify that with a lie. Of course I did, I just didn't have the courage.' He waited while Tam read the contents then, when he chuckled, said with some impatience, 'What does it say?'

Folding the paper the lawyer tapped it on his desk. 'Are you sure you want to know?'

'How long does it take to strangle a lawyer, Tam?'

Tam laughed. 'Lawyers are so inflated by their own rhetoric, I imagine it would take quite a long time before they ran out of air.'

Plucking the paper from Tam's fingers Dominic unfolded it.

Dear Robert,

You should be made aware that I've declined the opportunity to become Lady Challoner and will be returning home as soon as possible.

Agnes treated me shamefully by making me leave the safe home and hearth provided for me by my parents. Needless to say, your response to that was reprehensible. It was only through the goodness of a stranger that I survived that ordeal.

My father always told me never to put anything in writing that can be used against me. I will not, therefore, accuse you of being a liar or a cheat – or, indeed,

> *a thief who preyed on gullible women such as my ailing sister and myself.*

Now it was Dominic's turn to chuckle before he resumed reading.

> *Please take note, Robert. When I return to Edinburgh, unless you can give me a satisfactory accounting of my inheritance, past and present, my intention is to consult with a representative of the law to investigate the extent of the legal guardianship you hold, and whether my rights have been infringed in any way.*
>
> *Those who knew and respected my father will surely remember him and come to my aid.*
>
> *Yours faithfully,*
> *Kenna Mackenzie*

'Miss Mackenzie has a good turn of phrase and a lively mind. She'd make a good lawyer,' Tam remarked.

Dominic gave a half-smile. 'Kenna has a temper on her and it sounds like hot air to me. The last time I saw her she didn't have a penny in her pocket, so she wouldn't have been able to afford legal help.'

'Her father was well-respected. Had she but known it, there's a lot of truth in that last statement of hers. I wouldn't have turned her away if she'd come to me for help. I was appalled when you told me you'd found her half-dead on the street.'

Dominic gazed at him, anxiety filling his eyes. 'I hope she hasn't suffered a relapse. This letter is dated three weeks ago . . . so where is she?'

'There's always the possibility that she decided to marry the laird.'

The anxiety turned into alarm. 'But she said—'

'Women have been known to change their minds. Perhaps you're right, though, and she's been ill and is recuperating. There's only one way to find out.'

'Yes. I'm going up there, Tam.'

But when he got back to the hotel it was to find that a

message had been delivered from his mother. '*Come home as soon as possible, Dominic. Evelyn is gravely ill.*'

He had an hour to spare before the train left, so sent a note by messenger to Tam, and similar ones to the Stuarts and Mairi, his former housekeeper, who'd been made aware of the situation. If Kenna came back to Edinburgh she would go to the Ainsley Place house first. Inside the note to the Stuarts was one for Kenna, so she'd be left in no doubt of his feelings. She would be well looked after by Anna and George until he could see her in person. And as he hadn't sealed it, Anna wouldn't have to go to the trouble of steaming it open.

Quickly packing his bag, Dominic paid his bill and strode across to the station with minutes to spare. He purchased his ticket and settled himself in a carriage, his face lined with worry. Scarlet fever! He couldn't bear to think of Evelyn suffering, and refused to think of any other future for his daughter but a complete recovery.

Agnes Gilmore had found a room near the docks and had been earning her living the hard way.

One morning a knock came at her door. A nondescript-looking man of middle age stood outside.

'Agnes Gilmore?'

'Who wants to know?'

'My name is Joseph Duncan. I'm a private investigator.'

She felt a stab of alarm, but her curiosity led her to ask, 'What d'you want from me?'

'I'm looking for a man called Robert Gilmore. I understand you're married to him.'

She allowed him entrance, checking to make sure the place was tidy first. She might be forced to earn her living in a profession she detested but she liked to be clean. 'Aye, I am married to him,' she said bitterly. 'But someone should tell him that. He left me in London to fend for myself and went off without a word.'

'Do you know where?'

'If I did I wouldn't be hanging around here. He's a crafty one, is Robert. He planned it and would have covered his tracks. He might have left the country.'

The man slid some money into her hand along with a card. 'If you can think of anything else, please let me know.'

'I've got a photograph,' Agnes suddenly remembered. Opening a drawer she took out a stack of small photographic cards. She was pictured seated on a balustrade. Robert stood behind her. They looked well together, and Agnes felt a quick thrust of despair because she'd been duped into believing Robert's lies. She'd enjoyed the respectability of being married. Sadly, she said, 'We had it taken in London.'

'Ah, a *carte-de-visite*. May I keep it?'

She shrugged. 'I suppose so. Robert thought I'd only bought one, but I ordered a dozen because they worked out cheaper. I didn't tell him because he scratched himself off the one I showed him; said it didn't look like him. It does, though.' Her eyes narrowed thoughtfully. 'It will cost you sixpence if you want one. That's what it cost me. I don't know what I'll do with the others, though. It was a waste of money.' She stood one against a bottle of lavender water on the dresser.

'I'll take two of them if you don't mind, just in case I lose one.' He slid her the shilling and pocketed the cards. 'Thank, you, Mrs Gilmore.'

'You said you were a private investigator . . .'

'Yes.'

'Then you must be working for someone. What do you want with Robert?'

'He seems to have disappeared from Edinburgh.'

'Aye, I've noticed. Is somebody after him for money? If so, you can add me to the list. A husband should support his wife, and Robert had plenty tucked away. I suppose it's that haughty sister-in-law of his making trouble? She's a stubborn cow. He got rid of her, too, I imagine. He had plans to marry her off to some uplander. He took all her money first, I'll be bound. Robert's been fleecing her for years.'

Joseph Duncan's eyes narrowed. 'What d'you mean about him getting rid of her *too*?'

'I'm not saying anything more.' Agnes clamped her mouth shut, folded her arms over her chest and stared at him.

'I should perhaps tell you that there are rumours about Robert Gilmore.'

She'd said too much, and felt the colour drain from her face. 'What sort of rumours?'

'The nasty sort that warrant a thorough investigation. Being his wife, no doubt the police will question you. If there's anything you feel might be useful to their enquiries it might be a good idea for you to make a statement in advance – to a lawyer, perhaps.'

'Robert was a lawyer. He couldn't be trusted. Besides, I can't afford one.' She spread her hands. 'Take a look at this place. I'm a respectable married woman and I'm forced to live here, and to earn money by . . . well, I work in a tavern.'

He nodded and flicked a card on the table. 'This man will advise you free of charge if he thinks it will help our client.'

'I'm not saying nothing until you tell me who's paying you.'

'My client is Doctor Dominic Sterne, who is looking for Miss Kenna Mackenzie, who is a friend of his. Robert Gilmore's disappearance cropped up as part of the investigation.'

'I've never heard of him. What sort of *friends* are Kenna and this doctor?'

The man smiled. 'I'm given to understand they were once sweethearts.'

'Were they? That Kenna is a sly boots. She's never mentioned him and I've never heard of him. I'm pretty sure Robert hadn't either.'

Agnes thought for a moment. Robert had planned everything in advance. He'd sold the house and had intended to abandoned her right from the beginning. She began to wonder about Kenna. He might have killed her, same as the others. But no, it would have been too risky. Kenna might look on her kindly if she helped her get back together with her sweetheart. A doctor? Aye, that would be the respectable type of man Kenna would be attracted to. As for Robert, she owed him nothing; in fact, she'd had a lucky escape. Vengeance would be sweet, and she had the perfect revenge in mind.

'Is this doctor offering a reward?'

'I'm sure something could be arranged. A guinea perhaps.'

Agnes sniffed, but it was better than nothing. Let me see you get out of this one Robert Gilmore! She gazed triumphantly at the man, and lied, 'Robert killed his first wife . . . he fed her the arsenic he kept hidden in a secret compartment in the kitchen. She died in agony, she did. And he might have done for her father in the same way.'

Joseph held up his hand. 'Don't say anything more, Mrs Gilmore. Mr Fellowes will advise you of your rights first. You can then make your voluntary statement to him, or you might decide not to. If you decide to go ahead, your statement will be taken down by his clerk and a copy made, so you can read it before you sign it. We could go there now. Or we could go in the morning if you'd like to think things through first.'

Agnes threw caution to the winds. 'We'll go now. I want tae be back before dark. I have rent tae pay so must earn some money – at the tavern,' she added quickly.

Besides, she thought, there was an American clipper berthed at Victoria Dock and the foreign sailors always paid well for her services.

Sixteen

Kenna was dropped off at the railway station at Galashiels. It was a fine day, the air filled with a late April softness.

'On a day like this the countryside is so beautiful,' she remarked as Donald carried her trunk on to the platform.

Donald McTavish cleared his throat and said gruffly, 'Ye don't have to go, lassie. If you want tae change your mind I'll find room for ye and ye can give me a hand in the shop.'

It was kindly meant. 'Of course I have to go, Donald. Given why I came here in the first place, Fiona wouldn't feel easy with me living on her doorstep.'

'Aye, the laird is a flighty one.'

She remembered the kiss he'd given her on the night of his wedding. 'And he has a great deal of charm when he puts his mind to it. Fiona tells me you own half of Glenchallon?'

'Aye, I do. For generations bits and pieces of land has been sold off or mortgaged, and the McTavish family have invested in the estate. When I drop his grandfather's will off at the lawyer and the auld fart gets around to dealing with it, the Challoner will learn that he owns the other half of the estate free and clear because his grandfather sold his holdings in England and bought up most of the mortgages on Glenchallon, and more besides. Och, 'tis a complicated matter.'

'Does Rory know?'

'Mebbe, or mebbe not. Debt is commonplace on the big estates, and deeds might change hands several times over the generations. Hardly anyone pays any mind to it. He also stands to inherit a great deal of money when the will is proved. Then there's the insurance Magnus Fergusson has been paying all these years.'

She turned to him, smiling, because the irony of it appealed to her. The laird had gone looking for a wealthy woman when there was one under his nose all the time. She'd like to see his face when he realized that fact. 'Magnus made you one of the executors of his estate?'

'Aye, I've acted as his agent with his banker for years – for a small fee, of course.'

'Of course.'

'And I withdrew his allowance every month from his account and purchased anything he needed, though his needs were small. He was a frugal man.'

She'd like to meet one who wasn't in these parts. 'Rory and Maggie always wondered where his grandfather got the money to buy paints and whisky.'

The pair exchanged a conspiratorial grin, then Donald told her, 'Magnus knew he could trust me. I witnessed his last will and testament. Are you quite sure you'll nae stay, lassie?'

'No, thank you, Donald. I have something to sort out at home.'

'If you want tae come back you'll be welcome.'

'Thank you.'

He placed her luggage in the guard's van then helped her into the passenger compartment, closing the door behind her. 'Have ye got your basket, now?'

'I have, Donald, so stop fussing.' Inside it were some buttered buns, cheese, a slice of cold sausage and a bottle of tea.

'I'll be awi' then,' he said when the whistle blew. 'Don't forget tae close the window when you get going else ye'll get soot in your eyes.'

'Aye, Donald. Anything else?'

He laughed as the train jerked forward and paced alongside the carriage for the length of the platform. 'Just take care of yourself.'

'I will. Tell Fiona I'll write when I'm settled,' she shouted.

The train began to gather speed and left Donald behind. She gave him a final wave then withdrew her head and closed the window. The carriage she was in was empty of other passengers.

The sadness of parting was tempered by the thought that

she'd escaped from the situation Robert had placed her in. Her future seemed uncertain, though.

Dominic's housekeeper, Mairi, had once compared life to a bowl of scotch broth. 'You don't know what you're getting until it's been ladled into your bowl,' she'd said.

Gently twisting the bracelet Dominic had given her, Kenna traced over the names with the tip of her finger. Evelyn, Dominic, Hamish and Kenna, united by an etched sprig of rosemary for remembrance. Together for ever. It had been a short, but significant time in her young life, the memory captured in a gold band – a golden spark of brightness in the troubles that had beset her.

Perhaps Fiona had been right when she'd said that Kenna might fall in love again. But at the moment her heart ached for those she'd loved and lost.

She wondered if Robert had received her letter, and what sort of reception she'd get . . .

Later that day Kenna took a cab from the railway station to Ainsley Place. She looked at the house she'd grown up in and suddenly didn't want to go inside. Here, at different times, all of her family had prematurely died.

There were new curtains at the windows. One twitched to one side and a woman looked out. She was a stranger to Kenna. The pair gazed at each other, then a smile sped across the woman's face and she disappeared from view. A moment later the front door opened wide and she came out to stand on the doorstep. 'Are you Kenna Mackenzie?'

'Aye, I am. Who are you?'

'My name's Anna Stuart.'

'Are you the new housekeeper?'

The woman stepped forward and took her hands in hers. 'No, my dear. I live here.'

Puzzled, Kenna stared at her. 'You're renting the house from my brother-in-law . . .? I don't understand. Where's Robert? Is he still in London?'

'We actually bought the house from Mr Gilmore – who has since disappeared.' A frown of disapproval touched her brow. 'His wife was looking for him, too, a rather common young woman, I thought.'

Kenna could only nod in agreement as a thought generated in her brain. So Robert had abandoned Agnes as well as herself.

'Come inside, my dear. There's a lot for you to know, and I promised Doctor Sterne—'

Suddenly breathless, Kenna's heart lurched in all directions as she interjected, 'Dominic is still in Edinburgh?'

'Nae, lass. He came back here looking for you, but he received a message that his daughter has been taken ill and he's gone to her.'

'Evelyn? Oh, my God, the dear girl. What's the matter with her?'

'She has scarlet fever, I understand. But let's talk inside. I must say the doctor seemed very fond of you. In fact, the dear man is in love with you.'

A smile seemed to fix itself brightly to Kenna's face. 'Did he say so?'

'Aye, he did. He was beside himself when he couldn't find you, and was about to go to Glenchallon after I showed him the letter you sent. He thought he was too late, and you might have married the laird. Then the message came about his daughter. Doctor Sterne asked me to look after you if you turned up. He's such a dear, well-mannered man.'

Kenna burst into tears, despite her smile. 'I must go to them.'

'And so you shall. He's left a note with me for you. Take the other end of the trunk, would you, dear?' They picked the luggage up between them and carried it inside.

'Mrs Stuart, will you please tell me what's going on?' Kenna said. 'I'm totally confused. Where is Robert Gilmore?'

'I don't know, but others are looking for him too. There has been allegations . . .'

'What sort of allegations? What others?'

'Take a seat, my dear. This might come as a shock.'

Settling herself in the nearest chair, one which had once belonged to her mother, Kenna gazed at her. 'Tell me?'

'There's talk that Robert Gilmore murdered his late wife.'

'Jeanne!' She stared at the woman for a long moment, her heart thumping as the words sank in, then she said slowly, 'I don't believe it. Robert might be manipulative, and he's certainly dishonest, but he adored my sister. He was beside himself when she died. I'll never believe he killed her. Never!' She began to laugh, then when her laughter was spent she stared at Anna Stuart, tears prickling her eyes. 'It's not true. I just can't believe it.'

'No, I imagine you can't. A lawyer named Tam Fellowes seems to be at the forefront of the investigation. You must speak to him.'

'Tam Fellowes? I vaguely remember the name. I think he was a friend of my father.'

'I'm sorry, dear.' Anna heaved a sigh. 'I'll make us some tea then I'll show you where you can sleep.'

'I know where my room is.' She hesitated, then shrugged. 'I'm sorry. It's not my room any more, is it? I used to sleep in the one overlooking the street on the right.' She ran a finger over the velvet on the chair. 'It feels odd when I grew up with this furniture, to discover it now belongs to somebody else. I feel dispossessed.'

'Aye, you would do. But we bought the house and everything in it fair and square.' Anna Stuart bustled around, setting plates and cups on the table with pursed lips and an oddly determined air about her. Kenna knew she'd upset her.

'I'm not suggesting anything different, or trying to make you feel guilty, Mrs Stuart. If anyone cheated me out of anything it was Robert Gilmore.'

Anna relaxed. 'You're a fair-minded girl for one so young, I'll give you that. No doubt the law will sort the man out once they catch up with him. If it will make you feel more comfortable you can use your old room. And there are some things my George put in the attic that might hold sentimental value for you. Ornaments, and such. You can have those if you wish.'

'Thank you, you're very kind. What happened to the portrait of my mother?'

'Doctor Sterne took it away with him. He said it reminded him of you. I admit that the resemblance is strong.' She took an envelope from a box on the dresser and handed it to Kenna. 'Here's your note from the doctor. So romantic . . .'

Kenna's fingers trembled as she opened it.

Kenna, my dearest,

Can you forgive me? I'm not eloquent in the art of romance and can only express simply the emotion written on my heart. I hold you close in my affection and with the deepest respect. I miss you, my sweet sonsie girl.

Meanwhile, I have your brooch to remember you by, and I live with the hope that it will bring you back to me.

Dominic

Tears sprang to her eyes as she thought, So, Dominic, you fell in love with me despite thinking I was a fallen woman and decided to follow your heart. Perhaps leaving you proved to be the right thing to do, after all.

Jethro Kester had paid the girl for the use of her body. Now she reclined on the bed and watched him through slumberous dark eyes as he pulled on his boots.

He liked her. She wasn't hardened to her profession, for she'd enjoyed him as much as he'd enjoyed her. And she was clean.

'I haven't come across you in Edinburgh before. How long have you been doing this?'

'A week. It's the only way I can pay for a roof over my head.'

As he reached for his cap he dislodged a photograph leaning against the lamp. Retrieving it from the floor he stared at it through narrowed eyes. 'Who is the man with you?'

'My husband, Robert. At least, he *was* my husband,' she said bitterly. 'We were wed over the anvil, though I've got nothing to prove it since the smithy has closed down, and the witnesses gone. God only knows where Robert is now but the law is after him. Now you know why I'm doing what I'm doing. It's not by choice.'

'This Robert, does he have a second name?'

'Aye, it's Gilmore.' She swung her legs over the side of the bed and gazed sharply at him as she pulled on her bodice. 'What's it to you? D'you know where he is?'

'I might.' He sat down on the bed beside her. 'What's he wanted for?'

'Killing his first wife, amongst other things.'

Jethro sucked in a shocked breath. 'What other things?'

'Fraud.'

'I see. He resembles someone I've known for a short time. It might be a different man, though, he has a beard.'

'He grew one in London after the photograph was taken. But you recognized him in the picture. What was it about him?'

'Something about the shape of his eyes and the way he stands. Is your Robert a lawyer?'

'Aye,' she said in surprise.

'And could you positively identify him?'

'I could. In fact I've written a statement about him for some legal fellers. That will teach him to treat me like dirt.'

'Then get your bags packed. The ship sails for Boston on the evening tide.' He suddenly grinned. 'You can sleep in my cabin.'

She offered him a saucy look. 'Can I now?'

'You'll have to since all the passenger cabins are full. You won't see much of me, but I'll reimburse you for the income you'll lose.'

The seaman hadn't been at all bad. He liked to do things his way, and she liked the way he treated her, like a lover instead of a whore. He'd left her feeling satisfied. 'Och, it's not something I want to do fer a living. Just treat me with respect, is all I ask. If it is Robert, what will happen to him?'

'I'll bring him back to Edinburgh and hand him over to the authorities so he can face justice.'

'Why are you so interested in him?'

'He's courting my sister.'

Agnes sighed. 'Robert can be charming when he's dealing with women.'

'My sister is already taken with him. She's a very determined woman when she wants something.'

'If your man is my Robert, what is he calling himself?'

'Bart Parnell.'

Agnes pulled her bags out from under the bed. 'I'll lose my room if the rent's not paid up in advance, and I can't afford it in a lump.'

'He nodded. Eight weeks should cover it. And I'll buy you a couple of respectable gowns.'

'There's no need. I have respectable gowns. I tried to sell them but the pawn shop only offered a couple of shillings. Hardly worn, they were.'

'Then put one on. The gown you're wearing is far too provocative; the crew won't be able to keep their minds on their jobs.'

She smiled and undid her bodice, setting free her breasts. He leaned forward to cup their fullness in his hands, then kissed each brown nipple. 'You have a beautiful body. You should keep it for one man to enjoy.'

'Aye, I would if I could find a decent one.' Though it was probably too late for that now, she thought.

He removed her bodice then eased her skirt down over her hips so she stood in her stockings and a satin chemise. Her gaze was drawn to the apex of his thighs and she saw he liked what he saw. Agnes suddenly wanted him again.

'We've still got time to conduct a little business,' he murmured.

'Not business this time, pleasure. You treat a woman nice. What's your name?'

'Jethro Kester.'

'Mine is Agnes Gilmore.'

Jethro smiled to himself. Agnes was a pert little trollop, and her accent was delightful. He might keep her for a while if she suited him, and he couldn't wait to see the look on Parnell's face when the man set eyes on her.

The following day, accompanied by George Stuart, Kenna spent some time with Tam Fellowes and a private detective called Joseph Duncan.

She shook her head and repeated what she'd told Anna Stuart. 'Robert might have robbed me blind but he wouldn't have killed Jeanne. He wouldn't have had the stomach for it, especially using poison. Who made such a stupid accusation?'

'The wife he deserted, Agnes Gilmore.'

'Ah, that accounts for it, then. Agnes can be vindictive.'

'Nevertheless, the accusation is a serious one and must be investigated.'

Kenna gave a little cry of distress. 'Damn Agnes.'

'Mrs Gilmore has been most helpful. She recently sent a note by messenger to say that she thought that Robert might be using the name of Bart Parnell. We've checked, and the man was certainly one of his clients. He was about Gilmore's age and died without issue. He left all his worldly goods to the church. Robert could easily have stolen his identity to cover his tracks.'

'He didn't make a very good job of covering them, then.' She sighed. 'Where's Agnes now?'

'It appears she's paid her rent in advance for the next eight weeks and has gone on holiday.'

'Where?'

'She didn't tell her landlord where, but he said she went off with an officer from one of the clippers.'

'It would have been the *Atlantic Queen* out of Boston,' the detective said. 'That was the only clipper in port at the time.'

Kenna turned his way. 'So Robert might be in America. It's possible that he sent for her.'

'I hardly think she'd join him after making such serious accusations. She's made a statement and knows she'll be needed as a witness in court if this murder charge goes ahead.'

'I'll be the first to admit that Robert and I didn't like each other. But how can he be accused of murder when my sister was attended by a well-respected doctor for the duration of her disease? She had a growth which caused her a great deal of pain, and she died slowly and painfully. Jeanne was so brave, and Robert wept for several days after she died. I guarantee that his grief was genuine. Besides, Jeanne is buried. It will just be his word against that of Agnes.'

Tam Fellowes cleared his throat. 'My dear, there is already an order issued to have your sister's body exhumed and examined for traces of the poison. That's the only way we can prove that a crime was committed. If the test is positive Robert Gilmore will be arrested and charged – if he can be found.'

Kenna gave a cry of distress. 'You'd disturb Jeanne's resting place on the say so of Agnes? That's too cruel. If she's not being deliberately malicious then she must have totally misinterpreted what she observed. The only thing

Robert used poison for was to kill rats. He used to stir it in with the food scraps.'

'There were food scraps and an empty arsenic packet in the garden when we moved into the house,' George said, his mouth pursing with disapproval. 'Baiting with food attracts more rodents than it kills. '

Something else occurred to Kenna. 'If Agnes said she saw him poison my sister then she must have been there at the time. Wouldn't that make her just as guilty?'

The two men exchanged a look, and Tam nodded. 'Kenna has a point.'

'Mrs Gilmore didn't say she saw him in the act, merely that she saw some arsenic in a secret compartment in the cupboard in the kitchen. She thought he'd used it to kill his wife . . . and possibly his father-in-law.'

Kenna gave an exasperated sigh. '*My father?* He died in hospital from a burst appendix. I'm sure it's well-documented. Can't you see how ridiculous these accusations are? She'll be saying I poisoned them next. The rat poison was kept in a glass jar, then in the hidden compartment as a precaution. It was always clearly labelled. It wasn't just Robert who used it. My father impressed on me that it mustn't be touched when I was a child.' She gave George a frown. 'Neither my father nor Robert used baits foolishly. I imagine Robert threw the food out at the last minute, so it wouldn't go off and the smell attracted the rats inside.'

'A rational enough explanation, though an irresponsible practice, especially when children were due to move into the premises,' George said, and folded his arms over his chest with the air of one having the last word on the subject.

Kenna said into the silence, 'Please drop this line of enquiry. You'll simply make fools of yourself. Where is your evidence? You certainly won't find any by disturbing Jeanne's remains, and even if poison was found, there were three of us in the house that could have administered it – including Agnes.'

'I'm afraid it's too late for that.'

She'd hate to see Robert go to the gallows for something he hadn't done. But she *would* like him to be punished for what he *had* done.

'I would very much like my inheritance back from

Robert, and I'd like to gain full control of it. After all, it was my father who worked for it in the first place, and Robert turned out to be an irresponsible guardian. Can this be achieved?'

'As long as it's still in existence. Investigating fraud is interesting,' Tam said, and smiled. 'You get a sense of pitting your wits against a worthy adversary. We do have something concrete to go on now – a name. We'll get our facts straight then hand the dossier over to the police, who will issue a warrant for his arrest and that of his partner in this crime, the shady lawyer Malcolm Owen.'

Joseph smiled. 'Perhaps he could be persuaded to make a full confession, since he handled the sale of the house.'

'Not just yet, Joseph. This will take some time. Let's unscramble Robert Gilmore's nest of eggs before we start on Owen's. We don't want him to fly the coop, as well . . . and it's always possible that he's an accessory to a murder, too.'

Kenna gave a snort of disbelief. 'I'll guarantee that there was no murder. One thing, Mr Fellowes. I have no money until my inheritance is restored. I can't even give you a retainer. And I'd rather you didn't bill Doctor Sterne. He's been good to me. The debts I incur are not his responsibility.'

'Of course they're not. At least, not yet, eh?' The three men looked at each other and grinned when she blushed. 'Neither will you need to pay us, my dear. I'll do this as a favour to your father, whom I had great respect for. Now, can you write out a statement for my clerk to copy before you leave? Try and remember any documents you may have signed for Mr Gilmore in the past, no matter how long ago – and even if they seem unimportant. The bank would have been obliged to approve them. If you don't want to do it today, as soon as possible. I'll then call in some favours and we'll soon sort this out.'

'I'll write a statement today.' She smiled . . . in fact, she felt as though she was smiling inside as well as outside, as if she'd swallowed the sun. 'The day after tomorrow I'm going to Bournemouth to find Dominic and Evelyn. I can just about afford a one-way train ticket.'

'I'm sure I can scrape up some cash for your pocket. We'll call it an advance.'

And the advance turned out to be a generous one.

She said goodbye to her hosts two days later, and experienced a sense of freedom. Although they were good-hearted people they took the responsibility of her very seriously. She felt restricted, and obliged to be on her best behaviour in their presence.

With Anna in attendance she went through the goods that had been packed away in the attic, and chose a couple of small figurines that Jeanne had been particularly fond of. She discovered a brass kaleidoscope.

'It used to be my father's when he was a child,' she said to Anna. 'He gave it to me for my fifth birthday. I'd really like to keep it.'

It didn't take up much room in her luggage.

She gave her room one last look before she left it for good. She couldn't remember ever being really happy in this house of sorrow, and would be glad to see the back of it.

And oddly, although the southern uplands now seemed part of her past, since she'd been back in Edinburgh she'd missed the freedom that Glenchallon had afforded her.

But when George and Anna Stuart settled her on the train with well-stocked picnic basket and lots of fussing, excitement grew in her for what might lie ahead.

As soon as the train picked up speed she drew Dominic's note from her pocket and read it over and over again.

He loved her, that was all that mattered to her.

Evelyn was over the crisis and regaining her strength. Dominic had allowed her to enjoy some fresh air, tucked up in the daybed near the open French windows. Hamish slept at her feet except for the frequent forays into the garden, where he watered the daffodils or chased away the seagulls who'd trespassed on the property.

The wine-coloured rash that had covered Evelyn's arms was now fading. Soon her skin would begin to peel. Until that infectious process had been completed, her cousins would not be allowed near her.

'Am I still sick, Papa?'

'I'm afraid so, cherub. You're not as sick as you were yesterday, though. And tomorrow you'll be better still.'

She nodded. 'My head doesn't ache so much today.'

'Perhaps I should bang on it with my book.'

Smiling faintly at such a preposterous notion, Evelyn closed her eyes. 'I'm sleepy. When I close my eyes I can hear the sea; do you think mermaids are real?'

'Do you?'

'Yes . . . they've got flowing hair and lovely silver tails that thrash the water into froth. Hennie told me. She showed me a picture in a book, and the mermaid looked a bit like Miss Mackalenzie.'

Kenna certainly has a lovely tail, he thought with a smile, and kissed his daughter's flushed cheek. 'I'm taking the rig into town to see if there're any letters later. And I'm going to see the estate agent about purchasing Summertree Villa, since we both liked the house so much. Your grandmother will come and sit with you while I'm gone.'

Her eyes suddenly flew open. 'Miss Mackalenzie will come back to us one day, won't she, Papa? She hasn't forgotten us?'

'She won't be able to forget us, she's wearing the magic bracelet with our names etched into it and the springs of rosemary for remembrance.'

'But what if she takes it off?'

Remembering a kiss against his cheek and the soft whisper of her voice in his ear, his spirits rose. Kenna had told him she loved him before she'd walked out of his life. The words had penetrated his sleep – not deep enough to bring him fully to consciousness, but enough to leave him feeling warm and smug. It had taken time for it to sink in that she'd gone, and he remembered the feeling of hollowness inside him. 'She won't take it off.'

'Promise?'

He'd been so close to finding her . . . *so close*. 'You know I can't make promises like that, Evelyn. Kenna has a mind of her own. I can only pray that we mean something special to her, as she does to us.'

Evelyn reached out for his hand and turned her face against it. After a short while she fell asleep.

Love for his daughter was a warm river that flowed through him as he went in search of his mother.

Seventeen

By the time Kenna ran out of railway track, she was as close as she could get to her destination. She was sick of trains, and tired of changing from one to the other.

Luckily, she'd travelled from Edinburgh in the same compartment as a married couple heading for Southampton. On their advice she'd stayed the night with them in a boarding house in London before going to Waterloo Station to board the train to Southampton the next morning. There, they parted company. From there she caught another train to Dorchester, alighting with other passengers at a small station called Christchurch Road.

But the tedious journey wasn't yet over. Kenna bought a ticket on a horse-drawn coach of the Royal Blue company and was transported uncomfortably into Bournemouth. Deposited outside the Belle Vue Hotel along with her luggage, she was glad to be out of the jolting vehicle and finally at her destination.

She gazed around her. Opposite her was an expanse of curving sand and beyond, a jetty poking out a short distance into the sea. Boats of all types darted across the water, or were beached above the waterline. The area was thickly covered with heathland, though someone had had the foresight to plant pine trees, and there was a profusion of them in various stages of growth.

The scenery wasn't as spectacular as that of Glenchallon, but she didn't think anything would ever compare to the grandeur of the southern uplands of Scotland. The smell of pine resin in the air reminded her, though. Bournemouth was simply a small seaside town, she thought, with a slightly genteel and sedate look to it. But there were signs that the town was growing. The fine buildings had a prosperous look and so did the people. Plenty of building going on. It was a different world.

The shadows were beginning to lengthen as she approached a young lad with a cart. 'Can you tell me where Exeter Road is?'

He pointed behind them and a little to the left, where the cliff sloped gently upwards. 'Follow that track. There's only a few houses in Exeter Road, which one d'you want?'

'Seahaven Villa.'

'It's up there near the top. I can show you, and I can take your luggage up there for sixpence,' he said eagerly.

Kenna was so tired it would have been impossible to have carried her luggage that far by herself. The walk invigorated her a little after her long journey. She began to worry about what her reception would be as they neared the house. What if Evelyn had succumbed to the fever and they were in mourning? No, she must not think negatively. Dominic was a fine doctor. He adored his sweet daughter and wouldn't allow her to die. Even so, she prayed with each step that took her closer to them.

The building was constructed of white stone and had a steeply pitched roof. It looked pretty set amongst the pine trees and surrounded by a neatly clipped hedge. White pillars bordered three stone steps up to the garden path.

There was a quarantine notice on the gate.

'You'd better not come in. The daughter of the house is recovering from an infection,' she said to the boy.

The lad placed her trunk on the pavement, pocketed the sixpence she gave him and scurried off, whistling to himself.

Kenna's emotions were a mixture of excitement and despair. When she rang the doorbell a dog began to bark, then Hamish came tearing around the side of the house, his teeth bared. Catching sight of her he skidded to a halt and rolled on to his back, giving small, excited yips and yelps.

She laughed as she stooped to tickle his stomach. 'You idiot, I thought you were supposed to be a guard dog!'

She didn't hear the door open, but when she straightened up it was to the sight of Dominic standing there, tall and elegant. The grey eyes that sought hers expressed astonishment, then they filled with laughter as he said softly, 'Kenna Mackenzie. You received my note, then?'

Eyes rounding innocently, she said, 'No . . . what did it say?'

'That I had your brooch . . . and I asked you to forgive me.'

'Forgive you for what, Dominic?'

His eyes narrowed. 'You know damned well.'

She grinned. 'What else did it say?'

'That I missed you.'

'And?' she prompted.

His lips twitched. 'I think I said I held you in my affection and deepest respect.'

'Oh . . . *that* note.' She managed a faint smile before she said, 'Yes, I did receive it. Do you still hold me in your deepest affection?'

'Yes?'

'Good, because I love you too, Dominic. The last few weeks have been hell without you.'

The chuckle he gave was as warm as she remembered. 'I'm quite convinced that it couldn't have been that bad.' Taking a step forward he tipped her face up to his and kissed her with more tenderness than she'd ever thought possible, his mouth warm against hers.

She breathed in his scent and touched her palms gently against his face to reassure herself he was real. Then she slid her arms around him and hugged him tight, her face against his shoulder. 'At last, I feel as though I'm home.'

'I was worried you might have married the laird.'

'Aye, so was I. Glenchallon was pretty and I felt trapped for a while. So much has happened over the past few weeks. But we'll talk about that later. Tell me how Evelyn is faring?'

'She's much improved. She'll be glad to see you.'

'You don't often embrace young women on the doorstep, so I can only assume this is the young lady from Edinburgh you told me about. Won't you ask her inside, Dominic?' a woman said from behind him.

Kenna found herself drawn to one side. Dominic entwined her fingers with his as he said, 'Mother, may I present Miss Kenna Mackenzie? This is the woman I love, and intend to make my wife, if she'll have me. Kenna, this is my mother, Mrs Charlotte Sterne.'

Kenna had the impression of a graceful woman with high cheekbones and eyes like Dominic's before Charlotte kissed her on both cheeks. 'Welcome to my home. Did you come all this way from Edinburgh by yourself? How brave you are.' Her glance went to her son and she grinned. 'Do let the girl go. I promise not to allow her to run away from you again. You can go and fetch her luggage in.'

'Is Evelyn awake yet?'

'Yes . . . I was just about to ring for afternoon tea. You'll join us of course, Miss Mackenzie?'

'Aye, I'd like too. I haven't eaten anything since I left London this morning.' Her stomach grumbled at the reminder. Kenna felt Charlotte's scrutiny as she preceded her into the interior of the house, which gave an impression of spaciousness and light. A huge jar of daffodils glowed like a splash of sunshine on the highly polished surface of the hall table.

Catching a reflection of herself in the mirror, Kenna became conscious of her travel-worn appearance and dishevelled hair. 'I'm sorry I look so untidy.'

She could have hugged the woman when she said, 'I'm not surprised after travelling all that way. After tea your room will be ready. I'll have some hot water sent up so you can refresh yourself and rest before dinner.'

Kenna turned to her. 'I must apologize for turning up on your doorstep without a word and putting you to so much trouble.'

'Nonsense, my dear. We've been expecting you.' She threw open the door to a large drawing room. 'I must go to the kitchen and confer with the servants. Go in and say hello to Evelyn. I imagine it won't be long before Dominic joins you.'

A maid rose to her feet and quietly left the room when Mrs Sterne beckoned to her. Followed by Hamish, who was making self-important huffing noises, Kenna gazed down at the flushed little invalid. 'Hello, Evelyn Sterne.'

The girl's eyes fluttered open and she stared at her, then a smile edged across her face. 'Miss Mackalenzie! I knew you'd come one day.' She held out her arms and Kenna gently hugged her.

'I was sad when you went away, but I knew you'd come back,' Evelyn said, snuggling up against her. 'You won't go away again, will you?'

From the corner of her eye Kenna saw Dominic standing in the doorway. Her eyes met his and when he raised an eyebrow she laughed. 'Nothing will take me away from you again, I promise.'

Evelyn wriggled. 'I feel all tickly, Miss Mackalenzie.'

'I had scarlet fever when I was a child. The doctor told me that I had the tickles because my skin was damaged by the rash. It will tickle itself right off your body.'

'Like lots of ants?'

'It will look more like the wings from flying ants.'

Evelyn looked anxious. 'But my blood will run out if my skin flies away.'

'You don't need to worry about that, there's a brand new skin growing underneath the itchy one and it will look really soft and pretty.' She ignored Dominic's chuckle and changed the subject before she sank in any deeper. 'I think it's time you called me Kenna, don't you?'

'Or Mamma, perhaps,' Dominic suggested. 'Kenna and I are going to be married, then she *will* be your mamma.'

'But you haven't asked me yet, Dominic.'

'I'll get around to it before too long,' he said with a grin.

'This is the best day of my life,' Evelyn declared.

Dominic smiled and raised Kenna's hand to his lips. 'And mine, but no doubt there will be many more to come.'

The engagement of Bart Parnell to Jessica Moorehouse was reported in *Harper's Weekly*.

Jessica was rather a demanding creature, Robert realized. But she was now head over heels in love with him. She'd presented him with a solid gold card case inscribed with his initials to celebrate the event.

Robert had so far avoided setting the wedding date, but there was to be a ball at the weekend to formally announce the engagement. One hundred invitations had been sent out.

Judge Kester had invited him to his club and introduced him around.

'It's possible that Bart here might become my next partner if he plays his cards right,' he told everyone, and he'd smiled expansively when they'd settled down with their whisky to talk of the troubles.

As Robert dressed for the ball he felt a longing for the simplicity of his old life in Edinburgh. But he couldn't go back now, he'd burned his bridges.

The party had hardly started when Jethro Kester arrived with a woman, who was shielded by his body and immediately taken towards the back of the house.

The judge peeled off from the body of the guests and joined Jethro. The pair spoke together for a short time, their faces grave. On seeing Jethro, Jessica hurried across the dance floor. She was not built gracefully enough to move fast and resembled a lolloping puppy, Robert thought disparagingly as she hugged her brother and squealed with the delight of seeing him.

Jethro whispered something in her ear. She nodded and headed towards the library. Both men looked Robert's way, then the judge crooked his finger at him.

The imperious gesture annoyed Robert, but he supposed it was some sort of family conference and he followed them to the back of the house where the library was situated. A pair of brawny crew members took up position outside when Jethro closed the door.

'How mysterious you're being, Jethro. What is it, a surprise?' Jessica said happily as she slipped her arm possessively through Robert's.

Her brother didn't look in the least bit happy and Robert was filled with a sudden uneasiness. When he glanced towards the door the judge moved to lean back against the panels.

'Yes, I suppose you could say it's a surprise, but not a pleasant one for you, Jess. I'm afraid there's a person you must meet.' Jethro held out his hand to someone seated in a high-backed chair.

It was with a sense of dread that Robert watched a young woman rise to her feet and turn. '*Agnes*,' he whispered, and felt his face drain of colour. And even though he knew she was about to bring him down he couldn't help but admire her pert, pretty features.

She smiled intimately at Jethro then turned his way, saying, 'Robert . . . so we meet once again.'

Jessica stared from one to the other, then her nails dug into his forearm as she said harshly, 'Who is this woman, Bart? Why is she calling you by that name?'

Agnes's dark eyes filled with sympathy as she gazed at Jessica. 'Tell her, Robert . . . tell her that I'm your wife, Agnes Gilmore. Not that I want you back.'

The life Robert had envisaged for himself evaporated in a puff when Jessica released her grip on his arm and went to stand by the desk, a horrified look on her face.

He gave her an appealing look. 'The marriage was never a legal one, Jessica.'

Flatly, Agnes told him, 'It is in Scotland. I checked with a lawyer.'

'We're not in Scotland,' he pointed out, and there was silence for a couple of moments. 'Why are you doing this to me, Agnes?'

'Because you left me destitute. I want some of the fortune you cheated out of Kenna Mackenzie. After all, I did help you to acquire it.'

'Who's Kenna Mackenzie?' the judge asked.

'Robert's ward. She is his first wife's sister.'

'Leave Jeanne out of this.'

Agnes gave a nervous little giggle. 'Oh, I can't, Robert. I forgot to tell you . . . the authorities are after you. They think you poisoned Saint Jeanne with arsenic! I wonder what gave them that idea . . .'

Taking her by the shoulders Robert shook her and hissed, 'Don't you dare say such a wicked thing! Jeanne is the only woman I ever loved, or ever will love.'

From the corner of his eye Robert saw Jessica raise her arm. Light from the lamp glinted along the barrel of a silver pistol in her hand.

'No!' Jethro yelled, and lunged at his sister.

There was a sudden crack, a pain in his head, then Robert felt his knees buckle under him.

* * *

When Robert woke it was to pitch darkness. He was lying on something hard. When he tried to turn over he discovered that one of his hands and both his feet were manacled to a chain. Beneath him was hard wood. He managed to prop himself into a sitting position, his back against what seemed to be a barrel. His nose wrinkled against the stink around him, and his head ached abominably.

He could hear water slapping against his prison, and movement. He must be on the *Atlantic Queen*.

For a moment he experienced despair at being tracked down – especially by Agnes, who hadn't had much of an education. If it had been Kenna, he would have expected her to come after him when she realized there was no money. At least he wasn't dead, he thought wryly.

Nobody came near him for the next few hours, but there were thumps and voices up on deck as cargo was loaded. He grew thirsty and shouted out for a drink, but nobody came.

Mostly he slept, for when he was awake the darkness pressed in on him. Darkness reminded him of his childhood. His mother had locked him in a cupboard for hours on end. One night she hadn't come back. It had been days before he'd been discovered by a debt collector who'd broken into the hovel they'd lived in to remove goods to pay his mother's debts. He'd been a charming man – but a man without scruples who kept an eye on the main chance. But the man had given him a home and educated him, but in a brutal manner. He'd been a good teacher. Robert had proved it to him by robbing him of his savings when he left.

Robert was starving when Jethro came down to him, lamp held aloft. The man had a jug of water, which he placed in his free hand. 'Sorry I can't make you more comfortable.'

Gulping down the liquid, Robert said, 'You could if you tried. I'm thirsty and hungry, and my head hurts.'

'Your head's all right; the bullet just skimmed it. Agnes has put some salve on it.'

'This place stinks.'

'It's the tobacco bales, and there's a few bundles of skins. You'll soon get used to the smell.'

'How long are you keeping me locked in here?'

'Only until we put to sea. Then we'll allow you up for exercise now and again, so you can get some air and empty your bucket.' He called out, 'Billy!'

One of the crew members Robert had seen at the house appeared. He bought in a bucket, a plate of steaming stew and a chunk of bread.

'Eat hearty, there's no knowing when the next meal will be, since there's a bit of rough weather on the way.'

The two men exchanged a smile when Robert began to shovel the warm, greasy mess into his mouth.

While he was sopping up the gravy, Jethro said, 'Billy will be looking after you. I'll leave you in his gentle care.'

As soon as Jethro had gone, Robert said to the sailor, 'How much will it take for you to let me go?'

'More than you've got, mister.' Billy picked up the plate and headed off, leaving darkness to close in on him again.

A little later the ship began to move. When they reached open water the ship began to rear up, then slap down alarmingly. He guessed he was in the forward section. Water began to slosh back and forth, releasing into the air its vile smells. He shuddered when the squeak and scrabble of rats reached his ears. He'd always hated the creatures and waves of nausea roiled inside him.

It wasn't long before the stew in his stomach slopped and churned. Remembering the smile the two men had exchanged as he'd eaten the greasy stew, he muttered, 'Damn you conniving bastards!' just before he lost it all.

The voyage seemed never-ending, and it was the most uncomfortable few weeks Robert had ever spent. The weather was unfriendly for most of the time and he was tossed around, back and forth, as the front of the ship slapped into or over the waves. He lost weight in the first week, but the misery of his seasickness disappeared as he got used to the movement.

Jethro made sure he got some exercise most nights. The uncommunicative but ever-vigilant Billy took him up on deck.

The voyage was in its fourth week when his shackles were remove. He was provided with a broom, some soap and a bucket of salt water to scrub his quarters out with. The mess joined the slop in the bilge, but he'd grown used to the stink now.

The next day the ship docked. He listened to the passengers disembark and waited for somebody to come for him. That night, Billy took him up on deck and brought him a pail of water and a change of clothes.

The dark shape of the castle kept watch over Edinburgh.

Despite the cold wind Robert stripped off and sponged himself down, then dressed, dragging the clothes on to his damp body. He was shivering all over when he'd finished his ablutions, but at least he felt more human.

Jethro joined him on deck and handed him a cigar. The crewman disappeared, returning in a little while with a bottle and two glasses. Jethro poured a small amount in each. 'Brandy, it will warm you up.'

'Is Agnes on board?' Robert said, savouring his drink and thinking it might be a good idea to get back in her good books.

'Agnes is still in Boston. She's accommodated in a small house I own, and doesn't want to see you again.'

'I see.' Robert sneered. 'You're not beyond taking another man's wife into your bed, then.'

'By your own admission she's not your wife. Agnes is quite happy with the arrangement, especially now she knows that you're worth nothing. You don't have to worry about her. I'll treat her kindly.'

'I'm not worried, Agnes is very resourceful. I wish her luck.'

'She wants you to know she regrets having accused you of murder, and has retracted her statement. My father witnessed her signature.'

Robert's mind began to tick over. 'It would have been her word against mine, and a man is innocent until he's proven guilty. I didn't kill my wife.'

'I believe you. If the charge goes ahead, Agnes won't be there to testify against you.'

'Only to save her own neck. If the accusation had happened to be true and Agnes had known about it she'd have been charged with being an accessory. But it doesn't matter if she's there or not. If Jeanne's body is exhumed – and I'll insist on it – then they'll find no trace of poison. Agnes was involved with the fraud, though. She forged my sister-in-law's signature.'

'It's easy to manipulate a woman when she thinks she's in love with you. Don't blame your dishonesty on her, and be thankful I didn't drop you overboard in mid-Atlantic.'

Fingering the wound on his head, Robert grimaced. 'I couldn't manipulate your sister.'

Jethro grinned. 'I must admit Jess is a bit hard to manage when she's upset. You were lucky she missed. Usually she's a crack shot. Take my advice. Be a gentleman, Robert. Shoulder the blame and offer to pay back the money you stole. It was your ward's inheritance, I understand. How low can a man get?'

Robert had paid scant regard to either Agnes's or Kenna's feelings in his quest for wealth, and Jethro's scorn burned through him.

'You have to sink that low in the first place to find out. You were born with a silver spoon in your mouth so don't understand poverty.'

'I may have grown up with privileges but I earn my money and do understand honesty, mister.' Jethro stood. 'Your baggage is ashore. Good luck, Robert, I wish things could have been different. If you plan to return to America in the future I strongly suggest you make your destination New York rather than Boston.'

'How strongly?'

'I wouldn't advise you to test it and find out.'

Robert's baggage wasn't the only thing waiting ashore for him. Two burly men stepped out of the shadows. 'Robert Gilmore?' one of them said. 'We need to question you in connection with certain allegations. You're obliged to accompany us to the police station.'

Confession was good for the soul, it was said, and Robert knew that restitution would be looked on favourably.

He was the first to admit he'd often wished Jeanne dead during the course of her illness, but mostly so she'd be free of the pain she suffered. Murder could not be proved where it didn't exist. He had great faith in the judicial system, especially when applied to members of his own profession, and was almost certain he could talk his way around a jury.

He envisioned a short sentence for the fraud at the most.

He smiled to himself as he surrendered to his captors.

He'd left nothing to chance, and still had his contingency plans. Papers belonging to a second deceased male's identity and a small fortune in cash were stashed safely away in a London bank.

And as Jethro had thought to mention, there was always New York . . .

Eighteen

Kenna turned twenty-one late in August.

The weather was warm. Evelyn hopped excitedly from one foot to the other. She wore a skirt layered in pink ruffles, and matching satin bows kept her ringlets under control.

'Do try and stand still, dear, else you'll get creased,' Charlotte Sterne said to her granddaughter. 'Go down and join your aunt Adele and your cousins. The bridesmaids will go in the first carriage with myself and Adele. How pretty you'll all look in your different colours, like flowers.'

After Evelyn had scampered off, Kenna turned to her soon-to-be mother-in-law and kissed her cheek. 'Thank you for helping me, Charlotte.'

'It was a pleasure to stand in for your own mother, who would have been so proud of you, Kenna dear. Now you're ready you can look at your reflection.' She pulled a dust sheet from the mirror.

Kenna saw an image of herself in an ivory satin gown with lace and delicate rosebud decoration on the bodice. Layers of petticoats over a crinoline hoop gave it a graceful fullness. A long veil of guipure lace with a floral motif border flowed down over her shoulders. It was held in place with two creamy roses made of silk. They matched those on her bodice.

Butterflies attacked her stomach. 'Is it too plain? Will Dominic like it?'

'He'll adore it, Kenna. It's so elegant and unfussy, even the dressmaker said so. Besides, he'd still love you if you were dressed in a flour sack!' She turned to pick up a jewellery case, opening it to reveal a necklace glittering with diamonds. 'This is Dominic's gift to you.' She secured it around Kenna's neck and said with satisfaction, 'There, how pretty it looks.'

Giving in to a sudden urge to hug the woman, Kenna whispered, as she fingered the portrait brooch pinned in her bodice, 'If only my father was here to give me away.'

'You'll have to make do with Adrian as a substitute. I must go now, the bridesmaids are waiting in the carriage for me. I wish you much happiness, Kenna, and welcome you into my family as a beloved daughter. Look after my son. He's a good man.'

Kenna smiled at that. 'Dominic is a treasure, and I adore both him and Evelyn.'

'I know you do, my dear. I'm pleased he's found the happiness he deserves.'

The population of the quiet seaside town only numbered fifteen thousand people, yet Kenna felt as though most of them were in St Peter's Church as she walked up the aisle on Adrian Sterne's arm. Mostly she'd been contented to let Charlotte Sterne make the arrangements, since the only people she could call friends lived in Edinburgh. Charlotte had sought her opinion on most things, but Kenna alone had chosen the design for her gown. She was amazed at the number of people who'd managed to cram inside the church.

Dominic had turned to watch her come down the aisle. He blew a kiss to Evelyn, who, along with her cousins, enthusiastically strewed rose petals from a basket with a wide smile on her face. Then Dominic's eyes met Kenna's and his smile became one of such tenderness and love that she felt her heart might burst.

She hadn't seen Dominic for a while. For the sake of propriety he'd moved into the house he'd bought in Westover Road that would become their home. They would spend the first night of their marriage there, and every day thereafter.

His smile told everybody of Dominic's feelings for her. A blush crept under her skin, for while there had been no opportunity to be alone together – Charlotte had seen to that – she remembered the time she'd spent with him in Edinburgh, the quiet manner that concealed his passion and wickedness. She looked forward to the intimacy they would share.

I love you, she thought, slipping her hand inside his, and he raised her hand to his lips, kissed her palm and whispered, 'You're exquisite.'

The Reverend Bennet cleared his throat, stepped forward and said, 'Dearly beloved, we are gathered together here in the sight of God, and in the face of this congregation, to join this man and this woman in holy matrimony . . .'

The congregation's murmurs faded as they made their vows to one another.

Epilogue

September 1862

Autumn was a blaze of glory, and the warm weather had lingered.

Dominic had brought Kenna the mail and they were seated in the garden as the shadows lengthened.

'It's a letter from Fiona,' Kenna said. 'She says she's expecting another child. She's hoping for a daughter, this time.'

'Fiona should take a leaf from your book and produce two at once.'

She laughed. 'Stop looking so smug about the twins. You didn't do it all by yourself, you know. And next time I only want one. Twins are disconcerting, I can never tell one from the other and they look exactly like you.'

'Two exceedingly handsome boys, then. No, my love, they're not exactly like me. They have your honey-coloured eyes and voices like the wail of Scottish bagpipes.'

Kenna laughed. 'Especially when they're singing a duet. Oh . . . Fiona says the Challoner is having architectural plans drawn up for an addition to the lodge, using the stones from Glenchallon, now his grandfather's inheritance is through. He's certainly single-minded. Who's your letter from?'

'Tam Fellowes. He says Robert Gilmore was sentenced to eighteen months, but because he's already been in custody for over a year he'll be free in a month or two. The solicitor who helped him got a lighter sentence, because he didn't stand to profit as much.

'They didn't go ahead with the murder charge. The autopsy showed no traces of arsenic in your sister's body.'

'Poor Jeanne,' she murmured. 'I was certain Robert hadn't

killed her. For all his faults and his resentment of me, he always treated her with gentleness and love. I didn't like the thought of her being dug up and examined. I thought Agnes had sent a letter, signed and witnessed by an American judge, saying she'd lied because Robert had scorned her? Shouldn't that have been sufficient to negate the investigation?'

'Unfortunately, by the time somebody in charge decided to read it the autopsy had been carried out. The examining pathologist would have shown respect for your sister's remains, Kenna, and at least it had the effect of proving it conclusively. It's all over now and she can rest in peace. I wonder what your brother-in-law will do when he gets out of prison.'

'Oh, Robert will have a plan . . . he's always got a plan. I imagine he'll disappear from Edinburgh and start afresh somewhere else – abroad, I should imagine.'

'Gilmore won't have much to start over on since the proceeds of the house sale and all the monies from the accounts were signed over to you. I wonder if Agnes will be waiting for him.'

She laughed. 'After Robert rejected her in such a cruel manner? As for him handing over my inheritance – that was a well-planned, grand gesture, and a good move on his part. I doubt if Robert parted with everything.'

'Take a walk around the garden with me, Kenna.'

Arms around each other's waists they strolled together as the light began to darken to dusk. Dominic stopped to pick a late blooming red rose and handed it to her. 'I love you.'

She turned in to him and hugged him tight. 'I'm so happy I could dance.'

He drew her into the shadows of a tree and there, he kissed her. 'So could I. Do you remember that time in Edinburgh, my sonsie girl . . .' He drew her into his arms and, laughing, they whirled together across the garden.